BIGFOOT HUNTERS
NEVER LIE

A NOVEL

KATE E THOMPSON

TwoNewfs Publishing
Voices from the Great Pacific Northwest

ISBN 978-0-9906998-7-3
ISBN 978-0-9906998-9-7 (hardcover)
ISBN 978-0-9981564-0-8 (ebook)
Library of Congress Control Number: 2014916521

TwoNewfs Publishing
Voices from the Great Pacific Northwest

Seattle, Washington
www.TwoNewfs.com

For Hey Girl and Good Boy

Chapter One

I wasn't expecting this. I stop on the edge of the encampment, zip my coat and blow into my hands. Anthony was right when he said he'd owe me big-time for this favor.

Police are marching though camp kicking tents and barking into bullhorns. They have the place surrounded with high powered beams that lose their edge in the predawn fog, but shed enough light for the police to roust out the folks who live here.

A wakeup call far worse than the one that pulled me out of bed an hour before the alarm was set to go off. Grace will find my note when she wakes up. I didn't mention Anthony in it. I called the favor an errand. We'll argue about it when I get home.

Anthony didn't say much. Just that he was in P-Town for a few days and needed a favor now, right now. I'm supposed to find a guy named Mel and help him pack up and move before he gets arrested. Mel who lives in a Sears refrigerator box in Area 51.

I spot someone crawling out of a tent backwards on all fours. An officer hovers over the opening. Anthony said look for an orange and yellow safety vest. Mel always wears one. Tell him Commander Cathcart sent you. The guy emerges and the officer pulls his arm around to his back and starts handcuffing him. Unless he left his vest behind, this isn't Mel. I hope I find him before the police do. I wind my way down a slippery, pitted path. Commander Cathcart? The road above my head rumbles and groans.

I don't see anything that looks like an Area 51. I duck under a clothesline between a wool blanket and a threadbare towel and see an officer dragging a kid, who can't be any older than Anthony, out of a tent by the ankles.

He struggles and the officer pulls him to his knees and holds him there with a nightstick pressed against his throat. A second officer shines a flashlight in the tent and brings out an accordion.

"Get your hands off my property," the kid shouts.

The officer takes out handcuffs. "You and your squeezebox are trespassing on city property, punk." He handcuffs him and the other officer hurls the accordion. The thing opens like a wing and wheezes. The kid cries no and watches it bang into the side of a dumpster, drop and shudder.

Blue-gloved men move in, rip the tent out of the ground and throw it and everything in it away. The officer marches his barefoot prisoner through a mud puddle. I step back into a concrete pillar to get out of the way. An eviction notice to vacate the site is duct taped to it. A small weathered flyer with today's date, by eight a.m. and the threat – comply or go to jail.

The police are two hours early.

"Dolly, where are you?" A little girl, hands cupped around her mouth. "Dolly?" She's wearing pajamas. Panda bear slippers. She pads over to a tent and pokes her head in. "Are you in there?" Tugs on a man's fingers. "Have you see Dolly?"

She looks up at me and pushes a stocking cap two sizes too big off her eyes. "Have you?"

"I don't think so. Is Dolly a friend of yours?"

She studies me, her big dark eyes narrowed and her brow pinched.

"Where's your mommie?"

"I'm not supposed to talk to you. Ellie says never talk to people I don't know because they could be tweakers or serial killers or sex traders."

"Oh. I see. Well. Ellie's right about not talking to strangers. Is Ellie your sister?"

She stares at me tight lipped.

A bullhorn voice spews out a mess of condescending garble and the little girl looks up into the heavens and hollers. "I'm not leaving without Dolly."

"Ellie's looking for you, Miss Amelia." An old man lays a knotted hand on top of the girl's head. "She says it's time to go."

Amelia tugs on his kilt. "But Mr. Finn, I can't find Dolly." She sniffs and rubs her eyes with her fists.

"I'll find her, honey, don't you worry."

"There you are, Munchkin." A woman comes up from behind. Shoots me a wary glance, then clamps her hands over the girl's shoulders. "What have I told you about wandering off and talking to people you don't know?"

"But Dolly got lost."

The woman wipes off the girl's tears with her palms. "You're supposed to stay with me at all times. You scared me."

"Sorry." She wipes her nose on the side of her hand. "We can't leave until I find Dolly."

"We can't look any more. We have to get out of here."

"But Ellie."

"You don't want the cops to take you away from me, do you?" She shakes her head. "We're going on a little trip and we're taking the Greyhound bus. Won't that be fun?" Amelia shakes her head. "Yes, it will. Maybe Grandma will let us stay with her. Thank you Finn, you've been a good friend. We're going back to Portland. We can't live this way anymore." Ellie glances over her shoulder at an officer trying to manhandle a shopping cart away from a woman.

"You two take care," Mr. Finn says. He chokes up.

Ellie grabs Amelia by the hand and walks her, screaming and dragging her feet, up the hill to the street.

"Now that's a dirty rotten shame," Mr. Finn says and folds his arms over a holey Batman sweatshirt. "Ellie has been trying to get her and Amelia back on their feet. She worked at Cuppa Joes saving for their own place."

"They lived here in a tent?"

"No sir. They lived in Ellie's car. She parked it here and people watched over her, a single woman pretty as her isn't safe at night. Those pigs took her Toyota, the dirty rat bastards. Pardon my French."

"Why did the police take it?"

"The pigs gave her one chance to start it and when she couldn't get the old beater to turn over on the first crank they had it towed along with all her belongings inside. Took it to the impound place. It'll cost her four hundred bucks to get it back. She doesn't have money like that."

"It's shameful the way police are bullying these folks."

"They're used to it." He picks at a scab on his knobby knee. A foghorn blares and he makes a shivery sound. "Take my word. I lived here not that long ago."

"Maybe you know a guy named Mel?"

"Everyone knows Mel. You're Noah, aren't you?"

"Uh. Yes."

"Long time, no see. I met you at the 51st Street Mission when Anthony brought you that one time, you probably don't remember."

"Oh, I do." I think back to the one time.

"I called Anthony this morning soon as the pigs started busting up camp and arresting people. He's in Portland, of all days to be out of town, but said he'd send you in his place. Anthony's a good guy. Cares about people. He was just a kid living on the street when I met him. He made sure I went to all my AA meetings. I've been sober five years and three days."

"Congratulations."

He reaches for the baseball cap tucked in his waistband. "This way to Area 51." He dons the cap, Viet Nam Vet embroidered in red. "Watch where you're stepping." We walk around a sleeping bag and the guy snoring inside. "Did I tell you Dolly is Amelia's only doll?"

I say he didn't.

Tears roll down his cheeks into a scraggly beard. "Dolly is her only doll."

"That's too bad."

I think of Elmer, the scraggly no-eyed rabbit Gabe still talks to, the Christmas toys he's already tired of and all those video games.

"I saw Mel earlier," Mr. Finn says. "Hoo-boy, he was worked up. Did I say Amelia and Dolly are best friends? Well, they are. Mel was ranting about alien shape-shifters and government cover-up. Don't let him scare you. He's a little woo-woo in the head, but harmless. Good thing you came or he'd get himself thrown in the slammer again." He stops and points. "Mel's the next pillar over alongside the river. Call him Agent Mel, out of respect." Mr. Finn stands at attention and salutes. "I'm off on a mission to find Dolly. You're a good guy, Noah, like your brother. See you next time I see you."

I thank him and head toward the pillar. Skirt around a mud pit and walk down a slope covered in blackberry vines. Now I see it, Area 51 spray-painted vertically on the concrete pillar, and there's Mel, orange and yellow safety vest, tramping around a cardboard box cursing into a phone.

I wave and call his name, Agent Mel. He looks over and the phone slips out of his hand. I see now, the phone is a smashed plastic water bottle. "Anthony, I mean, Commander Cathcart asked me to give you a hand moving."

He scoops the water bottle phone off the ground and holds it to his ear. "Secret Agent Mel here. Come in, Commander. The aliens have landed. Can you hear me? The aliens have landed. I repeat the aliens have landed."

"I'm not an alien. I'm Commander Cathcart's brother."

"Duck and cover Commander. Aliens on your hindquarter." Mel's looking past me. I whirl around.

Several police officers come to a halt. The accordion basher is one of them. They pull out their sticks.

"Hello, Officers, I'm Noah Cathcart." I smile and gesture toward Mel. "I'll have him out of here in no time."

"Put down the weapon and hands up," one yells at Mel through the bullhorn. Apparently, not everyone knows Mel. "You, hands up."

He's talking to me. I raise my hands high like they do in the movies. "I'm clergy. I came to help."

He points the bullhorn in my direction. "Shut up."

"Stop, Aliens, don't come any closer." Mel holds up a stop sign hand. "You're trespassing on top secret government property."

"He's harmless," I say. "Agent Mel, set your phone on the ground. Please."

"I told you to shut up," the officer says and points the stick at Mel. "You, drop it and down on your knees now."

"With all due respect, the man's not armed. He's mentally ill, obviously," I say.

"What are my orders, Commander?" Mel stomps around the box.

"On the ground now." The officers march toward him.

"Wait, don't hurt him," I say.

"The aliens are going to take over the world, Commander. We have to stop them."

"Please, no violence. Let me help. I'm Associate Pastor of Rolling River Ministries."

The next thing I know, I'm face down on the ground, the accordion basher's knee pressed into my spine. "You can't arrest me. Mel's sick, I came to help," I say and he punches me in the face, once, twice, three times.

He handcuffed me and arrested me and now he's walking me to the police van. I stumble and he picks up the pace.

"Mel's sick, I told you, he needs help, not jail," I say and his beefy hand tightens around my arm. "Why am I under arrest? I didn't break the law."

He stops at a police van and passes me off to another officer who pats me down a second time.

"I'm a pastor, I haven't committed a crime."

He yells in my face to shut up and opens the back of the van revealing a second door made out of heavy duty steel that locks down like a prison cell.

Inside, another officer orders the prisoners to make room for me on the bench where there isn't room.

"I'm a pastor. I came here to help. I didn't do anything wrong."

"If you know what's good for you, Pastor, you'll help yourself by sitting here nice and praying silently." He shoves me onto the bench and the others grumble and vie for space.

I hang my head. I can't see out of one eye. I can't feel my cheek or nose or wrists. The guy on my right reeks of urine. I smell wood smoke and mildew. I smell unwashed bodies.

"I'd say it's little late for prayer," the guy on my left says under his breath. I notice his feet, bare and muddy.

"It's never too late," I whisper.

"The coppers sure did a number on your face. You must not be praying enough."

"God gives us our trials."

"Yeah right. Like letting bastard cops smash my grandpa's accordion? They had no right."

"I'm sorry."

"My accordion was my livelihood. I have a permanent job at the Moulin Rouge, guaranteed, soon as I get there. I'm saving up. My name's Justice, as in liberty and justice for all." He guffaws. "Ironic, don't you think – a name like Justice, when justice isn't for poor dirty street people like me." He wiggles his toes. "You got a name besides Pastor?"

"Noah."

He snorts. "Pastor Noah's Ark – there's no irony in your name."

The officer tells him to shut up and crams in five more prisoners and locks the door. The engine starts. My stomach clenches.

"If I were you, Pastor Noah's Ark, I wouldn't worry," Justice whispers. "The cops in booking will see you aren't one of us, no need for God to intervene on this one, and they'll send you home to your electric blanket, your suit and tie, your Bible and blueberry pancakes."

The officer leaves me standing in the lobby, a manila envelope in my hand, and undecided whether I should call Grace now or walk to my car and drive home. I open the envelope, reach for my keys and hear my name. Across the lobby, Charlee waves and drops a pile of papers along with her glasses into her teacher bag.

"Am I glad to see you," I say.

"I'm not glad to see you in jail." She slings the bag onto her shoulder and walks over, a big relieved smile, open arms. The smile goes slack. "Oh my God – your face."

"I must look pretty scary."

She brushes her fingers down my jawline. "I have a cold pack in the first aid kit. Did the homeless guy beat you up?"

"No. Who told you I was in jail?"

"Anthony. How'd this happen?"

"I'll tell you everything, but first, let's get out of here."

"Good plan, I'm parked out front."

"Thanks for breaking me out."

"We have an oath." She pulls me into a tight hug and for the first time in hours, I feel like I'm going to be okay.

"Bigfoot Hunters forever," I say the same time she does.

Charlee parks behind my car. "You really think it's a good idea to drive home?"

I set the cold pack on the dash. "I can drive a few blocks."

I look out over the abandoned camp, the neon orange no-trespassing signs the city staked around the perimeter, crows pecking at bits of trash, a gull hopping around a pile of scrap wood.

"Did Mr. Finn tell Anthony they hauled me off to jail?" I ask.

"I don't know who told him. Did they arrest everyone?"

"I think mostly stragglers and those who wouldn't comply."

"Like you?" I nod. "Where'd the rest go?"

"Shelters, I guess."

"So that's Area 51?" She points to the pillar, which stands out in the late afternoon sun.

"Yep, Mel's place. I hope he's all right. I feel responsible."

"You don't know the guy."

"He's sick. I kept telling the police. I wish I knew what they did to him."

"I would imagine they sent him off to the psych ward at the hospital."

"I hope you're right."

On the way over, I told Charlee everything. When we were kids, we told each other our nightmares and that's what telling her felt like. I lean against the head rest and she puts the cold pack over my eye again. "You didn't leave this on long enough. I can't believe our Rivers Edge police did this to you. I tell my students to trust them. I'll have to rethink that one."

"Not all of the police beat up people."

"Only those you encountered."

I think of the officer's fist connecting with my face. My hands were raised when he tackled me, weren't they?

"I hope they didn't beat up Mel," I say. "Did Anthony call Grace?"

She rolls her eyes. "I truly doubt it. Why didn't you call her?"

"A prisoner has the right to one phone call must be in the movies. I think my face will explain better in person anyway."

"You mean distract Grace from the fact that you spent the day in jail because you did Anthony a favor?"

"Good plan?"

"Your face will only get you so far."

I kiss her on the cheek and open the door. "I'd better get my face home."

I drop my keys while I'm trying to unlock my car. My head weighs a hundred pounds. I lean my forehead against the window for a moment and Charlee powers her window down.

"Let me drive you."

"No, I'm fine." I pick up the keys.

She watches me unlock, watches me open the door. I turn to wave her on and see movement on the pier over at the old cannery. A glint of silver, a flash of red, someone's over there, maybe they know what happened to Mel. I shut and lock the car, turn up my collar and tell Charlee I'm going to check out the cannery real quick. She says she's coming with me.

We cross the tracks. The road to the cannery is

broken up and overgrown. The place shut down the year before we were born. The year Dad drowned and came out of the river saved.

We stop at the steps that lead up to the pier. Underneath, waves roll in and break on the rocky bank.

"I'd be surprised if the cannery doesn't fall down before the city gets around to demolishing it." Charlee points out a sagging roof.

I inspect the crumbly steps and the sign hanging by one nail – Danger Sea Lions on Docks. My stomach clenches. I hear them barking, but it's hard to tell where the sound's coming from. "Do you see any?"

She glances right, left. "No, are you going up?"

"Yeah, I'm going up." A street lamp crackles overhead. "It'll be dark soon."

She follows me up the steps. On the farthest end of the pier, we see a person spray painting on the building.

"Is that Mel or some punk tagging the cannery?" she asks.

"Doesn't look like Mel." We look at each other and I wonder if going out there is a good idea. Whoever it is could be crazier than Mel, or worse, dangerous. "Why don't you wait here? If they stab me, run for it."

"No way, we're doing this together."

We walk a brisk clip through rust puddles and patches of seaweed slime over to the painter.

The painter is a woman, a scar under her ear a mile wide, steel toed boots. She stands back to scrutinize the lofty broad strokes. Shakes the can, touches up a spot and tosses it in the river.

"Admiring my artistic rendition of a red cross or did you come for nursing?" she asks.

"Do you know a guy named Mel, orange and yellow safety vest?" I ask.

"Everybody knows Mel. You're the pastor the cops beat the shit out of, aren't you?" I say I am. "Why don't you give me your names and what business you have with Mel?"

I do while she puts on thick black-framed glasses. She scrutinizes my face. "You certainly do need some nursing. My name's Akim Appleton, but people around here call me The Nurse."

"The Nurse?" She nods. "Nice to meet you, but I don't need nursing. Do you know what happened to Mel after the police raid?"

She clomps over to a shelter made out of tarps and bricks, bungees and bright colored rope. One end is secured to a stack of rusty crab pots, the other to a piece of driftwood she crammed into a shopping cart full of newspapers and garbage bags and one of the city's no trespassing signs on a stick.

"If it wasn't for you diverting the cop's attention this morning, they would have took my cart away. I'm appreciative." She pulls back the tarp door. "All righty, that's enough nicey-nice. Let's get you inside and clean out those nasty cuts before they get infected."

"No that isn't necessary."

"You want to know about Mel, don't you? I'm not talking to you out here in the cold. Hurry up and get inside before my heat goes out."

We duck inside. There's no heat to let out. She pulls the sweater off over her head, revealing an AC/DC t-shirt over a thermal.

Charlee sidles up beside me and looks around wide-eyed. I don't think she's ever talked to a street person, except to give them a buck or two if they're panhandling.

"Sit." The Nurse points to the ground and turns on a propane lantern hanging in the corner. In the light I see the tattoo on her hand. Love is Pain. Charlee sees it too and gives me the eyebrows.

"Did you hear me?" The Nurse rummages through an overstuffed backpack. "Sit while I look for my first aid supplies."

"No need for first aide, Charlee took care of me. If you could just tell us about Mel –"

"Look at your face, the girl has no nursing experience."

The Nurse pulls mismatched socks out of her bag, pants and scarves. A pill bottle drops out of a towel and she grabs for it, misses and it rolls into my foot. I pick it up.

"Don't want my vitamins rolling away." She holds out her hand and I give it back. "I had to pack up quick. Made a mess of everything, it will take me days to get it all sorted out. Will you two just sit down?"

"All right, but we can't stay long." I sit on a patch of black moss. "What can you tell us about Mel?"

"You young people these days are too impatient. One thing at a time."

Charlee squats in her designer jeans and leans into me. "We don't want to walk back in the dark," she whispers.

"Don't blame you," The Nurse says. "The boogie man's out there, I seen him. I'm all out of Band-Aids. But I found plenty of swabs." She sits cross-legged in front of me and rips open one of the packages, takes me firmly by the chin and starts swabbing.

"Ouch." I jerk and she pulls my face closer. "It's going to sting. Alcohol is for killing germs. Now hold still. You and Charlee married?"

"Not to each other," Charlee says.

"We're friends. We grew up together." I push The Nurse's hand away. "Thank you. You've done plenty. You said you know Mel?"

She opens another package. "It's not good nursing to start something and not finish. I'm a certified RN, in case you're worried if I know my nursing shit or not. You'll have to take my word though, I haven't had a chance to hang my license in my new abode." The wind whistles through the gaps in the tarp and she growls like a bear. "My back's been giving me fits this winter. For 12 years, I worked as an RN in the busiest Chicago ER, until I wrenched the back. Before I had a chance to heal, my loving and devoted husband left with my kids and I haven't seen head nor hair of them since."

"I'm so sorry," I say and Charlee squeezes my shoulder.

"That's life, I suppose," The Nurse says, "and not worth talking about. Tell me what you do for a living, Mrs. Charlee."

She scrubs out another cut. "Not so hard," I say.

"Hold on just a little bit longer. Go on Charlee."

"I teach third grade."

"You got to be a saint to be a school teacher."

"Ouch. My son Gabe's in Saint Charlee's class."

She laughs. "How old is your boy?"

"Eight."

"Lordy, kids can suck the life out of you. You got any, Charlee?"

"Only the 32 in my class."

"Not a bad deal having kids you can send home at the end of the day. Speaking of kids and nasty cuts, Amelia had a terrible skinned knee a while back. You know her and her sister, Ellie?"

"I met them briefly this morning," I say. "The little girl lost her doll."

"Oh me, her and that doll was inseparable. I took care of Amelia's knee and got it all bandaged up and do you know what, she didn't flinch once and she's just a little girl."

"Tough kid. Did you tell that story for any particular reason?" I ask.

"No reason. I hear the father's abusive. It's a shame she had to go back home to him. All right, I patched you up the best I can." She admires her work. "Now you put Band-Aids on these cuts soon as you get home."

"I will. Thank you. Are you sure about Amelia's dad?"

She takes off the glasses and props them on top of her head. "As sure as I can be. Did you know 30-some people lost their homes today? More than 30, so the rich man who owns most all the buildings downtown can make himself a pretty park under the bridge."

"We have shelters for the homeless," Charlee says.

"Waiting lists at the shelters are a mile long. I don't even try to get in anymore. Nowadays, I put up my own shelter where I can and open it to people who are in need of nursing."

"God bless you," I say.

"I realize you're a pastor and it's your duty to go around God-blessing all us poor souls, but you should know, I've never seen the likes of God on any of the streets I've lived on."

"God's with every one of us, including you."

Charlee rolls her eyes.

"I don't much like a God who stands by watching bigheaded cops beat up a pastor for no good reason," The Nurse says.

"The scratches I got today are nothing compared to how Jesus suffered and died for us. God loves all of His children. He loves you and he loves you, Charlee, even when you roll your eyes. All you have to do is believe. Repent of your sins and you'll be saved. The gospel of Jesus is the way to happiness."

"No disrespect, but that's a load of bullshit," The Nurse says. "I was a church-going woman until I found out that God is not only a hypocrite, but a mean man, and that Bible of His is one long and boring contradiction."

"God's way is complex, a mystery. One day He will open your eyes and you'll understand."

"That's just a bunch of talk-talk, not an explanation. You don't understand God any better than I do."

"Let's get back on point," Charlee says to me and turns to The Nurse. "What can you tell us about Mel?"

"He either got arrested or didn't. Say he did, hypothetically speaking. Being crazy isn't illegal and the cops don't care about helping the man so they let him go. Whether he got arrested or not, Mel will come back to Area 51, I can tell you that. He's got no place else to go."

"Thank you for the information," Charlee says.

The Nurse opens the tarp door. "Do either of you have any spare cash you don't mind parting with?"

I look at Charlee and she gestures that she has nothing on her.

"Oh Lordy, what am I thinking? Asking a preacher and a teacher if they have money to spare, of course, you don't. You're in two of the worst paid jobs in the country."

I reach for my wallet. "I believe I have a couple of dollars." I leave the ten and pull out three.

She lays her hand over mine. "God bless you, Pastor."

The tarp closes behind us and I brush off the seat of my pants. A foghorn blares in the distance.

"It's dark," Charlee says.

"Not entirely, our eyes will adjust. Let's go."

"Before you leave." The Nurse is standing in her tarp doorway shining a flashlight in our faces. "Thought you folks might need one of these."

"We can't take it. We'll be fine," I say.

"I won't miss it. I have another fancier one. You'll find this one in perfect working condition." She turns it on and off and on. "Matter of fact, it's brand new, a bargain at ten bucks. Now it's none of my business, but I would think you'd need a reliable light if you're planning on escorting a pretty young woman through these parts."

The flashlight stops working before we get to the main road. "Some bargain." I smack the thing against my palm and fiddle with the switch. "That ten was the last of my gas money until payday."

"I'll buy your next tank. You think she's going to buy drugs with your money?"

"I don't know. Besides, it's no longer my money. I gave it to her."

"Were those vitamins of hers really vitamins?"

"Oxycodone."

"She's an addict."

"One bottle doesn't make her an addict."

"Then why'd she lie about them?"

"How would I know?"

"You talk to God don't you?" She smirks and the flashlight flickers and comes back on.

We cross the tracks and stop on the sidewalk. The row of streetlights cast a dim yellow light over the empty space under the bridge. I throw the flashlight in a dumpster the city left behind. Kick a plastic water bottle and it bounces off the Area 51 pillar.

"Don't be hard on yourself. You tried. Come on, let's go home," Charlee says.

"Hallo Commander. Over here."

A half-block down I see an orange and yellow glow.

"Is that Mel?" Charlee sounds as excited as I feel.

"That's him, all right." I wave. "Agent Mel."

"We'll debrief when I get back to Headquarters, Commander." He's dragging a refrigerator box and waving one of the no trespassing signs over his head.

He parks his box in Area 51 and props the sign against the pillar.

"Welcome back Agent Mel," I say.

"Thank you, Sir. I'm happy to report that I've secured Area 51."

"Well done. Are you all right?"

"The aliens took me hostage, but I didn't divulge any top secrets."

"Oh, well, that's good."

"I have more to report. Does the woman have

top-secret security clearance?"

I look at Charlee. "Yeah, of course she does. This is Agent uh Agent 99."

"Agent 99?" she asks.

"It's all I could think of," I say under my breath. "She's one of us. What else do you have to report?"

He spots the water bottle I kicked. He stomps on it before he picks it up and puts it to his ear. "Commander, come in. I've detained an extraterrestrial, an alien by the name of Dolly. I'm awaiting further instructions."

I think of Amelia wandering through camp calling for her lost doll.

"What can you tell me about Dolly?" I ask.

"Dolly is a code name and her mission is to take the world hostage. Other than that, she's tight lipped."

"I see. Show me your prisoner."

Mel crawls inside the box and comes out holding a little rag doll by an arm.

"Is that the lost doll?" Charlee whispers.

"It must be." We look at each other and smile.

"I've got our prisoner on video, can you see her?" Mel aims the bottle at the doll.

"Yes, I can. I'll take her in for further questioning."

"Yes Sir. If you don't mind me asking, Sir, did one of Dolly's alien compatriots do that to your face? They're known to torture their victims."

I touch my face; the skin is hot and tight. "No, one of our own did this."

"The aliens knocked me around too, but I'm happy to report that I'm not a casualty." Mel gives me the doll. "Be careful, Commander. She looks sweet and

innocent, but don't let that fool you, she's one dangerous cookie."

"I won't. Agent, you've done an outstanding job."

"Yes Sir, I'm awaiting further orders, Sir."

"Okay. Do you have any blankets in there?" I nod
toward the box.

"I do not. The aliens confiscated the last Headquarters and everything in it, Sir."

I give the doll to Charlee and take off my coat, it's
an old one, and hand it to Mel. "All agents in the field
are required to wear one of these." He puts it on over
the vest. "Looks like a good fit. Now get some sleep.
That's an order, over and out."

Mel flashes us the peace sign, climbs in his box
and disappears.

"Well done, Commander Cathcart." Charlee
plops Dolly in my hand.

Chapter Two

Grace breaks eggs into a skillet. They sizzle and she stabs them with the corner of a spatula. She is beautiful, messy haired, a silky robe. I slip my arms around her waist and press my good cheek against hers. "You feel nice."

She nestles back in my arms and we watch the eggs cook.

"How are you feeling?" she asks.

"You aren't wearing anything under this."

"You're peeking."

"Uh-huh." I reach inside the robe and we make the same breathy sounds. I turn her around and we kiss. I try to ignore the throbbing side of my face, but I must wince, because she wriggles out of my arms.

"You aren't up for this." She slides the eggs onto a plate. Sets it on the table and goes through the junk drawer until she finds a miniature bottle of pain relievers. She gives me a glass of water, shakes four pills into my hand. "Take these and get some ice on your face." She adjusts the robe and reties the belt. "Like

I told you last night, ice will make the swelling go down and you'll feel better."

I take the pills and set the glass in the sink. "I do feel better."

She puts her finger under my chin. "You're lying. Besides, Gabe's going to walk in on us."

"He's in his room."

"Maybe not." She tugs on one end of my tie. "Want me to tie this?"

Justice said I'd go home to my suit and tie. He was right about that. "I'll tie it later." I find mugs in the dishwasher and pour coffee.

"Your dad called."

"Did you tell him?"

"That his son went to jail yesterday? No, but I'd be surprised if he hasn't already heard." She carries plates and forks over to the table.

I bring the coffees and we sit across from each other. "I hope Sister Monk didn't find out. She'd go running to Dad making what happened into a big deal."

"It is a big deal. Your gay brother almost got you killed."

"Why do you bring up Anthony's sexual orientation every time you mention him? He's my brother, your brother-in-law, and the fact that he's gay has nothing to do with us. Call him Anthony. And he didn't almost get me killed."

"Look at you." She leans over the table. "All it took was one phone call from – Anthony, and you ran off to help those people."

"Since when is helping someone a crime?"

"Those vagrants you went to help were breaking

the law. They're dangerous."

"They didn't hurt me."

"The police were doing their job. You should have stayed out of their way."

"Perhaps." I lift the mug up to my lips, but the coffee's too hot to drink. "I was trying to explain that Mel was harmless. I told the officers I was clergy. They wouldn't listen."

"Yes, you told me. If the police hadn't taken you down, the crazy guy probably would have."

"I don't think so. There must have been a way other than violence to get the people to leave."

"The homeless are the city's problem, not yours."

"I did what I felt was right."

"You should do what God says is right, not what you think is right." She reaches for my hand and laces her fingers through mine. "God called you to serve Him in Rolling River."

"I'm well aware of His expectations."

"Good." She pokes at the eggs. "Don't ruin it. Breakfast is getting cold. Take one." She glances toward the stairs. "I woke Gabe a half hour ago. If he doesn't get his butt down here, he's going to miss the bus again." She pushes away from the table. "I forgot to make toast." She puts four slices of bread in the toaster. "You distracted me. Watch this while I go up."

"Okay." I watch her until she reaches the top of the stairs.

I put an egg on a plate and eat a rubbery bite. Grab my Bible off the corner of the table where I left it yesterday and leaf through looking for a passage that will grab the interest of my youth group for Sunday's lesson. The Nurse's words come back to me,

"This is all bullshit."

The dogs pound down the stairs. Henry stops at the bottom waving his red feathery tail waiting for his good morning kiss on the nose from Grace. Hercules shoots around him and is about to leap into my lap when he sees my face, backs off and growls.

"Hey, it's me. Look." I show him my good side and he stands on his hind legs, rests his one front paw on my knee and studies my face.

I smell something burning.

I rush over to the toaster, press eject and four burnt pieces fly out onto the counter. "That's just great. Well, Hercules, this is what you do when you burn toast." I get a knife and scrape the black off over the sink and slather on margarine. "Good as new. Gabe won't even notice." I stack the slices on a plate.

Coraline hisses. I look over my shoulder. Hercules is trying to push his way onto the white pillow that's covered with a black blanket of Coraline's own fur. "She doesn't want to play, buddy. Come here." I sit down and he trots over and jumps in my lap, burrows under my arm and goes to sleep.

I close the Bible. Grace is right. God knows what's best for His children. I've known this since before I could read and Dad read the Bible to me.

"He was still in bed." Grace is marching Gabe down the stairs.

"I'm sick." He holds his stomach. "I can't go to school."

Grace shakes her head. "You aren't sick, mister. Eat your breakfast." She points him toward the table and bends down to give Henry his kiss.

"I'm gonna puke at school and it's gonna be all

your fault." Grace isn't listening. Gabe stomps over. "Dad, Dad, don't make me go."

"Weren't you sick last week?"

"Last Thursday." Grace is wiping her face with a kitchen towel. Henry is looking up at her smiling.

"Last Thursday, huh?"

Gabe fiddles with his fingers.

"Could this be the Thursday flu?" I press my hand against his forehead. "I believe it is. A full day of school is the only cure for this illness."

Gabe slumps. "It's not fair. You get to stay home because you got beat up."

"My beat up face is going to work today and you're going to school."

"Don't blame me if I puke inside my backpack and all over my desk and the floor and on Ms. Radcliff-Aunt Charlee's shoes and in the drinking fountain and –"

"Gabriel, enough," Grace says and puts an egg and a slice of toast on a plate for him. "Sit down and eat."

"Does your face hurt?" He cups a moist sticky hand over my good cheek and studies my eye and the cuts and bruises.

"A little bit. Now do what Mom said."

"You look like one of the monsters I fight in my video game."

I didn't tell him who did this to me and I'm not going to. I raise my arms and make monster sounds and he screeches and turns to run, but Grace is standing there and she grabs his arm and forces him into a chair.

She pushes his breakfast in front of him. "The bus

will be here in a few minutes. Eat fast." She picks up her coffee and hovers over him.

"You burnt the toast, Mom."

"No. Dad did."

"It's not that burnt," I say.

Gabe's brow wrinkles. "You scraped off the black part and covered up the scrape marks with butter."

"I made it edible. Eat and be thankful you have food. Not everyone is as blessed."

"Do what Dad says." Grace sets her empty mug on the counter, pulls open the blinds and sun pours in. "What a beautiful day." She breaks into smiles. "Days like this make me want to get out in the garden. I can't wait for spring. The crocus will bloom, then the daffodils. I think I'll plant more dahlias, what do you think?"

"Sure, I guess, if you want to." I finish my coffee.

"You could at least act interested." She peers out the window in the direction the bus comes from. Then she brings the coffeepot over.

"Thank you. I am interested."

"Dad, Dad. Who's going to bless the food?"

"You are. Make it snappy," Grace says and we fold our hands.

"...and thank you God that Dad isn't dead. Help the police catch the bad men who beat him up and just help them find Jesus while they're in jail." Gabe smiles out of the corner of his mouth.

"Thanks Gabe, I –"

"I'm not done. God, I forgive Dad for leaving me at school last night."

"I left you?"

"Yes, you did," Grace says. "I had a committee meeting and you promised to pick him up after school. He sat on the curb waiting for you until dark. Until the principal came out and discovered him there and called me."

"I'm sorry. Sorry, buddy." I squeeze his arm and Grace glares.

"God. Tell Mom and Dad if they let me have my own cell phone, I could call home whenever I'm in danger." He looks over to see if we're listening. I shake my head and he goes back to praying. "God. Dad tries to be a good dad, really he does. Please make him happy. Tell Mom to let Dad keep Hercules and tell Hercules to not be so hyper. Amen."

Grace's eyes slide over to me.

"You forgot to bless the food," I say.

"Oh. Bless the food and the hands that prepared it."

"Amen," Grace and I say.

"And God please help Ms. Radcliff-Aunt Charlee not be mean today. Help her find God and help Uncle Anthony find God too. Amen. Oh no, I forgot to pray for Henry and Coraline. God, please –"

"The prayer is over. Finish your breakfast." Grace starts putting his coat on him. "Did Ms. Radcliff-Aunt Charlee put you in detention again?"

"He's in detention again?" I ask. Grace doesn't answer. "Why?"

"I don't know." She scowls. "We don't have time for this discussion right now."

Gabe pokes his egg. "It's going to be another bad, bad day."

"Eat your toast." Grace tries to put Gabe's backpack on him. "Noah, you have to find that dog a home."

"I'm working on it. Finish your toast, Gabe."

"I don't like it." He sticks his finger through the middle of it.

"Get that off your finger young man," Grace says. "You promised you'd find him a home two weeks ago."

"It's not easy finding a handicapped dog the right home."

"He gets around on three legs as well as any four-legged dog. He chewed up another washcloth and one of your socks. And he peed on the carpet again." Grace brushes crumbs off Gabe's face.

I look down at Hercules and frown. "You're not making this easy, buddy," I whisper.

"The bus." Gabe shoots out of his seat, the back-pack hanging off one arm and the straps dragging.

The bus driver waits. We wave.

"Chihuahuas aren't the most popular dog these days. Poor little guy." Hercules shivers and I hug him close. "You think he needs a sweater?"

Hercules cranes his neck and looks over at Grace with the big soulful eyes.

She shakes her head. "No, Noah. I don't think he needs a sweater. He needs a home. Don't give up looking, we have enough pets."

"I won't."

Grace clears the table and starts washing it.

Her robe is coming loose in the front. I take the sponge out of her hand.

"What are you doing?"

"Come here." I tug on her damp hand until she comes around. I kiss her palm and try to pull her into my lap. "No one's going to walk in on us now."

"No." She pulls away.

"I feel better. The pain relievers helped."

"I'm glad to hear, but it's getting late. I have to clean up and get ready for my meeting."

"What meeting?"

"The Downtown Improvement Committee."

"What do you do on that committee?" I put my mug in the sink.

She gives me the eyes. "I told you. Margaret Simmons, the president of the River County Master Gardeners, recommended me to the committee and they invited me to be a consultant in sustainable landscaping for the old cannery renovation."

I lean my back against the counter. "Isn't the park under the bridge part of the renovation?"

"Yes." She opens the dishwasher and unloads clean plates.

I take the pile from her and put them away. "Did you know the city was going to evict the homeless from that space?"

"I knew the city was helping them find shelters, subsidized housing and food stamps before they evicted them."

"I think the only housing they arranged were rooms in the jail."

"Excuse me." She's trying to open a drawer I'm blocking. I move out of the way. "Josh promised they'd be taken care of. They'll be better off in the long run. No one should live under a bridge."

"I agree. But I heard the shelters are full."

She unloads the silverware. "Social services tried to step in and help. Josh said most of the homeless didn't want their help."

"Who is Josh?"

"Josh Barrett. He's funding the cannery renovation and is president of the Downtown Improvement Committee."

"Is he the guy who owns most of the buildings downtown?"

"He owns many of them."

"His renovation displaces the homeless while it makes him richer."

"They don't belong under the bridge. The renovation is good for the community. It will bring tourists to town. The new park will be welcoming and safe for regular families."

She glares in the silverware drawer for a moment, then slams it shut. "Now I have to explain how my husband got himself arrested while trying to thwart the committee's efforts."

"Wait a minute; you're making this into something that it's not."

"What this is – is embarrassing."

"You're embarrassed of a husband who has compassion for the mentally ill? Isn't that what Jesus did?"

She shuts the dishwasher. "I have to shower. Josh asked me to come early to look over some proposals." She heads over to the stairs.

I follow. "If you're meeting with your Downtown Improvement Committee today, who'd you meet with yesterday?"

"The Downtown Improvement Committee."

"How many days a week does this committee meet?"

"When needed."

"No wonder you don't know why Gabe's in detention again."

"What do you mean by that?"

"I mean if your community obligations distract you from family obligations, like taking care of your son, maybe you should consider cutting back."

"Maybe you should consider spending more time with your son. If you picked him up yesterday like you were supposed to, you could have talked to him about detention. But you were in jail."

"That was uncalled for."

"Questioning how I care for our son was uncalled for. Who has gone to every standing parent-teacher meeting since September? I have. Who helps Gabe with his homework? I do. This conversation is over." She whirls around and stomps upstairs.

I hear dresser drawers banging, her feet coming down hard on the floor.

I think back to the eggs cooking. How nice she felt in my arms. How did our morning turn out like this? I think about going upstairs, but I would end up apologizing.

I call on God. Lord – a pastor and his wife should get along peaceably and set the example for others. Any suggestions on how to do this would be welcomed. I close my eyes and wait.

I hear tic-tic-tic and open my eyes and there's Hercules dancing on his hind legs, scratching the air with his one paw.

Dad removes his reading glasses and sets them on his open Bible. "Shut the door and have a seat."

I pull the door closed and sit in the armchair. "Hi Dad."

He glares over the massive mahogany desk. "Son."

"I imagine you've heard." I point to my face. "I can explain."

He picks up a folded newspaper, comes around and slams it on the desk in front of me. "Explain this." He breathes down my neck while I unfold it.

My picture's on the front page. I don't look anything like myself. The headline reads – Rolling River's Maverick Pastor Arrested in River Street Brawl.

"I've never been on the front page before." I glance up at Dad. Face made of stone, the steel blue eyes.

The reporter snapped my picture after the officer dropped me, after he beat me and cuffed me, after I lost track of up and down. I read the headline again and wonder if Dad would have recognized me in the picture without it.

"It wasn't a brawl. The story is misleading." I slap the paper back on his desk.

"Brawl or not, the truth of the matter is Rolling River's Associate Pastor was arrested yesterday, were you not?"

"Yes, I was, but the charges were unfounded and dropped."

He thunks my newspaper face with his knuckles. "This type of publicity reflects badly on the church. My phone started ringing before dawn."

"Let me explain."

"No, I'll explain. Several board members phoned. Brother Jacobs went as far to suggest that I should pray more diligently about my pending retirement. You see, he doesn't believe a maverick pastor should be left to run the church."

"I'm not a maverick pastor. I went to help someone on my own time, not Rolling River's. I didn't commit a crime. The newspaper sensationalized the story."

"People think what they think. It's a matter of perception." He chucks the paper into the trashcan and returns to his seat. "Sister Monk was among the many who phoned."

I cringe when I hear her name.

"She threatened to pull Brian and Naomi out of your youth program."

"Because of a story she read in the paper?"

"Yes and I assured her there'd be no repeat of the incident, or one like it. I asked Brother Stan to teach the youth this Sunday."

"Why? I'm capable of teaching."

Dad holds up his hand. "I also invited Sister Monk to sit in on your classes when you return and thankfully, she agreed not to withdraw the children."

"That's just great."

"I want you to pray diligently, repent, and get yourself closer to God. You might work on humbling yourself as well. By the way, your pay for Sunday will be adjusted accordingly."

"My pay?"

"How else will Brother Stan be compensated?"

"I see. You haven't even heard my side of the story. Thanks for the vote of confidence."

I start to spring out of the chair and Dad stops me. "We aren't finished. Sister Monk is an influential member of Rolling River. I'm not taking this lightly and you shouldn't either."

"She's influential, all right, she pushed and you buckled before you talked to me. Where's God in all of this?"

"Sister Monk has been a faithful member of Rolling River for many years. I prayed long and hard over this situation and God concurs. You'd be wise to remember that Sister Monk pays a third of your salary in tithing."

"This is about money?"

"Rolling River is a business and as you know full well, one of a pastor's jobs is to direct and maintain a profitable ministry." He leans back in his chair for a moment. Then he folds his hands and rests them on the desk. "A pastor's work is never done. There is no such thing as your own time. You represent God's church, Rolling River Ministries of JESUS Church of the Mighty Miracles, at all times."

Dad walks over to the picture window and gazes out over the choppy river. He wants me to think.

I think how Grace is going to flip out when the next paycheck comes up short. I tip my head into my hand.

"That eye's got to be painful. Tell me what happened," Dad says.

I look past Dad out the window. A gull lands on the railing. Others follow. Waves roll in and break on the pylons. Clouds are stacking up. Dad is waiting for an answer. I wonder how long he would wait. Two minutes, one?

He comes over and lays his hands over my shoulders. "Take the day off. Get some ice on your face. I love you, Son. A day doesn't go by that I don't get down on my knees and thank God for sending you to me. Thank you Jesus. Be diligent and brave. Satan wants you bad. You are Rolling River's miracle. You are Rolling River's future."

Chapter Three

Charlee pokes Elmer in the belly. "This is going to be awkward." She sits on a table and crosses her ankles. Looks Elmer in the face where his eyes used to be. "All right, this is the plan."

The door to her classroom is wide open. I shouldn't interrupt her conversation. I pick up Hercules and lean against the doorjamb.

"First off, I'll go through all the blah blah I go through every week with Grace," Charlee says. "Next, she will make her excuses, the same tired excuses she made last week, just reworded. Normally, we end there, but not today." She looks over at a plastic grocery bag on the other side of the table. "Or should I bring the incident up first?"

That's just great. I wonder what Gabe did this time.

"I'm thinking a straightforward approach will work best with Grace. It will be awkward, like I said, but okay." She pauses. "The upside will be the expression on Grace's face when she finds out what Gabe shared with his classmates today. Just thinking about this makes me smile a little."

"You and Elmer start the meeting without me?" I ask from where I'm standing.

Elmer falls out of her hands onto the floor. "What are you doing here?" She hops off the table and straightens her skirt.

"Grace got tied up in a meeting and asked me to come in her place. Your door was open. I guess I should have knocked."

"Yes, you should have. Did you bring Gabe?"

"No, I left him at the church with Granddad."

She bends down and picks Elmer up by a leg and tosses him on the table. "The rabbit and I were having a private conversation." She chuckles and her cheeks pink up. "Well, don't just stand there."

I put Hercules down and he follows me inside.

"What's up with the sunglasses?" she asks.

I give her a hug. "They distract from the monster face." I pull them off. "Don't you think?"

"Uh. No. But your face looks much better than it did two days ago."

"It feels more like a face."

"Did you file a complaint with the police department yet?"

"I'm not going to. I heard our local police didn't have the manpower to conduct the raid and called in volunteers. Several officers were from other parts of the county."

"Are you saying Rivers Edge police wouldn't beat up a pastor?"

"I don't know who beat me up and if I file a complaint, they'll say I got in the way. Maybe I did. Jesus said turn the other cheek and that's what I'm going to do."

"Pfft. Jesus got himself killed. But it is your word against them and your only witness believes he's a secret agent." She pulls out a kid sized chair. "Have a seat and we'll get started." She sits across the table from me and picks through some papers, looks up and chuckles. "Would you like a grownup chair?"

My legs are sprawled out under the table. "No, this one's fine." I push away from the table, sit straighter, and glance over at the plastic bag.

"If you say so." She grabs Elmer around the waist. "The rabbit came to school again." She gives him to me. "This is Gabe's second offense. Next time, Elmer stays locked in my desk until the end of the year."

"He loves Elmer. He tells him everything."

"I know. Gabe has been packing Elmer around since he was a toddler. But those are the rules."

I push the stuffing back in Elmer's knee. "Is it weird? Isn't Gabe too old to be this attached to a baby toy?"

"Kids who are attached to their security blanket or rabbit, as in Gabe's case, let go of them, some just take longer than others. It's better not to force it."

"You think?" She nods. "Of course he shouldn't bring Elmer to school. We'll talk to him about it."

"Good."

My eyes have wandered back to the bag. I can't imagine what's in it.

"This is a list of all the assignments Gabe hasn't turned in. I gave Grace the list last week and Gabe only made up one." She hands me a paper.

Apparently, Grace's claim that she helps Gabe

with all of his homework all of the time was a bit exaggerated. I fold the list and slip it in my coat pocket. "I'll talk to her."

"Don't just give the list to Grace." Charlee wags her finger at my coat. "Gabe's progress is as much your responsibility as hers."

"Grace takes care of all the school stuff."

"Yeah, I know. Maybe it's time you and Grace and Gabe have a conversation. An open line of communication between the child and family, along with the teacher, is key to a child's success. We all want Gabe to succeed."

"Of course we do, I know. I'll talk to Grace."

Charlee looks over at the grocery bag.

"Is that for me?" I ask.

"Yes, it's Gabe's show and tell."

"There was a problem with it?"

"Yes." She shoves the bag into my hands. The handles are tied in a bow. "He brought a Golden Bullet to school."

"You mean a weapon of some sort?" I'm alarmed and she looks at me like I'm being ridiculous.

"No, a Golden Bullet isn't a weapon. Just open it."

I untie the bag and look inside. I don't know what it is at first. Until it's in my hand and I see the words Golden Bullet on the side written in fancy script. Until I feel the shape and the size and find a switch on the end, then it dawns on me what the thing is and I drop it back in the bag.

"This can't be Gabe's show and tell." I try giving the bag back to her and she won't take it. "You must have it mixed up –"

"No, it's Gabe's, all right. He gave the class a demo."

My mouth drops open and I wonder if this is the expression she anticipated from Grace. It isn't making Charlee smile like she thought, not even a little.

She continues. "Gabe said the Golden Bullet was for killing monsters. He pulled it out of the bag vibrating, pointed it at the class, pew – pew, he said. Oh, the class was fascinated, especially the boys. I told Gabe to drop it and of course, he didn't. Hillary spoke up then. It's not a bullet, she said, it's a vibrator, I know because my mom has one just like it." Charlee stops to scowl. "The class wanted to know what a vibrator was, naturally, and Hillary would have been happy to tell them, but the bell rang to go home and the vibrator was forgotten."

I hear what she's saying, but I still feel there must be a mix-up, a misunderstanding, something other than what it is. "Where'd he get it?"

"His mom."

"Who?"

She looks at the bag hanging from my fingertips, dangling between my legs. "He said he borrowed it from his mom, which I'm pretty sure, wasn't the case."

"You mean Grace?" I tie the handles in a knot and set the bag on the table.

"Well, yeah, Grace. Gabe's mom, you know, Grace Cathcart."

"This thing belongs to Grace?"

"I don't know anything about it except that Gabe had better not bring it to school again."

The grocery bag feels like a third arm. It swings

between me and Charlee as we walk to our cars. Another moonless night and the woods behind the school are restless, an icy nip in the breeze.

She tells me about the teacher's refrigerator, how no one cleans it and the unlabeled containers of mold. I half listen. I'm thinking about my wife's vibrator. Why would she want one? She has me.

"Who steals salad?" Charlee asks.

I look at her. "Someone stole salad?"

"Yes, someone ate mine today when it was clearly labeled. Are you thinking about that thing?" She nods toward the bag.

"I guess."

We stop at my car. Hercules barks and squirms while I unlock.

"When are you going to admit that you're keeping this little yapper?"

"I'm not keeping him. It takes time to find a proper home." I open the door and he jumps inside.

"You think you'll find a proper home without looking for one?"

"I'm not giving the little guy to just anyone. I have to be sure they won't put him back out on the street the first time he pees on their pillow or chews up their underwear."

"Still chewing on Grace's panties?" She bursts out laughing.

I try not to laugh, but I remember the red lacy ones I found in Hercules' dog bed and chuckle. "Not funny. Those incidents only move him higher up Grace's crap list."

"Him and you."

"Yeah. Do you have a few minutes?"

She cocks her head and frowns. "Why don't you just go home and talk to Grace about the vibrator and get it over with?"

"It's not about that. I planned on calling you tonight, but since we're here –"

"In that case, what's up?"

"Let's talk in my car so I can keep an eye on Hercules."

I toss Elmer into the backseat and put Gabe's show and tell surprise between the front seats. Hercules sits on top of the bag and glares at Charlee.

"Remember Dolly?" I ask.

"The extraterrestrial?"

"Yes. And you remember The Nurse saying Ellie and her sister, Amelia, went back to live with their abusive father?"

"I do, but – The Nurse isn't exactly a reliable source."

Hercules comes over and nuzzles in my coat. "What if she's right? And what if I could help them?"

"Help them, you don't even know them."

"Hear me out. I talked to Ellie's boss at Cuppa Joes this morning. He went on about what a good worker she is and how much he'll miss her. He said he'd take her back in a minute."

"Yeah, so?"

"He gave me her forwarding address."

"So you can put Dolly in the mail?"

I shake my head. "I also talked to Catholic Services. They have a room at St. Mary's that Ellie and Amelia are welcome to use until Ellie can afford a place of their own."

"Did you talk this over with Ellie?"

"No. I have an address, not a phone."

"You took it upon yourself to set up housing without asking her?"

"I heard St. Mary's has rooms from time to time. I didn't think it would hurt to ask."

"Isn't that rather presumptuous? What if she wants to stay in Portland?"

"Why would she?"

"I don't know and you don't either."

Hercules springs off my chest and jumps in the backseat barking at shadows. "After the police confiscated her car, she may have felt she had no options, but she does. I'm going to P-Town in the morning to see her and I want you to go with me. You're a woman. It wouldn't be right for me to go there alone."

"It wouldn't be right to go at all."

"Dolly is Amelia's only doll. The least I can do is return it, and while I'm there, I'll tell Ellie about St. Mary's and that her boss wants her back. She should know, right? If I can help them, in any other way, I think I should. After all, I'm a pastor and God put the doll into my hands."

"No, God didn't, crazy Agent Mel did. You don't know what you'll find at the forwarding address. Maybe her dad will answer the door. He could be beefy and big and mean. Maybe he has a gun. Or he's a drug dealer."

"I'm trying to do the right thing. I thought you'd give me some support."

"I do support you. That's why I'm telling you straight. I'm not going and I don't think you should either."

I run my hand through my hair. "I have to do

this."

"Okay." She opens the door and the overhead light comes on. "Be careful."

"I will." In the light, the grocery bag catches my eye. The thing is glaring. "Why would Grace want one of these?"

Charlee pauses, her hand on the door. "Having a vibrator isn't a big deal." She pulls the door closed. "Lots of women have them."

"If it isn't a big deal, why keep it a secret?"

"A vibrator is personal. Something a woman may not share with a husband."

"Why would a married woman need one?"

"There are lots of reasons a woman, married or not, would want one."

"Like what?"

"Like. Like self-discovery. Or just for fun. Pleasure, I don't know. Grace must have her reasons and the only way you're going to find out what they are is by asking. You have to talk to her about it anyway, because Gabe took hers to school and that's not something you can ignore."

We hear growling coming from the backseat and we turn and there Hercules is, his pointed teeth sunk deep in Elmer's head, and he's shaking poor Elmer, shaking him like a grizzly bear would.

As I drive, I try to form an image of Ellie in my mind. Her height, build, hair, the way she dresses.

I take off my sunglasses and set them on the dash. In the distance, an angry cloud bank envelops

P-Town. "Looks like rain."

"No big surprise," Charlee says without looking up from her book.

She hasn't been very chatty. She said Michael's note about a last minute business trip wasn't getting to her. I think it is. She flips a page.

The Ellie I finally conjure up in my mind looks more like a mannequin at JC Penney than a real woman. Charlee's right, I don't know her, but I'm a pastor, and knowing her isn't required to help. I reminded Charlee that Jesus helped people he didn't know.

"We're about ten minutes out." I turn on the wipers and pull in the left lane and pass a truck I got stuck in back of as we were coming off the mountain.

Charlee shuts the book. "What a dreary day." She pulls her tablet out from between the seats where Hercules is sitting. He growls under his breath. "You think you're such a big dog," Charlee says.

"Be nice," I say to Hercules and he puts his paw on my leg and looks at me, the pointed ears back slightly, heavy lidded eyes.

"I mapped out her address," Charlee says. "It's in the north end." She reaches over and locks her door.

"I'm glad you changed your mind and came with me."

"Better than sitting home all alone." She stares out the window. "Oh, it's the next exit. How'd the vibrator talk go with Grace?"

"What lane do I need?"

"The right."

"We didn't have the talk, not yet. Grace was late getting home from her meeting and then there was dinner and bed. We were tired. I'll tell her tonight."

"Uh-huh. Take a left at the next light."

The address is a townhouse apartment complex on a busy road with no on-street parking. I park a block north of it, between a car with smashed windows and an empty cab the driver left running. We put up our hoods. It's raining hard now. I put the leash on Hercules and grab my sunglasses.

A woman opens the chained door wide enough to see a slice of her, a bloodshot eyeball, dingy nightgown, toenails painted green. "I'm sick and tired of telling you Jehovah's," she says, "I don't want you coming to my door every Saturday morning. Beat it."

"Wait," I say. She's shutting the door on us. "We're not Jehovah's. We came to see Ellie, does she live here?"

"Are you the police?"

"No. We're friends."

"What's your business with her?"

I introduce me and Charlee without mentioning I'm a pastor. "We came to return her sister's doll."

"Her sister?"

I open my jacket and pull Dolly out. "Yes, I believe the doll belongs to Amelia."

"Wait here." She shuts the door and double bolts, leaving us huddled out here on the porch, a broken slab of concrete overgrown with crabgrass and rain pelting a narrow, cobweb infested gable.

"I wonder who that lovely lady was," Charlee says.

A fire truck blasts its horn and comes around the corner of the Quick Mart next door and Hercules yips and tries to climb up my leg with his muddy paws. The doorknob jiggles and Charlee jabs me in the side. We hear one dead-bolt unlock.

"Lose the sunglasses, you look like a gangster," Charlee says and I pocket them.

She opens the door as far as the chain will allow. She has a nose full of piercings I don't remember, but this is the woman from the police raid.

"Marge said you have Dolly?"

"Yes, Ellie, how are you?" I sound too friendly. I don't see a spark of recognition in her eyes. I take off the hood and hold Dolly up where she can see her. "Agent Mel found her. Do you know Agent Mel?" She says everyone knows Agent Mel. "I'm Noah Cathcart and this is Charlee. I was at the raid on River Street a couple days ago. We met briefly. Mr. Finn was trying to find Dolly."

"How do you know where we live?"

"Mr. Finn said you worked at Cuppa Joes. I went there and asked the owner if he knew how to reach you so I could return Dolly and he gave me this address. He said you were his best barista. He asked me to say hello and tell you he'd give you your job back in a heartbeat."

She pushes the bangs out of her eyes. Eyebrow piercings. "You can tell John I'm not coming back."

Inside, feet are pounding and children are squealing. "Who are you talking to?" a little shrill voice asks. "Who's out there?"

Ellie looks over her shoulder. "Go upstairs, Munchkin, and play with your cousins until I'm finished. Then we'll go get Big Macs."

"I want to know who you're talking to. Is it Daddy?"

"That's enough sass, upstairs with you." The booming voice of the first woman.

"No, Grandma, I don't want to. I don't want to."

"We have the cousins today. It's a circus around here. Amelia will be happy Dolly came home."

"I'm glad. If you decide to come back to Rivers Edge, St Mary's has a room available."

"I said I won't." She unlatches the door and reaches for the doll.

"If you ever need anything, please give me a call. I'm a pastor." I try to give her my business card and she won't take it, but she takes the doll.

"We don't need a pastor."

"Okay. God bless you and Amelia."

A shiny red, double cab, pickup pulls in the yard and stops in the patch of crabgrass lawn.

"You have to go," Ellie says.

We step off the porch and Ellie follows. The door shuts behind her.

A guy with a buzz cut hops out of the truck. Pauses to look us over. I notice a gun rack and rifle in his back window.

"We have company?" the guy asks and saunters over.

"They were just leaving," she says.

"Don't rush off on my account." He dons a baseball cap backwards.

"Daddy!" A little girl darts out of the house, shoves her way past us, and gloms onto his leg. He calls her Munchkin and picks her up and kisses her.

"Who are your friends?" he asks Ellie.

"They're not friends. They were returning Amelia's doll." Ellie holds Dolly up for Amelia to see.

"Dolly, you came home," Amelia cries road squirms out of her dad's arms.

She grabs the doll and kisses it all over the face.

"That's quite a shiner you got there," the guy says to me.

"I got in somebody's way."

"I bet you don't get in their way again." He chuckles. "Thanks for taking the time to bring my daughter's doll back. She's pretty attached to it."

Ellie pulls her sweater together and folds her arms over it. "Tell them thank you, Munchkin."

Amelia hugs Dolly to her chest. "Thank you guy and lady." She leans back into Ellie.

"You're welcome. My name is Noah and this is Charlee. Agent Mel found Dolly."

"I know Agent Mel. He lives in a big box. He's funny. Can we visit him and Mr. Finn, Ellie?"

"No."

Amelia sticks out her bottom lip. "Why not?"

"We're not going back. We're staying right where we are," Ellie says.

"With Daddy?"

"You betcha," her daddy says.

"Yay! This is my Daddy," Amelia says and we shake her daddy's hand.

"I'm also known as Steve. Steve Rawlins, Ellie's husband."

We leave a black veil of rain behind. Open road ahead. Charlee offered to drive home. Hercules is sitting on my lap staring at her, the heavy lidded eyes.

I think of Ellie and Steve standing on the porch as we walked away, his arm slung around her neck, holding Amelia on his hip. I try to remember if Ellie was smiling or not, but I don't recall.

I take off the sunglasses and set them on the dash. "Do you think The Nurse got her facts mixed up and meant Ellie's husband, Steve, abuses them?"

My wimpy car lugs down on the grade and Charlee sighs and moves into the slow lane.

"The Nurse, who by the way isn't a nurse, didn't have the facts. She was wrong about Ellie and Amelia being sisters. She didn't say anything about a husband. What she led you to assume turned out to be completely different."

"But why would Ellie leave home and go to Rivers Edge to live in her car?"

"Maybe she doesn't get along with the grouchy old lady. Maybe she's Ellie's mother-in-law. Wives don't always get along with mother-in-laws. Mine doesn't like me, you know. Living in a car would be a better than living with her."

"I know. I guess Grace doesn't realize how lucky she is not having a mother-in-law to deal with."

"That's for sure." Charlee comes up behind a truck, looks over her shoulder and pulls into the passing lane. The car sputters and she gives it gas.

"Did you think Ellie and Steve seemed tense?" I ask.

"We were strangers intruding on their privacy."

"I thought I was doing the right thing."

"Amelia was happy to see her doll."

"I wish I could have done more. Help Ellie move,

find a better job." Hercules snuggles in the crook of my arm.

"You did what you could. She didn't ask for help. You can't fix her problems. You don't even know what they are."

"I guess God is the only one who can really help her. It's God who heals. It's God who will turn her life around. Not me." I point to my face. "Maybe this is God telling me to help people find Jesus, not jobs and housing."

"God didn't do that to you. The cops did. And God can't fix Ellie's problems either. She can. She's perfectly capable of weighing her options and making her decisions without you or God butting in."

"I'm a pastor. Butting in is what pastors do." Hercules scrambles up my chest to see over the headrest. I make him get in the backseat.

For the next twenty minutes, I listen to him gnaw on his squeaky clown and the engine straining, while I think about Dolly and the raid, the husband and The Nurse and try and figure out where God wants me in all of this.

We reach the summit and Charlee pulls into the wayside.

"You still stop here on your way home from P-Town?" I sit up straighter and stretch.

"Not for years, I'm either in a rush or Michael's driving and he never stops for breaks. I think the last time I was here was with you." She opens her door. "Are you coming?"

The pavement is slick with moss and the forest an umbrella of cedar branches and firs, heavy and dripping. She zips her coat and we walk up a gravelly path to the end. To a high mountain stream and a ledge built out of river rock, the place where we sat dangling our legs while our parents stretched theirs all those years ago.

I sit on the ledge and set Hercules in my lap. "Remember, Charlee, we'd sit right here and peer into the forest looking for shadows that weren't shadows, for two deep-set eyes."

"I remember. Wanting to see Bigfoot and at the same time, scared we would."

She sits beside me and we dangle our legs over the swollen stream raging with early snowmelt.

"Are you listening for the great-horned owl?" I ask.

"Two hoots followed by an eerie quiet means Bigfoot is near, according to the Bigfoot Man. Does he still own the Little Bigfoot Mercantile & Museum?"

"I think he was 100 years old when we were kids. He probably passed a long time ago."

"You're right. I bet he's fishing in high-mountain streams alongside a family of Bigfoot now."

"He did when he was alive."

"So he said." She points to a mossy boulder. "Bigfoot could be standing right there and we wouldn't see him unless he wanted to be seen –"

"Because Bigfoot have magical hypnotic powers."

She hums a bar of the Twilight Zone. "The only way to see Bigfoot is to live by the code. What happened to our Bigfoot Hunter's Journal? Do you have it?" She picks up a stone and throws it in the stream and we don't hear the plop for the roar of rushing water.

"I haven't seen it for years." I pick up a stone and

rub my thumb over the smooth surface. "I haven't been to the wayside since we were kids either. When Grace and I are on the road home from P-Town, Gabe's on our last nerve and nobody feels like stopping then."

She chuckles. "Your mom always called Portland P-Town, like you do, remember?"

My stomach clenches. "Why are you bringing my mother up?"

"I thought of her when I pulled into the wayside. Your dad never wanted to stop here, she made him. Remember?"

"No." I pitch the stone and it bounces off a pine on the other side of the stream.

"You do too remember. The drinking fountain is still here. Did you see it?" I nod and she swings her legs around. "First one there gets the first drink." She darts down the path.

"Hey, I wasn't ready." I put Hercules down. "Let's go, buddy, we can catch her." Me and Hercules veer off the path and cut through a clearing and touch the fountain one second before Charlee.

"Cheater, you didn't stay on the path," she says.

"Me cheater?"

"Yeah, you, and cheating, if you remember is totally against the Bigfoot Hunter's Code."

"You cheated too. You had an unfair advantage. My dog is handicapped. Poor little guy."

We look down and there he is prancing in puddles. We break out laughing.

"I guess that makes us both cheaters," she says.

"Yep, we won't be seeing Bigfoot today."

Water is spilling over the fountain's river rock

sides and splattering our shoes. We lean over the burbling towers and gulp down crisp, mountain cold water and come up gasping.

"Brain freeze." Charlee wipes her mouth on her sleeve. "I don't remember it being this cold."

"Me either."

It isn't long before we're back in town standing on the edge of Charlee's driveway.

I look out over the river, the mountains, forest and ocean. "It feels like the top of the world up here. I never get tired of your view."

"It's always there. We don't even see it anymore. I think Michael is having an affair." She looks at me for a moment. "You look like I slapped you. I think he's had an affair going on for a while, with the ex."

"Why didn't you tell me?"

"I'm telling you now."

Chapter Four

Anthony rocks on his heels and turns one of his massive rings around and around. I'm not sure why he and Mark came to see me. I ask them to sit in the metal chairs in front of my desk and they decline.

"You didn't have to come to my office. I would have met you for coffee."

"No time for coffee. I have to be at work in a few minutes," Anthony says. "Did I ever thank you for helping Mel out? I mean, after what the cops did to you."

"That was over a month ago. You already thanked me."

He points to my face. "I can't even tell you got beat up."

"Do you want another favor?" I ask.

"Yes," Mark says.

"No," Anthony says. He grins and takes Mark's hand. "We came to tell you we're getting married."

"Oh, well, good. I mean congratulations." I shake

Mark's hand, then Anthony's. "I'm happy for you."

"We want to spend the rest of our lives together," Anthony says.

"That's great." I sit on the corner of my desk. "Wonderful news. When's the big day?"

"October 7th, the anniversary of the day we met three years ago," Anthony says and he and Mark linger in the moment.

"We've rented a little community church on the Washington side of the river," Mark says.

"You're having a wedding?"

"Yeah, Bro, didn't you hear? We're getting married. This isn't just some vow exchange where we're presented a pretty license a friend made on his computer. This is the real thing. We'll be just as married as you and Grace."

"Uh-huh." If only he understood the reality of marriage. The point where you've settled in your roles and time starts slowing down. I wonder if I have an obligation to tell him, since I'm his big brother, but I put the thought aside. I haven't told Grace about my pay getting docked, since she didn't notice, and I know I should. I haven't found a good time to confront her about that Golden Bullet that's locked in my desk.

"Noah?" Anthony asks. "If you have a problem with this, just be upfront with it."

"No, I don't, not at all." I smile. "I'm glad you and Mark can get married like everyone else."

"I hoped we could count on your support." Anthony breaks out in smiles. "You're the first we've told. I figure you'll tell Charlee before I get a chance, but I set up a coffee date with her anyway."

"I won't spoil your news," I say.

Anthony cocks his head and narrows his eyes. "Yeah, right."

I probably will tell her, if not in person, over the phone. I've been worried about her since she unloaded her news about Michael's suspicious behavior. I wouldn't be surprised if he turned out to be a philandering husband. I've never liked him. I pray he isn't, for her sake. Betrayal isn't something you come back from or get over. Unless you're Dad.

Anthony checks the time on his phone. "We have to go."

"Isn't there something else?" Mark lays his hand on Anthony's shoulder.

"There's more?" I ask.

Anthony takes in a deep breath and lets it go. "Should we leave out the back door? Last person I want to run into is Dad."

"Aren't you planning on telling him?"

"Why would I? He doesn't want to have anything to do with me until I give up my evil lifestyle."

I wish Anthony was wrong. I sling my arm around his neck. "I'll walk you to the front door."

Anthony was 15 when Dad found him with a guy from Biology class. I remember Dad filled with God's wrath, the fire in his eyes. Anthony left. Dad didn't know where he went. Dad sat me down in his office. I pray you won't disappointment me is what he said.

We stop in the foyer under the painting of Jesus the Shepherd. "Dad doesn't matter," I say. "You and Mark are committed and in love and that's all that's important."

"Absolutely," Mark says. "Our wedding is going to

be grand. Isn't it, Anthony? Why don't you ask Noah now?"

"I was getting around to it." Anthony pushes up his glasses. "We have something to ask you."

"All right."

"Mark and I would like you to be the officiating pastor for our wedding." My mouth falls open and Anthony raises his hand. "We don't want an answer now. Please think it over. You can say no. We don't want to cause you any trouble with Dad or Grace."

"There'd be no hard feelings if you decline. But we'd be honored if you can," Mark says.

I hear Grace in my head – don't ruin it, Noah. I hear Dad – think hard, think very hard.

I think of drowning for all eternity in Satan's frigid bottomless sea.

I clear my throat. "I'll pray about this and give you an answer as soon as I can."

"Take all the time you need, Bro." Anthony zips his leather jacket over the Pooh Bear scrubs.

I want to say yes right now, I'll perform the ceremony, I'd be honored. Instead, I thank them for asking me.

Anthony pulls a hat out of his jacket pocket. "A Chullo hat, handcrafted in Peru out of Alpaca wool, you like it?"

"Yeah, nice hat."

Mark adjusts the flaps so they cover Anthony's ears. "We have a wedding to plan. I don't want you coming down with a cold."

Mark buttons the top button of his flannel shirt and zips his raincoat. "Again, thank you for considering our request."

Mark is shaking my hand when I catch a glimpse of movement. I glance over my shoulder.

Dad.

"I won't keep you guys any longer." I open the door wide. "I'll talk to you soon. Thanks for coming. Goodbye."

They leave without noticing Dad. Thankfully, Dad didn't make a big scene. How could I not have seen him before? The pure white hair. The height. Red tie. Sister Monk, of all people, is with him and she's looking at me like I'm a movie she's about to walk out of.

From my window, I watch Sister Monk drive her Mercedes away. The gold trim winks in the sunshine. Seconds later, Dad's rapping on my door. "I want to see you in my office." He doesn't bother to come in. "Now."

No big surprise.

Dad's hands are locked together and resting on his desk. He tells me to sit. "Your brother plans on marrying that man, does he not?"

"The man's name is Mark Dickerson. And yes, as you overheard, Anthony plans on marrying him."

"Sister Monk was appalled. She wanted to know why my associate pastor, a man of God, would agree to ponder a request to participate in something as blasphemous. Why don't you enlighten me?"

I fold my hands and lean back in the chair.

Dad thumps his knuckles on the Bible. "Pastor Noah, you represent Rolling River Ministries of JE-SUS Church of the Mighty Miracles at all times. I believe we had this discussion after you got yourself arrested. Sister Monk got over it. She's happy with your youth program. Brian and Naomi are growing in Christ. Naomi applied to Oral Roberts University." He bangs his hands down on the desk. "I had the situation smoothed over and now this."

"I've done nothing that Sister Monk should be concerned with."

"Frankly, I'm as concerned as she is, aside from your – Dad doesn't matter – comment, hearing you offering up your complete support to the homosexual lifestyle was disturbing, to say the least."

"Frankly, I didn't know we had an audience. It's Anthony we're talking about. You know, Anthony Cathcart, your son. He and Mark are in love and want to start a life together, not a lifestyle, and yes, I do support them and their commitment to each other, as I would any committed heterosexual couple."

Dad walks around the desk and sits on the edge. "I love Anthony as much as you do and I want him to find happiness."

"Then why are we having this conversation?" I stand and Dad wraps his arm around my shoulders and walks me over to the couch. "We aren't finished."

I'm not as committed as I let on. Anthony and Mark are happy together, I know, but whether marriage between same-sex couples, whoever they are, is an abomination or not, I don't know.

"I don't believe you feel the full weight of your duties as a pastor," Dad says. "It's a pastor's job to reprove ungodliness. Show sinners their misery. Warn those who are walking in slippery places. You want to ignore Anthony's sins because he's your brother and you love him. But Anthony is hanging by a thread over Satan's raging sea and if he doesn't turn his life over to God, snip, he will be lost."

"Anthony doesn't have a sinful bone in his body. Why would God cut him off for wanting to marry the person he loves?"

"A man lying with another man is sinful as you well know, Leviticus 20. One man, one woman, this is the law and God's law is not up for interpretation." He gives me a moment to chime in and agree. When I don't he lets out an exasperated sigh. "Listen to me. I couldn't bear to watch my son, my flesh and blood, fall into the watery depths of Hell. I've been there. I know firsthand. How slippery the docks are. How frigid the water. In Hell you never stop drowning."

My stomach clenches. "I know."

"You would be sorely grieved if this was Anthony's lot. Think about it. Think hard." Dad walks over to his desk and opens the Bible.

Think Noah. He wants me to think back to when he was a sinner. It's all in the story I've heard dozens of times. When the thread he was hanging from snapped and Satan glommed on and swam all the way down to Hell with him. He wants me to remember that Jesus pulled him out. This was the first miracle, the mighty miracle that turned Dad's brown hair white.

Dad clamps his hands over my shoulders. "You must warn Anthony. Tell your brother how close he is to Hell. How there is no return. Call him to his knees. I've tried. Believe me, I have. He'll listen to you. Tell him to repent and ask God for forgiveness. Tell him, make him understand. This is love, Noah.

This is compassion. Only in Jesus will Anthony find true happiness."

I wake up to Grace jabbing me in the arm and Hercules growling at her. She's talking about Bible study. It didn't go well. I feel like I've been asleep for a while. I've sunk deep into the couch cushions. My Bible is lying open on my chest.

She wags her finger at Hercules. "You stop that growling right now, you little monster."

I tell him to stop and he buries his snout behind my back and grumbles. "He's just a little dog. Maybe you could try to be nicer."

She shuts off the TV. "I am nice."

I close the Bible. I don't have an answer for Anthony and Mark, yet. I fell asleep before I found one.

"Did you remember?" Grace is bent over unstrapping her heels and showing white lacy panties.

"What? Did I remember what?"

"Don't tell me you forgot to pick Gabe up."

"Gabe's in bed."

I try shaking off this grogginess. I sit up straighter and my foot bumps the grocery bag.

The vibrator.

"I've never been so humiliated," Grace says.

"Why?"

She puts her hands on her hips. "Tonight the topic at Bible study was my pastor husband who is going to officiate his gay brother's wedding. Everyone was horrified. They all looked at me for an explanation, and you know what, I didn't have one because I didn't know anything about it."

"Who told you?"

"Sister Monk."

"Figures."

"I should have heard it from you. Why didn't you tell me?"

"There was nothing to tell. I said I'd think about officiating, not that I'd do it."

"What's there to think about?"

"He's my brother. Why shouldn't I marry them? They're in love. What's so wrong with it?"

"One man one woman. It's the way it is and you know it."

"What if it isn't the way?"

"God says it is."

Hercules pulls his head out and growls. I tell him to go to bed and he's slow getting off the couch. I stand, stab my finger toward the laundry room where Grace makes him sleep and tell him to go to bed now. One more grumble and he scampers away.

"Look, I said I'd think about it, that's all. Sister Monk blew it all out of proportion. You know how she gossips." I try to embrace Grace. "I'm sorry she ruined your Bible study."

Grace pushes me off.

"Come on. Let's not fight."

"People are still talking about when you went to jail."

"You don't have to listen."

"Yes I do. They talk to me about you. It's embarrassing."

"Embarrassing, huh?" I see the grocery bag on the floor and snap it up. "I'll show you embarrassing."

I take the vibrator out. "This, Grace, is embarrassing. Your Golden Bullet is embarrassing."

"Where did you get that?" she screeches and tries to yank it out of my hand. "How dare you go through my things."

"I didn't go through your things. I didn't know you owned a vibrator until Gabe took it to school for show-and-tell. Yes, you heard right. He told the class it was a Golden Bullet, a secret weapon. He got the secret part right, didn't he?"

"Charlee should have stopped him. What kind of teacher would allow a student to show off a thing like that?"

"We aren't talking about her teaching abilities. We're talking about you leaving this thing out where your son could find it."

"Give it to me." She holds out her hand.

"But you haven't heard the whole story. Gabe turned it on and demonstrated its monster killing abilities. What do you think about that?" Her mouth opens, but no words come out. "A little embarrassing? How do you think I felt when Charlee handed me a grocery bag containing my wife's vibrator? Embarrassed, you think?"

"Give it."

"Not until you tell me why you have it."

"None of your business."

"Charlee said that's what you might say."

She throws her arms up. "I can't believe you talk to her about our intimate lives."

"You mean your intimate life, not ours. Apparently, I'm not good enough for you." I slap the thing in her hand. "You must have missed this. I'll just leave you alone with it."

I grab my coat and get Hercules and his leash. While I'm clipping it on his collar I hear a thump in the stairwell. "Go back to bed, Henry." I look over my shoulder for his snout sticking out between the rails, but Henry isn't there. Gabe is. He's climbing the stairs. He reaches the top and disappears.

Grace touches my shoulder and whispers my name. "Noah? Honey, are you awake?"

Of course I'm awake. I've been lying here on the couch since I got back from the walk thinking about me and her and another Grace I don't know. "What do you want?"

"I want to explain. The vibrator was a Valentine's Day surprise."

"You woke me up to lie to me? Go back to bed. I don't want to talk to you."

She's wrapped in our quilt up to her neck. A bare arm comes out and she sits on the edge of the couch. Lays her hand on my cheek. "I'm not lying. The surprise went all wrong. I'm sorry."

"Gabe heard us arguing."

She sighs and a strand of hair falls out of her ponytail. "You said he was in bed."

"I saw him on the stairs."

"How much did he hear?"

"I don't know."

"I'll try and talk to him in the morning."

"You'd better do more than try."

"All right." She rests her forehead on mine. "I

bought the Golden Bullet online from a Christian sex shop."

"Sex shops aren't Christian."

"This one is." She nudges me. "Scoot over."

"No, you have our bed all to yourself."

"But I want you next to me."

"I'm sleeping on the couch tonight."

"Then so am I." She pokes me until I roll onto my side and she stretches out, her back pressed against my front.

I think of the morning she was dressed in the robe and nothing else. I wonder if she's wearing anything under the quilt.

"The Christian sex shop is called Fire in the Bed."

"Are you kidding me?"

She giggles. "No. That's what it's called. Like the song, Fire in the Blood, you know?"

"I got the reference."

"There's nothing pornographic on their website. It's all about sexual well-being for Christian couples. A fulfilling sex life is part of God's plan."

"I believe the plan you're speaking of includes a husband and a wife, not a wife and a vibrator. We don't need that stuff. We have a fulfilling sex life."

She pulls my arm around her middle. "Between Gabe and church duties, household responsibilities and community outreach, there's little time or energy left for a sex life. Admit it, lately, all we've had is hurry-up sex or we agree to do it later and then we're too tired. I thought adding something fun would spice up our relationship."

"Fun for you."

"No, for us."

"How did you find your online sex shop?"

"Sister Pam sent me a link."

"Sister Pam?" I suppress the urge to laugh. "Are you serious?"

"I know, it's hard to imagine her and Brother Lew doing it at their age."

"What were you doing talking to Sister Pam about our sex life?"

"I wasn't exactly. She and her husband took a sex class for Christian couples in Portland and she told our Bible study group all about it a couple months ago. She said her sex life has been heavenly ever since." Grace giggles. "She said unfulfilled marriages are Satan's playground. Sex toys are all right. God is concerned about our sex life as much as he's concerned about our souls. I bought the vibrator for our marriage, for both of us. When it came in the mail, I opened it to read how it worked. I was going to wrap it for Valentine's Day. But it went missing. I looked all over. I thought it would pop up eventually."

"You were right about that." I press my nose in her hair. I think about it long, not tied, and falling into my face.

"It never crossed my mind that Gabe had the Golden Bullet. I thought Hercules snagged it." She starts laughing. "I looked for it in his bed."

I think of the day she found the bra that went with the red panties in his bed and called him a little pervert. I can't help it. I burst out laughing and she turns and kisses me long and wet and breathy.

"It's after midnight, which means it's officially Valentine's Day," she says. "I bought candles and oil for the occasion. Come upstairs and I'll give you a massage."

She hasn't offered a massage for a long time. She gives the best massages. I think of slipping my hands inside her quilt cocoon. Then I think of the vibrator in the grocery bag. Not knowing she had one.

She swings her legs around and I get a glimpse of bare thigh. She stands over me. "There's one more gift. Would you like it now?"

"I guess."

"You'll like it." She opens the quilt and lets it drop on the floor.

She's wearing the gift. It's tiny and see-through.

"Think you'd like to come to bed now?"

I don't think whether I will or won't. I think past that to when I'm in bed with my beautiful wife and the tiny gift is on the floor.

Chapter Five

I'm nervous about preaching tonight, a bit of stage fright, I think. I've been to the 51st Street Mission before, the one time Anthony brought me, but being a guest pastor is far different than being a guest. I drive past people huddled together in clouds of their own breath waiting in a line that snakes around the block, to the pretty part of the building where I was told to park, in the lot reserved for staff and guests.

Pastor Green meets me at the door and puts a Styrofoam cup of hot coffee in my cold hands. "God bless you for volunteering. I'll show you around and fill you in."

"I didn't volunteer, actually I –"

"We ask our guest pastor to also be a greeter, if you're willing."

"I'm willing." I sip the coffee and burn my tongue.

"Doors open at six, not a minute before or a minute after. The homeless can be a pushy group. You're probably used to standing at Rolling River's door shaking hands and chatting with members of your congregation. Here our greeters are more like shepherds herding people into the chapel, reining in stragglers and those who would rather start a line at the cafeteria than listen to a sermon. To be frank, they come for food, not the word."

"Why not feed them first? It is dinnertime."

"Helping the needy transform their lives is the mission's main objective and that begins with God. The homeless tend to eat and run."

"I see."

"Tell them to park their carts and bags and anything that won't fit in their laps or under the pews over there before they come in the chapel." He points. "A heads up, they don't come bathed and dressed in their Sunday best. Thanks again. I have some business to tend to. Feel free to spend the next half hour in the chapel gathering your thoughts. No one will bother you."

"I'm prepared. I noticed a long line of people waiting outside. I'd be happy to pass out coffee."

"We can't afford to do that on the funds we receive. They're lucky to get one hot meal a day."

"It's awfully cold outside."

"We do what we can."

Pastor Green opens the doors when its time and they pour inside. Naomi looks over at me, the eyes outlined in black. "I've never been around bums before," she whispers. "Mom says not to give them money because they spend it on drugs and alcohol."

I think of The Nurse and the ten dollar flashlight. "Let's not call them bums. They're people like you and me, who are down on their luck."

Naomi volunteering to be one of the greeters took some guts. The rest of my youth group ducked in the chapel saying they'd save a block of seats. She welcomes a couple of men with bedrolls tied on their backs and shakes their grimy hands. I offer an encouraging smile.

"Well, if it isn't Noah Cathcart." Mr. Finn comes inside and shakes my hand. "Anthony said you were preaching tonight."

"Good to see you again, Mr. Finn," I say and he tells me to call him Finn.

"Welcome to the 51st Street Mission," Naomi says and Finn clicks the heels of his polished black dress shoes together and salutes. "Gordon Finley reporting for mess duty." He holds the pose for a moment, then chuckles. "That's military verbiage meaning I came to help serve up tonight's supper. After all the meals I got from this place; I figure I ought to give back."

"Volunteers don't have to wait in line," Naomi says. "They use the front door."

"Nah, this door's just fine. I can wait my turn same as everyone else."

"Oh," Naomi says.

"Do you know this lovely greeter?" Finn asks.

"This is Naomi, from my church, a member of my youth group."

"Naomi Monk, we came to hear Pastor Noah speak." She smoothes her shiny dress.

"About time you took a turn at the pulpit, Pastor," Finn says. "Count me in when it comes time for the altar call."

"Sure. To be honest, Anthony volunteered me."

"Everyone will thank me." Anthony's shrugging out of his coat and Mark is helping. "If not for you, Bro, Pastor Green would be speaking and he's incredibly long winded."

"Since it's Valentine's Day, the topic is love. I could speak for hours about love," I say and Naomi giggles. "Naomi? Have you met my brother?" Her face hardens. Anthony says hello and she says hello.

"Speaking of love," Finn says. "It's in the air tonight, for me and my woman."

"Your woman? Have you been holding out on us?" Anthony slaps Finn across the back. "Give us details. Who is she?"

"Dorothy, you know her from the Seabird Café." Finn is grinning like a kid.

"Are you talking about Dorothy and her dogs?" Anthony asks.

"The one and only."

"Well, my man, you're looking debonair for the lovely, one and only, Dorothy. Love the bowtie."

"Red and white for the occasion," Finn says. "Do you love my new shirt from the Goodwill?" Finn puffs out his chest and points out the words on the pink t-shirt – Make Love Not War.

Anthony whistles. "A peace loving man is a catch for any guy. Or woman."

Finn chuckles. "Did I tell you, unbeknownst to me, Dorothy lives in my building? One day last month, she took her trash out to the dumpster the same time I did and the rest is history."

"Dumpster love, it sounds serious," Mark says

and hums the wedding march.

Finn raises his eyebrows. "Hoo-boy, not so fast, I've been a bachelor longer than you've been alive. Dorothy and me are taking our relationship one day at a time. Tonight we're celebrating the holiday at my place. I bought candles at the Goodwill and I washed the sheets and –"

"TMI, Brother Finn," Anthony says and holds up his hand. "TMI."

We start laughing. Finn's puzzled. Then he sees Dorothy come in and nods in her direction. "Over there's my woman."

A pony-tail is sprouting out of the top of her head. Two tiny dogs peek over the side of her bag and sniff the air. Finn pulls his sagging dingy white socks up to his knees.

"Wish me luck, boys."

We wish him luck and he hurries over to greet her.

"I'm lucky I found my one and only." Mark gives Anthony a squeeze.

I've never seen Anthony as happy as when he is with Mark. Would a loving compassionate God deny these two a life together?

A young man comes up from behind and drapes his arms around them. "I brought the crew." He gestures over his shoulder to several teens.

"Sweet." Anthony turns and high-fives him. "Great turnout Julian. Noah, this is our man in charge, president of the high school's Gay Straight Alliance. The GSA volunteered to serve and clean up tonight."

Julian straightens his thin red tie and shakes my hand. "Your brother talks about you all the time."

"I give him plenty to talk about."

"Oh, it's all cool. Anthony told us the real story behind the picture of you in the paper."

Anthony introduces the others. The turquoise Mohawk is Bobbie. He points out A.J., Tammy, Tyler and Jen who say Anthony is the best advisor the GSA's ever had.

"I'm not surprised," I say and Anthony grins and pushes up his glasses. "He has a knack for recruiting volunteers."

Everyone chuckles, except for Anthony who gets my reference and looks a little bit sheepish. Julian turns to Naomi and asks about a Math test their teacher sprung on them today. Naomi is cold, yet, polite.

Anthony takes me aside. "Sorry Bro, about volunteering you. Honest, it all happened so fast. One minute I was talking to Pastor Green about scheduling the GSA and the next thing I knew I was telling him you'd speak. I owe you one."

"I believe you owe me more than one – so you'd be fine with walking Hercules every morning?"

He laughs. "Yeah right."

"We also need a babysitter once a week, then there's the garage and I'm behind on the yard."

His eyes narrow. "I don't know, actually, I've been pretty busy with work and the wedding and…"

His voice trails off and I shake my head. "You don't owe me. Okay? Just don't volunteer me again."

"Pastor Noah's Ark?" The kid from the police van strides across the lobby waving.

"You know Justice?" Anthony asks.

"Of course the good pastor knows me," Justice

says. "We go way back, right, man?" He's wearing a top hat, a mangy crow pinned on the brim.

"Uh, yeah, way back."

He guffaws. "What brings you to our poverty stricken part of town?"

"I was asked to speak. Did you find a place to live?"

"Hell yeah, I have friends. What do you say; I start the food line to the cafeteria?"

"Sorry, the sermon's first."

"I'm starving, man, and me and you were jail-mates, surely you have an in."

"Pastor Green runs things here, not me."

Anthony invites Justice to sit with them. As they walk away, Justice turns and calls out. "Break a leg, Pastor Noah's Ark."

"Pastor Noah's Ark?" Naomi asks and I nod. "My mom's going to be pissed off, oh sorry Pastor, I mean mad, about them coming."

"Who?"

"The GSA."

Anthony told me about Sister Monk's campaign to run the GSA out of the high school. "I'm sorry she feels that way. The mission is open to all."

"But they're gay. You know?"

"Gay or straight, it doesn't matter. We're all made in God's image."

"That's not what Mom says."

I want to say how ignorant her mom is.

"She said you were going to perform the gay mar-riage of your brother."

I start to correct her – I only agreed to think about it. But that would make me the ignorant one, since I just finished telling her gay or straight doesn't matter.

"We're all human," I say. "We're people. People fall in love. People get married."

Dinah comes out of the chapel holding a baby. "Isn't she cute?" she asks.

"Yeah, cute kid," I say.

"Where'd you get that baby?" Naomi asks. The baby holds out a slobbery hand and Naomi steps back out of reach.

"I told her mom, Dawn, how much I love babies and we got to talking." Dinah wipes off the baby's hand and dabs at her chin. "Matilda, this is Matilda, was fussing. I offered to hold her and Dawn let me, and Matilda, she'll be one year old next week, stopped crying, just like that. She likes me, I have a way with babies and someday I'll have lots of them. Don't worry, I'll get married first, Pastor Noah."

"Glad to hear."

I always imagined Grace and I would have two or three kids, a girl would be nice. Until after Gabe came along and Grace said, no more, no way. The topic isn't up for discussion.

"Dawn lives in a shelter for single moms," Dinah says. "Matilda, there's your mommy over there. See? She's looking for you." Dinah waves Matilda's hand up and down and a girl who doesn't look any older than Dinah smiles. "I'd better get you back to Mommy. Is it all right if I sit with them?" She tickles Matilda and both start giggling.

"Of course it's all right."

"My mom wants lots of grandbabies," Naomi says and makes a sour face. "She's got my life planned out." Naomi directs a woman to park her cart with the others. "Mom insists that I'm going to Oral Roberts University, the same college my whole family has gone to. Find a worthy man with a good work ethic, marry him and pop out babies. The end."

"The end?"

"It has been the plan my whole life."

"Is it what you want?"

"I don't know. Does it really matter?" She scowls. "I'm going in." She takes a bottle of hand sanitizer out of her purse and squirts a dollop in her palm. "See you inside."

I think of God's plan for me. How I have no say in it. How Dad won't let me forget it.

Pastor Green asks if I'll check outside for stragglers and meet him in the chapel. I say I will and I turn and there's Ellie and Amelia. Amelia with Dolly hugged tight to her chest. The door shuts behind them. Ellie unzips Amelia's coat and holds Dolly while Amelia slips out of it. "I remember this place," Amelia says. "Do you think we're having hamburgers for dinner?"

"I don't know. We won't find out until after the –"

"God talk." Amelia slumps and sticks out her tongue.

"Those are the rules, Munchkin. Let's go inside." Ellie reaches for Amelia's hand and they see me standing here, like a creepy stalker.

"I know you." Amelia runs over. "Dolly says thank you for saving her life."

"I'm glad she found her way back to you."

It's been over a month since Charlee and I went to P-Town. I didn't think I'd ever see Ellie again. I haven't thought about her much.

"I'm the one giving the God talk tonight," I say.

"You really are a pastor," Ellie says.

"Yes, I am, and tonight, I'm a guest speaker here, but normally, I'm Associate Pastor of Rolling River Ministries." She takes her phone out of her pocket while I'm talking and looks at it. I turn to Amelia. "I saw some red and pink frosted cupcakes in the kitchen."

"Pink is Dolly's favorite cupcake color."

"We'll see what we can do to get Dolly a pink one."

"Really?" she asks and I say I'll do my best.

"The room at St Mary's was still available." Ellie drops the phone back in her pocket. "John gave me my old job back. Maybe things will work out this time. No one's ever gone out of their way like you did to help us." She hugs me.

"Guess what?" Amelia asks.

"I don't know," I say. "Why don't you tell me?"

"My daddy went to jail."

"Oh. I'm sorry." I glance over at Ellie and she sighs.

"Amelia, we've discussed what's okay to share and what's not, have you forgotten?"

"No." She looks down at her feet.

"Kids," Ellie says.

"Yeah, kids. If you'd ever like to talk, my door's open."

"I don't need to unload on a pastor."

"There you are, Pastor." Finn walks out of the chapel. "Oh my heavens, Miss Amelia is that really you or am I dreaming?"

"I'm not a dream girl. See?" Amelia dances circles in front of Finn. "I'm a real girl."

"No question about it." Finn laughs. "You're the real Amelia deal. I'm so glad to see you two." Finn gives Amelia and Ellie a hug. "Come sit with us. Me and Dorothy will make you room. We got the primo pew in the front. When the altar call comes, I'll be first up."

"First or last, it's all the same with God," I say.

"At my age, I have a lot of sinning to make up for and I sure as hell, oh pardon my French, don't want to end up in Hell with Old Scratch as my taskmaster."

"Is Hell in France?" Amelia asks.

Finn laughs. "Oh no, honey, Hell isn't anywhere near France, Hell is – down there." He points and Amelia eyes the threadbare carpet.

"Did I mention that I got a girlfriend while you were gone?" Finn asks as they're walking into the chapel. I hear Finn mention the dumpster and Amelia's singsong voice. "Mr. Finn has a girlfriend. Mr. Finn has a girlfriend."

The chapel is full. Backpacks are crammed under chairs. People are hacking and blowing their noses. The kids in my youth group are sitting shoulder to shoulder. Naomi's red dress marks the spot. When I pass, they break into polite laughter, if you call laughing at your pastor polite, and lean into one another. Have they pranked me again?

The pulpit is defined with pink and white streamers. I don't see anything odd. Pastor Green calls me up to the stage and invites me to sit beside him. He offers the invocation. While he prays, I remember a few of their pranks; the caramel onion they said was an apple, the donuts filled with mayo, and my desk filled with cheese puffs, some of their better ones. I'll be watchful tonight.

We're invited to sing, *Love Lifted Me*, number 142 in the hymnbook, a perfect lead-in for my sermon. Anthony and Mark belt out the lyrics. "When nothing else could help, love lifted me."

After the song, Pastor Green invites me to the pulpit. I look out over all the faces. Grace's isn't one of them. I thought she'd skip her meeting to come hear me speak. I wanted to take her out to a late candlelight dinner after, but she said we celebrated last night and she had business.

Justice gives me a thumbs up and I smile and say I'm grateful to be here. A woman in a puffy red coat shouts out amen. "Amen, Sister," I say and she grins. No teeth. I open my bag and take out my Bible. Pink and red construction paper hearts are taped all over the front and the back. Each heart has a message. Surprise is written on one, this is not a prank on another. And we love you Pastor Noah. So this is what they were up to. I touch the hearts and start tearing up. Naomi waves her fingers. I raise the Bible over my head and shout out, "The power of love is in this book."

I've talked for 20 minutes about love. Love as the center of the gospel of Jesus Christ. Love for one another. The greatest love of all, Jesus died that we might live. The four chapel walls are bare except for a black and white framed print of Jesus Knocking. I refer to it and most don't look.

I invited the straggler I found sitting on the ground under the cross that's lit up on the side of the building, Jesus Saves, it says, to come inside and he wouldn't. He believes in science, when you're dead you're worm food and that's all you are, and the only reason he was here was because it was slow today on the corner of Golden and Vine and he has found, if he waits outside the mission at dinnertime, someone usually brings him out a plate. I said I'd make sure he got a meal.

The aroma of cafeteria food has permeated the chapel. They've heard enough from me. "The power of love is in you." I close my Bible and the pianist starts playing *Just as I Am.*

Finn's ready to come forward and repent. I give the word and he'll spring to his feet.

"…though tossed about with many a conflict, many a doubt, fightings and fears within, without. Oh Lamb of God, I come."

Everyone expects the altar call. The pianist glances over her shoulder for my cue.

Dad starts with a favorite line – when you see Jesus coming out of the clouds, it's too late. I've used it. I know what I'm supposed to say – we're living in the dark end days. Jesus is on His way. He'll come when you least expect. He'll scoop up the righteous and hold them safe in the cup of His hand while He calls forth a tsunami, one the likes you've never seen, and unleashes it upon the world. For sinners, it's a one-way wave to Hell. You don't want to be on it.

This feels like the wrong thing to say.

Telling the old man in the back row who's wearing a Burger King Crown that Satan keeps his flock immersed in his frigid bottomless sea feels wrong.

Finn teeters on the edge of the pew. Call him to his knees, it's what he wants. He'll come. He'll come out of fear. Fear of God's vengeance. Fear he'll never measure up. Fear of the tsunami, of the devil and his frigid bottomless sea. The pianist clears her throat and I ask her to continue playing.

There is no fear in love. It says so right in the Bible. He that fears is not made perfect in love. I touch the paper hearts. God is love is written on one of them, Jesus loves you on another.

I think of the man outside waiting for a meal. The University of Oregon sweatshirt, the tiny round glasses and earmuffs. Before I came inside, I asked what his name was and he lifted one earmuff and asked if I'd repeat myself and I did. No one ever asks my name, he said, but it's Samuel Jackson, not to be confused with Samuel L. Jackson, the actor. He acted in a commercial for dog food a long time ago. He played the part of the vet. Maybe I'd seen it, he asked, and I said maybe I had.

The pianist is clearing her throat again. I hold up my hand and ask her to stop playing. "Thank you, Sister. We're going to do something different tonight."

I hop off the stage, rather than take the steps, there are only three. I'm reminded of Dad all riled up and red faced hollering for his flock to repent now or face the devil in hell. Dad comes down off Rolling River's stage and our bones rattle.

My bones are rattling right now with anticipation. We're going to do something different. "Brothers and

Sisters, there will be no altar call tonight."

I wait for God to strike me down.

He doesn't. I take a breath. "That's right. You heard me. There will be no confessing, no repenting or begging of forgiveness tonight. You're wondering why not. Has Pastor Noah gone off the deep end or what? Stay with me. I'm going to tell you like it is. You're already saved. You're saved by the grace of God."

The power in my voice startles me. I stop to let what I said soak in. I glance over at Pastor Green and he raises his eyebrows. I try not to think about Dad.

"Grace is a gift. This is important. I want you all to understand. Jesus paid the price. You can't earn grace, you can't pay Jesus back. Grace is non-returnable. Jesus gave it to everyone. He gave it to you and you and you. He gave the gift of grace to every single one of us."

"Amen, Brother," the toothless woman shouts.

"Amen," I say. "This is what God wants you to do. It's a simple thing, really. He wants you to stop worrying about getting to heaven. He wants you to stop worrying about going to hell."

"But we'll sin." Brian Monk stands. "Everyone sins and sinners aren't welcome in heaven. We do have to worry about repenting. It's the only way in."

"Everyone sins, you're right, Brian. We try to do better and we sin again. It goes on like this for a lifetime. We're human. God made us this way. We can't stop sinning. Thank God, He has unconditional love for each and every one of us. He will never stop loving you and there's nothing you can do that will change that. God is here tonight and he's asking you to accept his love. Accept it and start loving more. Love yourselves better. Love others better. Who can do this?" A few hands go up.

I pluck the heart off my Bible that says Jesus is Love. "Who wrote this? Jesus is love. Who wrote it?"

Brian raises his hand without raising his arm. I walk over, take his hand and bring him up front.

"Jesus is love, you know it, Brother. Jesus is all about love." I clap Brian across the back. "The way of love is the way of Christ. Remember this. Love is in you Brian." He mumbles and makes a move to return to his seat. "You're not going anywhere just yet," I say and the girls giggle.

"Love is in everyone," I say and look out over the congregation. Anthony grins. "There are no exceptions. This is what I want you to do, Brian. Find one person here that you don't know. Ask their name, tell them yours. Welcome them and bring them up here. Can you do this?"

He thinks about it. Then he walks up on the stage and comes down with Pastor Green. They catch on fast. Pastor Green goes after Dorothy and her dogs, Amelia and Ellie. Amelia brings Finn and goes back for more. She skips through the chapel swinging her arms. Dinah and Matilda and Dawn come up. Dawn brings the toothless woman, Ali's her name, and she brings Justice. Justice with the top hat cradled in his arm. Justice brings Naomi and Naomi brings Jen and Tyler and Tyler brings Mark and it isn't long before I can't tell who is bringing who.

I have to smile. Tonight couldn't have gone better. The spirit stayed with us through dinner. People lingered. I took a plate out to Samuel Jackson, but he was gone. I looked around and couldn't find him. I came in the chapel to pick up my things and Pastor Green followed. He thanked me for the sermon, however unconventional. People need positive affirmation too, he said. They need connection.

I put on my coat and check around the pulpit to see if I left anything. I pick up my bag and walk down the steps.

Anthony walks in grinning. "I just saw A.J. and Julian and Naomi and Brian leaving."

"So?"

"So they were leaving together and they were talking like regular teenagers."

"That's good." I pick up a hot pink baby hat someone left behind in the pew.

"Oh my God, Noah, they would hardly look at each other before the service. You shined tonight. Congratulations. You made a difference."

"Thanks, Bro. God was here. No doubt about it. He filled me with His spirit and I knew what to do and I knew what to say. His love entered into every heart that was here tonight."

"Your message of love hit home. You made a difference. Come on. Own it Noah. You left out Dad's hate and said what was in your heart."

"You found my kid's hat. What a relief, course it's the last place I looked." Dawn, Dinah's new friend, walks in and takes the hat out of my hand. Her baby's on her shoulder snoring under a blanket. "I got all the way home without the damn thing. That'd be my dumb luck, having to pay out for a winter hat when there's only a month of winter left."

"I'm glad it's found. God bless you and your little girl."

"There's more. I should a told you this right after your talk, but I got all stupid and me and my kid went home after we ate. So, see, I left the church I grew up in, after I got pregnant and my pastor tried to pray the devil out of me. There's nothing evil about my baby." The baby whimpers and Dawn rocks her. "I'll never go back to that place. I'm between checks or I wouldn't a been here tonight either, but I came to feed the kid, you know, not listen to the God blah-blah by some geezer pastor who's all judging on me because I'm 15 and have a kid. Maybe you're new or something, but you're different."

"I'm glad you got something out of the service." I give her my card. "In case you ever want to talk."

She shoves it in her back pocket without looking at it and leaves.

Anthony is grinning. "What?" I ask.

"What did I tell you? You made a difference."

"Pastor Green asked me back."

"That's great news." We bump fists. "When you announced there'd be no alter call, I thought his eyes were going to pop out." Anthony snorts and we both start laughing.

Mark walks in. "Ready to go?"

"If you two could stay for minute," I say, "I've made a decision."

Marrying Anthony and Mark is the right thing to do. Love was the answer. I have God on board now. If I needed confirmation, it came when Mark hugged me right off the ground, when Anthony broke out bawling.

I zip my coat. "I'll walk you guys out."

"No, wait," Anthony says and looks over at Mark. Mark raises an eyebrow.

"There's something I have to tell you. I've been waiting for a good time. This seems as good as any, especially after your sermon about love being in everyone. Maybe you should sit down." He gestures toward the pew.

No one is ever asked to sit down for good news. "Can it wait? I have to pick Gabe up at Charlee's."

He glances over at Mark who has made himself comfortable a few pews back. He has his phone out and he's scrolling.

That was selfish of me. Not wanting the news. Not wanting to end the night on a bad note.

"I found Mom," Anthony blurts out and looks at me over his glasses.

They're words, just words, three words that don't make any sense.

"Noah?"

"You found our mother?"

"Yes."

"No. You're wrong. She wasn't lost. That woman left us and she has been silent for the last 25 years."

He twists that big ring of his around and around. "We've been talking online for a few months now. She found me."

"Online?"

"Yes."

"No one online is real." I'm relieved. He's wrong and I'm relieved. "Our mother didn't find you. No one is who they say they are online; you should be internet savvy enough to know that."

"She has a profile with pictures."

"She left when you were three. You've never seen her picture. You have no idea what she looked like then or what she looks like now. The pictures you're looking at could be anybody."

"She told me stories about us."

"That's what online predators do. They pretend they're someone else. They post false information."

"I'm not stupid. I know what catfishing is. And I know this isn't the case. Mom sent me this from Peru." He tugs on the alpaca hat he wears every day.

"You gave out your home address? How old are you? Even Gabe knows not to give out personal information."

"Don't insult me. I'm not an eight year old. I found Mom. She's real and I have proof."

He takes my hand and slaps a picture in it.

"I suppose you got this off her profile?"

"Will you shut up and look at it? She sent the picture with the hat."

The picture is wrinkled. Years of handling has made it soft and the edges fuzzy. I turn it over. There's a woman, sunglasses resting on top of her head, and with her is a little boy. He can't be more than three. They're squatting beside a drinking fountain made of river rock. Heads close together, they're examining a mossy stick. I feel Anthony breathing over my shoulder. I look up and he doesn't leave. There's an older boy in the picture, ten years old, a girl the same age and they're pressed against the fountain standing on their toes, drinking from two burbling towers.

Chapter Six

Iscoop up a raggedy Doug Fir cone and toss it into the churchyard. "Go get it, boy." Hercules flashes me the eyes, the eyelashes, and goes back to drilling his way between me and Charlee.

"Impressive," she says.

I chuckle. "We're working on that one."

We've been sitting on the steps for a while. The church is locked. Anthony and Mark are running late. So is their wedding planner.

"It's pretty up here," I say.

"The view is incredible. The wildest part of the river, the coastline goes on and on."

We gaze out over brackish water heaving and churning and thick with herring. A mess of gulls are circling and vying for fish.

"Think they're late because a car stalled on the bridge?" Charlee asks.

"Or Anthony's just late." I push Hercules away, tell him to lie down and he doesn't.

"The churchyard could use some work before the

wedding, don't you think?"

Patches of tulips, brilliant red and wide-open, are growing out of the tall weeds. The white picket fence is peeling and weathered and so are the steps.

"There's plenty of time. The wedding isn't for months."

A car comes around the bend and slows for the sharp curve.

"Remember me talking about Sister Monk?" I ask.

"The old biddy?"

"I don't remember calling her that. Anyway, remember how she pulled Naomi and Brian out of my youth group?"

"Because you're participating in a gay wedding and turning her children gay, yeah, that was a couple months ago."

"Now she told Dad she's going to lead a protest at the wedding."

"How Christian of her."

"Dad told me to pull out of the wedding and threatened if I don't, I'll face serious repercussions."

"Like what?"

"He didn't go into them."

"He's just bullying you."

I lean into my hands. "I know."

"You're not pulling out, are you?"

"I said I'd marry them didn't I?" I sound angry, but I'm not, not at her. "Don't mention the protest to Anthony, okay?"

"Okay." She rubs her hand up and down my back.

"I keep thinking Dad will come around."

"He won't."

We're quiet for a while. I scoot over and Hercules sits his bottom down between us.

"You know how I've been speaking at the 51st Street Mission on Saturday nights?"

"Yes. Saturday is the mission's biggest night of the week because of you."

"It's because of God, not me."

"No it's not, it's because of you."

"God. They're going to close the mission on weekends due to lack of funding."

"That's too bad."

Hercules presses his head in the palm of her hand and she scratches behind his ear.

"Pastor Green felt bad about it. He said the Saturday night goers were beginning to forge a community. So he went to the board and got authorization to start a small outreach. He made a deal with the owner of the empty building over on River Street; you know where the bicycle shop used to be, to use it on Sundays for free, until the owner fills the space."

"The building next door to the strip club?"

"It's the building on the corner, across the street, not next door. Pastor Green asked me to preach there."

"For free?"

"Yeah, I don't care about the money."

"You said you'd do it?"

I break out smiling. "I said I would, in the afternoon between Rolling River's services. So what do you think?"

"I think you're going to like having your own congregation. Congratulations. I'm excited for you."

A Subaru neither of us recognizes pulls into the

gravel parking lot. "Must be the wedding planner," I say and we stand. "I'm glad you're excited. Does that mean you'll come?"

"To church?"

"Yeah."

"Pfft – no."

We're laughing when Mark and a woman climb out of the car, look up here and wave.

The woman extends her hand. "I'm Mari Yew, Mark and Anthony's wedding planner. You must be Noah and Charlee. It's always a pleasure to meet the family."

We say it's nice to meet her and I ask Mark where Anthony is.

"I don't know." Mark is scrolling and doesn't look up from his phone. "He should be here by now."

"I know. I know." Mari raises her hand to get our attention and the tweed coat she's wearing draped over her shoulders slips off one side. "You're wondering if Mari Yew is my real name." She tugs the coat back to where it was.

"No messages or missed calls," Mark says.

"Everyone asks," Mari says. "Mari Yew is indeed my real name, I swear." She chuckles. "I'll let you in on a little secret. I started my wedding planning business straight out of college, eight years ago, before I met and married the man of my dreams, Phillip Yew. Yes, Yew is my married name and no, don't get the wrong idea, I didn't marry him for his name, but let me tell you, after I became a Yew, my business skyrocketed. I have to turn couples away."

"Anthony said they were lucky to get you," Charlee says.

"A mutual friend referred them. This is my first gay men's wedding. I'm excited. Mark and Anthony are a lovely couple."

"Mari and I have been at Bard's all morning making catering arrangements," Mark says. "Anthony was supposed to meet us here at the church after work. I'm a little worried."

"He's just fine," Mari says. "My sister works in a hospital and she rarely leaves on time. You can't just drop your patient when your shift's over. I won't start without him. Isn't this a beautiful chapel? Do you know its history? Don't answer Mark, I know you do."

I saw a plaque in the parking lot, a brief history etched on it, but I didn't bother to read it. Charlee and I shake our heads.

"It's quite fascinating. The chapel was built over a hundred years ago by Jesuits. It's unfortunate; however, that they built this peaceful unassuming chapel in an area called Cape Disappointment and with such a lovely view of the Graveyard of the Pacific. The chapel was never used for weddings, can you blame them, until the county purchased it ten years ago and started renting it out for joyous occasions. I don't normally share the disappointment or death piece of history with my clients since it's rather glum and some would consider it an omen. I say phooey on superstitious nonsense. The location is apropos in Mark and Anthony's case, since the Graveyard of the Pacific, ironically, brought the boys together." Mari grins at Mark and he nods. "Mark told me the whole story. I'm sure you know it." We nod. "His job as a River Bar Pilot is a dangerous one, as we are all aware, and we're very grateful Mark didn't end up buried in the great Pacific. But we are happy he was admitted to the hospital with a few non-life threatening boo-boos after an unfortunate accident, since that's where the love of his life was waiting." Mari checks her watch. "Mark, why don't you try calling Anthony again?" Mark jogs down the steps to make the call. "I couldn't help but notice your ring, Charlee. Exquisite. Wedding ring, I assume?"

Charlee checks her finger. "Yeah, I'm married."

"Tell me how you and your husband met, if you don't mind, it's a little thing I ask everyone I meet."

"There's not much to the story." Charlee stares at her feet.

"Don't be shy, there's always a story."

Charlee looks up frowning. "My dad used to sell insurance, if you remember Radcliff Insurance that was across the street from McDonalds?" Mari nods. "When Michael moved to Rivers Edge he bought business insurance from Dad. Dad got to know him, asked me and him out to lunch and introduced us over Big Macs."

"Would you like fries with that?" Mari chuckles and Charlee doesn't. "Oh forgive me, funny how those catch phrases stick. Winning the father's approval early on is an excellent way to begin a courtship with his daughter, and that's a fact."

"Dad approved of Michael's business sense and stability and that's a fact. We got married a month after we met and that's about it."

Mari clasps her hands together. "Sounds to me

like love at first sight. Those marriages always survive, contrary to popular belief." Charlee looks over at me and I offer a sympathetic look and Mari goes on. "The little spark that ignited when they met ends up burning hot for a lifetime. Did you have a big wedding?"

"No. We got married at the courthouse. Noah, on the other hand, had a mega-wedding."

"How lovely, you went all out," Mari says.

"No, Grace went all out, not me," I say. "She and her sisters planned the whole thing."

"All Noah had to do was show up," Charlee says.

"I like to see the bride and the groom, or in Mark and Anthony's case, the groom and the groom, plan their wedding together," Mari says. "Along with them, I try to bring in as much of the family who would like to participate. You know what they say, the family who toils never foils."

"Is that what they say?" Charlee asks and Mari says it is indeed.

"Anthony was terribly disappointed that your parents, Charlee, won't be able to make it to the wedding."

"They've been in Budapest the last two years working in a Christian outreach."

"Anthony told me all about them. I hope I can meet Mr. and Mrs. Radcliff someday, may I call them Samuel and Twila?"

"Call them what you want," Charlee says.

"If you ask me, they're saints. Anthony told me how they got him off the street and gave him a home when he wasn't welcome in his own. How they helped send him to nursing school. It's not easy raising a troubled teen, I know. Twila may not be Anthony's mom by blood, but she's mom where it counts." Mari thunks herself on the chest over her heart. Then she touches my sleeve. "Anthony said your boy is eight. How long have you and your wife been married?"

"Going on ten years."

"Ten years is longer than most make it these days. Congratulations. How did you meet?"

"We met in college. She was a senior, a TA in the music department, and I was an incoming freshman."

"Ah, so she's older?"

"Only three years."

"I'm always surprised how many men marry older women."

"Three years isn't that much older."

"At the end of his freshman year, Noah married the – Pinup Girl of Pastors' Wives," Charlee says and smirks.

"Aren't you a lucky man?" Mari says and I agree. "Personally," she says, "I believe beauty only runs skin deep. I must say, I do admire those who marry in college and have the wherewithal to stick it out and finish their degrees."

"Grace finished and we came home to do the Lord's work here in Rolling River Ministries," I say.

"Oh, that's too bad. These days, more and more older adults go back to school to finish what they started. Maybe you will too."

"Soon, I will have a church to run and I won't have time for anything else."

"Noah doesn't need a degree," Charlee says, the same smirk. "He got what he wanted from college."

"Anthony is on his way," Mark says. He's jogging

up the steps looking relieved.

"What held him up?" I ask.

"I don't know. He sounded rushed and said he'd explain when he got here. It was kind of weird, but I'm glad he's okay."

"Mystery solved," Mari says and starts unlocking the chapel. Inside, she brings out a tablet and stylus. "First on the agenda, the churchyard. I've got a call in to the county, Mark, don't you worry, the grounds will be a marvelous sight to behold come wedding time, I'll see to it. We'll have some lovely fall color that time of year." She leads Mark over to the window.

"Anthony asked if I'd suggest music for the ceremony," I say. Charlee and I walk to the front of the chapel with Hercules prancing between us. "What do you think about Pachelbel's Canon for the procession?" I open the piano and plunk on it.

"That was the music at your wedding."

"Yeah, I guess it was." Hercules is whining. I pick him up and he plops his chin down on my arm.

"I think they should have a quartet perform the Canon like you and Grace did."

I think back. "I don't remember that."

"Grace's nieces, the oldest was on cello and the triplets on violins?"

I nod. I vaguely remember. "I was pretty nervous that day."

"Uh-huh, a little more than nervous, if I recall."

"Everyone has cold feet before the wedding, right?"

"Is that what it was?"

"God told Grace we were meant to be together."

"But He didn't tell you."

"Telling her was enough for me."

Hercules flies out of my arms and zips down the aisle barking, his toenails tic-tic-tic on the wooden floor. I go after him and pick him up the same time the church doors open and Anthony walks in, followed by a woman. The woman removes her sunglasses.

She walked right out of Anthony's picture, except her clothes are different and her face is tanned. She turns to me and smiles. She says my name. Noah. Her voice is tender. I step back and Hercules growls.

The day she left comes to mind. Dad and Charlee's parents whispering in the kitchen. Me and Charlee in our pajamas all day, eating leftover cake for breakfast. Anthony's wet stinking diaper. Your mother went on a trip is what Dad told me. She is coming back.

Charlee steps in beside me and loops her arm through mine. The woman brushes a strand of hair off her cheek and calls Charlee by name. I know her voice. She read to us every day, back then, Winnie the Pooh and Captain Hook. The Legend of Sasquatch.

She left a note. I found it months after she wrote it, wrinkled and smeared, in Dad's bible. I remember taking the note and hiding it in my Math book. I thought I was going to Hell for stealing. I read the note to Charlee. It didn't say much. Not a clue to my mother's goings-on or whereabouts, only instructions to look after the children. Anthony and I were the children. Why. Everyone asked why. Why God. Why now. Why would a mother leave her children?

"Why are you here?" I ask and she starts to answer, but I turn to Anthony. "How could you invite that woman?"

"I didn't," he says.

"I wasn't invited," my mother says. "I flew in from Peru yesterday and –"

I stab my finger toward her. "You've been silent for the last 25 years. No one wants to hear from you now."

"I came home from work and she was there. I was as surprised as you," Anthony says.

"I can't believe you, Anthony. She wouldn't be here if you hadn't been talking to her online. I have to get out of here."

Mari Yew steps in front of the doors before I get to them and belts out the kind of whistle that stops taxis and calls home the dogs. Her fingers slide out of her mouth and she uses them to signal timeout. "Let's take a little breather, folks."

My mother steps forward. "You don't have to leave, Noah. I will."

Mari Yew doesn't budge.

I think of Anthony's picture. In it, he's wearing plaid shorts and canvas shoes, glasses bigger than his face, and he's looking up at this woman like she's his world. Was she thinking of leaving then? Was her plan already in motion?

"Thank you, folks." Mari turns her palms up and raises them as she inhales.

Charlee's mom tried her best to cut our mother out of all the Radcliff's and Cathcart's photos, but the one survived. It has haunted me since the day Anthony slapped it in my hand.

Palms down and Mari exhales and grins. "We're in a better place now." She makes a sweeping gesture toward Mark. "I have to say, you're marrying into a truly remarkable family and I'm not being facetious here, I mean it, this is a high spirited, good hearted bunch. You're a lucky man."

He agrees and winks at Anthony and of course, Anthony breaks into smiles.

"The experts are absolutely right when they say getting married can stir up the dregs at the bottom of the old emotional kettle." Mari nods and Charlee rolls her eyes. "So family, listen up. In October, Anthony and Mark will be walking down this aisle to pledge a lifetime of love to one other. This will be a glorious day." Anthony is tearing up. "Save that for the wedding. This is what I need from all of you. Put aside your disputes, whatever they are, they'll keep, believe me. We have wedding plans to finalize. Before we get started, I need some helpers. First and foremost, I need two grooms. Any takers?" Anthony and Mark chuckle and step forward holding hands. Mari taps Charlee on the shoulder. "You be an attendant. Now we need a preacher. Is there a preacher in the house?" She turns on her heel and points to me. "You'll do."

"I said I have to go."

"Look, Pastor, you can do what you want, but it would mean the world to your brother if you stayed. Our planning session will take 30 minutes max. Anyone can be civil for 30 minutes, don't you agree?" She folds her arms and nods once. "All right, then. Anthony, I haven't had the pleasure of meeting this lovely woman you came with."

Anthony's eyes slide over to me and I look away.

"This is Libby Cathcart. My mom, our mom," Anthony says.

Mari welcomes her like they're old friends.

"I have something I'd like to say," our mother says. "If you don't mind, I won't take much of your time." Mari asks her to please go on. "Noah, you have every right to hate me. I hurt you, I know. I hurt all of you. I didn't come here to redeem myself. I'm not exactly sure why I came, to tell you the truth. But I'm grateful for this opportunity to see my children grown up and happy and beautiful." She claps her hands together and takes a moment to gaze upon each one of us. "That aside, I'm going to wait in the car. Noah you don't have to leave. Anthony, don't blame your brother. He's in your corner. Blame me. It's my blame."

I'm down on one knee tying Hercules to a pew. Mari and the grooms went downstairs without me and Charlee.

Charlee lays a hand over my shoulder and crouches beside me. "You okay?"

"Yeah." I wipe my eyes. "I lost it."

"No one blames you."

"I'm a pastor. I should at least be civil."

"You're Noah James Cathcart. Your mom left you when you were a little boy."

"I feel like a horrible person."

"You feel how you feel."

I clear my throat. "She used to say that."

"Oh. I didn't remember."

"I remember so much right now that I don't want to remember."

"I know."

"Should I go out to the car and get her?"

She shakes her head. "No."

"All those years we waited for her to come back."

"I know."

"I guess we'd better join the planning session, if Anthony wants me there."

"When you're ready."

We stay crouched in the aisle for a while. Hercules looks at me, then Charlee and back to me.

They don't see us coming down the stairs. Mark is pointing. "We were thinking the band could set up over there. We need plenty of room for dancing."

Anthony's head moves up and down and Mari makes notes with her stylus.

"Country, a little soft rock, some folk, the Rivertown Boy Band is the best," Anthony says. "We'll dance until the wee hours, right, Mark?"

"I plan on dancing a lifetime with you," Mark says and winks and Mari breaks into syrupy babble.

We come off the stairs and Anthony turns. The mushy grin disappears and he fiddles with one of his rings.

"I'll leave if you want," I say.

"No, don't. Thank you both for staying."

Mari gives us each a checklist and stubby pencil. "Make notes. As I was saying, the Rivertown Boy Band took some finagling to book."

"We'd like the food over here, several long tables heaped with it." Anthony walks back and forth in the space and Mark writes on his checklist.

"Are you absolutely sure about salmon fish and chips?" Mari asks and turns to me and Charlee. "I've tried talking the boys out of it. Steaks would be a classier choice, and more manly."

"We're still on with the salmon, right, Mark?" Anthony asks.

"You bet we are. It's Bard's specialty, rated number one on the west coast five years straight. And we want an open bar."

"Which we could all use about now," Mari says and we chuckle politely. "You might want to think about putting a limit on the bar. You never know how much booze family and friends can put away until you have an open bar."

Mark and Anthony have a conference and turn around smiling. "This is our first and last wedding and we're going to celebrate big-time so the open bar stays," Mark says and high-fives Anthony.

Mari claps and hoots. "What a party. Let's move on to décor, my favorite part of a wedding." She looks up at the ceiling. "Imagine a clear crisp night in October and the sky is a blanket of twinkling stars. Look, there's the big dipper. And over there is Orion." She gazes into her imaginary night-sky ceiling. "Beautiful, isn't it?" We nod. "Now imagine an old growth forest under that sky." She makes a sweeping gesture. "Intimate seating, the tables covered with a deep earthy brown, candles burning bright and all the flowers are white, think of it, white flowers all around, there's alabaster amaryllis, calla lilies and orchids, clusters of baby's breath and lily of the valley. Think accents of purple iris, pink anemone, and dark eyes' fuchsia. Can you see it?" Mari takes in a deep breath. "Can you smell it?" We nod. "As long as this meets everyone's approval, we'll move upstairs to go over the wedding ceremony. It will be lovely, not a dry eye in the house, I promise you that." She brings us into a group hug. "This is going to be the wedding of the year."

Chapter Seven

She slipped in after I started the service. Red poncho, jeans, boots. We are a work in progress is what I was telling the congregation when the door opened and the bell, a remnant of the bicycle shop, jangled. She sat behind two burly bikers and disappeared from my sight.

I want to tell her to get out, but of course, I can't. I look down at my notes and they're in a language I can't read. This is my third Sunday preaching for River Street, that's what we call the outreach, and attendance has doubled. I won't let them down.

"No one is perfect," I say and some cock their heads, others lean forward a bit. "Uh, Brothers and Sisters, all God asks of us is to love each other better." I start choking up. I'm not sure why, if it's God touching my heart or the sight of that woman. She should have turned around that first day and flown back to where she came from.

A flash of red and my head snaps around and I see one of the bikers, a red bandana covering his head, whispering to the other. Anthony turns and looks over his shoulder and then he shoots me a look like – what's going on, as if he doesn't know what's going on.

I close my eyes and try to remember where I was in my sermon. Hercules noses my leg and when I glance down, he scurries back to his blanket and lies down.

Anthony encouraged our mother to stay. Her plans didn't extend past the year she spent in Peru. She didn't have anywhere else to be. I told him to tell her to stay away from me and my family. But Grace has been asking about her. She says talk to your mother. She won't let up and we argue.

I called on God to give me the words and I talked for 30 minutes. I don't know what I said. After the closing prayer, I look for her. I don't know why. I see a big red bow tied in Amelia's hair. I see Finn's red and white kilt. I step off the platform and walk toward the back checking every row. I stop next to the row the bikers were sitting in. Empty. The row behind it is empty.

Anthony grabs my arm from behind. "What happened up there?" He sweeps his hand toward the makeshift pulpit. "You were fine and then all the sudden, you weren't."

"She came to the service."

"Who came?"

"After I made it clear that I didn't want to have anything to do with her, you went and invited her."

"Mom was here?"

"You knew she was coming."

"I did not. What did she say?"

"Nothing."

"Why would she come and say nothing? Where did she sit?"

"In the back." I glance around. I see Justice. I see people I don't know. I don't see her.

"If it really was Mom you saw, I can't keep her away from you. If you don't want to see her, you tell her. She rented a room on the top floor of the Sears building."

"I said I don't want to have anything to do with her."

I need some air. I pick up the brick I use to prop open the door and put it in place and stand just outside. As people leave, I thank them for coming. I thank the woman with no teeth. I try to remember her name. I can't and she's gone before I think to ask. The sun is bright, but it's deceiving, the breeze cuts through my clothes.

People leave in spurts. I try to remember to ask for their names. Brad strides past. He talked to me at length last Sunday. He looks older than a teenager, sunken cheeks and puffy eyes.

The guy wearing the Burger King crown, Jim, stops to tell me he's moving in with his daughter in St. Louis this week. He told me the same thing last week and the week before.

"I came late and stood in the back." Mark says as he and Anthony are leaving. "I didn't see your mom anywhere."

The two bikers reach around to shake my hand. "Thank you Pastor, we enjoyed your sermon." I invite them to come next week and notice neither is wearing a red bandana.

"She was wearing a red poncho," I say. Mark considers this for a moment, then says he didn't see anyone wearing a red poncho.

"Are you sure it was Mom?" Anthony asks.

I watch Anthony and Mark walk to their car. I believe Anthony. He didn't invite our mother. I don't know why she came or if she came at all.

"You're nothing like your father." A woman wearing a floppy pink hat is standing in front of me.

"Do I know you?"

"We haven't met. My name's Annabelle. Your dad and I go way back." The wind gusts and she checks her hat. "I enjoyed your sermon."

"Thank you. You're speaking of Paul Cathcart?"

"Yes, the one and only. We were close back in the day."

Anthony beeps his horn as he pulls away from the curb and I raise my hand.

"We were drinking buddies and we, well, like I said, we were close. Good Lord, that was 36 years ago, before I went into a 12 step program and before Paul went into the river and came out a high and mighty preacher." Annabelle touches her cheek and chuckles. "Oh my, Paul was quite a storyteller. His wicked blue beast story, Satan and the sea lions – all alcoholic induced hallucinations, obviously, yet, look at all the people he convinced they were true."

"Dad's ministry has touched the lives and souls of thousands."

"Well, more power to him." She rears back her head and laughs and starts coughing.

Annabelle's wrong. Dad's conversion wasn't a hallucination. Jesus pulled Dad out of the river. Go forth and build my kingdom is what Jesus said and the mighty Columbia began to churn and boil and the water turned a brilliant red and Jesus walked out onto it, as if it were a carpet unfurled.

"Don't ever start smoking," Annabelle says and wads a Kleenex up in her hand. "Like I was saying, only Paul could build himself a lucrative business out of nothing but a story."

"My father's stories are true."

She smiles and nods. "Of course you believe your father. You grew up with his stories." She starts hacking again and steps aside.

"Can I get you some water?" I ask and she shakes her head.

Every member of Rolling River knows Dad was a vile sinner. They know the story by heart. The before and the after. They know Dad was given the call. It was Dad God wanted. This was Dad's conversion, the great and mighty change, the backbone of Rolling River, the story that turns hearts with every telling.

"Hoo-boy, a stupendous sermon today," Finn says. He and Dorothy, the bag of dogs slung over her shoulder, squint and shade their eyes.

"Thanks, Brother. You're being kind."

"I am? Well, thank you for saying so. Uh-huh. Did you notice inside? Lots of people stuck around to visit. Me and Dorothy have to get the dogs home or we would have stayed longer." He shoots Dorothy a look of disapproval. "Me and her like what you're doing here with the outreach. Ellie was telling us she thinks she can get her boss to donate sandwiches once a month."

"That would be great. God is at work. We're becoming a community."

I see Ellie inside helping Justice put chairs away. They're laughing about something. Amelia, the red bow undone, is running circles around Hercules. Ellie turns her head and sees me looking in and smiles. I look away. I didn't mean to stare.

"I was saying to Dorothy this building makes a fine meeting place," Finn says. "It's a little dingy though. Don't you think it would be nice if we spruced it up? Maybe we can get a crew together to paint. I'm handy with a paintbrush."

"I'm not sure how much we can do. We only have the space until the owner finds a paying tenant."

Annabelle, who has been standing off to the side listening, clears her throat. "Mr. Finn, sprucing up this place is a brilliant idea. You should do it."

"I don't know the owner," I say. "But I can talk to Pastor Green and see if he can set it up."

"I own this building as well as Annabelle's," Annabelle says.

"You own – this building?" I gesture toward the brick façade.

"I sure do, Paul and I may have gone in far different directions, but we did well for ourselves. A nice looking joint might help get it leased quicker. If you want to get a painting crew together, I'll pitch in the paint. I have a ton of odds and ends in the basement. I'll help too. I can wield a paintbrush as well as old Mr. Finn here." She pinches his cheek. "You haven't been over to Annabelle's for a while, you'll have to drop by and see us real soon."

"Maybe I will one of these days." Finn grins and his cheeks turn the color of his shirt.

"Pastor Noah may say God loves you no matter what you do," Dorothy says. "But I'm not God, Mr. Finn." She glares at him. "The dogs and I are ready to go."

"I haven't been to the nudie bar since we started dating. You know I wouldn't go back. I was just being polite." Finn kisses at her, but she has turned her back on him and she's walking away. He hurries to catch up.

Annabelle laughs a throaty laugh. "Women don't like me much. But their men keep coming. I should be going. Please do forgive my reminiscing. I'm glad to have met you. You don't have the stories like your dad, but it seems you put your heart into it and you're doing an important work."

"Thanks," I say.

She runs her finger along my jaw. "I was wrong saying you weren't anything like your dad. You have his good looks."

Her finger stops on my chin. She smiles and I step back.

"Goodbye, Pastor Cathcart. I wish you the best with your endeavor." She crosses the street and waves.

In Dad's conversion story, Annabelle doesn't have a name. She's a harlot, an agent of the Devil. And now I'm preaching in her building. Dad isn't going to like this one bit. He says Satan lurks in the shallows waiting for the foolish ones, who walk on the edges of docks or play on the rocks or riverbanks, to slip or trip or get pushed and go in. I can hear Dad now. Don't go near the water, Noah.

Amelia smacks me in the chest with Dolly. "Dolly thinks Hercules is funny. He gave her a kiss on the mouth."

I remember the teeth marks Hercules left in Elmer. Grace didn't bother to mend him, but Gabe still packs him around. She found Elmer in Gabe's backpack last week.

"Tell Dolly to watch out, Hercules likes to chew up things." I remove the brick and the door shuts behind us.

Ellie is putting the last chair away. "All done." She's grinning. "I'm glad you talked me into coming on Sundays. Me and Munchkin feel at home here."

"I'm glad. You've been a great help today. Where'd Justice go?"

"I don't know. He left out the back. Did I say how much we like Saint Mary's? The nuns don't ask questions. They give Amelia little things to do to help out. Hanging out with nuns, who would've guessed, but what the hell, right? John gave me more hours at the coffee shop and he helped me get on at the Chowder House working weekends. You know what? I think we're going to be all right."

"I know you are."

She pulls the bill of her cap around and there's Chowder House's happy lobster, a toothy grin and his eyeballs about to pop out. "Let's go Munchkin."

"I have to say goodbye to Hercules." Amelia hugs him around the neck.

"I'm leaving now, are you coming?"

"I have to say goodbye to Pastor Noah."

She turns my hand palm up and slaps it. "Good." She slaps it again harder. "Bye."

I hold the door for Ellie and she kisses me on the cheek.

Chapter Eight

A burst of laughter, the buzz of voices, and the warm greasy smell of fried chicken welcomes me home. Henry trots out and noses my leg.

I hear Gabe snort and giggle. "This is so, so cool."

I don't recall Grace mentioning company coming for dinner. I put Hercules down and set my bag on the couch.

"I'm home."

"In the kitchen," Grace answers.

"Sounds like a party in there," I say to Henry and ruffle his fur.

Hercules is tearing around in circles chasing the ends of the bow Amelia tied around his neck after church, a blue and white one she brought especially for him. She sure lit up when the Chowder House delivered clam chowder and bags of rolls before the service today. She asked if we could eat before the God talk. I thought of the mission's objective – helping the needy transform their lives and decided a full belly comes first and we ate. Some left after lunch like

Pastor Green said they would, but most stayed for the sermon.

Lord. You're working miracles in River Street.

Gabe clomps in wearing bright green boots and a red knitted hat that's resting just above his eyebrows. His face is flushed, a grin stretched from one ear to the other. "She's so cool." He grabs onto my coat sleeve and tugs. "Come on, she's in the dining room with Mom."

"Who is? Who's cool?" I take off my jacket.

"I have the greatest idea. She could come to show and tell – she climbed Mt. Andy, you know, all the way to the top and she's older than you are and nobody at school ever climbed Mt. Andy, I'm pretty sure. At the top of the mountain, it's like outer space, she said so, and you can't be rowdy and run around because you'll puke and llamas spit, did you know that? She had one called Rosy who wore a red hat with one white flower in it, not a real flower, of course. Rosy carried her supplies around for her, a llama would be so cool, it would carry my backpack to school, can I get one, please, and Dad, Dad, look, she gave me this cool hat made out of an alpaca." He points to the hat and skips ahead.

The hat is like Anthony's, except for the color. "Wait, who gave that to you?"

I come around the corner and Gabe makes a sweeping gesture toward the dining room chair with a red poncho draped over the back.

"Grandma Libby did, Grandma gave me the hat," Gabe says and it slips down over his eyes.

❁

The table is covered with pictures and papers and maps that are open. Gabe picks up one of the maps and the thing is bigger than he is. "Look at all the places Grandma Libby's been."

"Hello Noah," she says.

Gabe steps in front of her and holds up the map. "In Peru, she helped kids who didn't have houses and lived in the street. I know where Peru is. See." He points and the map folds up on itself.

"Let me help." She takes one side.

"Right here," he says and stabs the map with his finger. "Peru is here and a long, long way away is Rivers Edge. Grandma Libby showed me."

I feel my head move up and down. "Why did you come to my house?" I ask.

"I invited her." Grace takes my coat and hangs it over a chair. Slips her arm around my back and mashes up beside me. "Don't you think it's interesting that your mom worked with the homeless, same as you? Why don't you sit down with us? I'll pour you a cup of coffee."

"We need to talk," I whisper.

She whispers back. "We don't have anything to talk about."

"If you two would like to take a moment? Gabe and I have plenty of pictures to look through."

Gabe is leaning on his fist picking through the piles.

"We don't need a moment," Grace says. "We're fine. As I was saying, I wanted to meet your mom. She has been in town for a month, one month Noah, and since you hadn't introduced me to her, I decided to introduce myself." She offers me a pointed look.

"Family is so important."

"Is this a real snake?" Gabe waves one of the pictures in my mother's face.

"Oh, yes, it's real, all right, a real anaconda." She taps it with a fingernail. "This one was the biggest I'd ever seen, about 40 feet long and 500 pounds."

"Wow. That's as much as Mr. King weighs."

"Gabriel James," Grace says. "It's rude to comment about someone's weight."

"Mr. King is still the principal?" my mother asks and Grace says he is. "Your mom's absolutely right, Gabe, how much someone weighs is a touchy subject and one best left alone. It must be hard to imagine though, just how big 500 pounds is until you come face to face with one of these giants." She tosses the picture back into the pile. Lays her hand on Gabe's head and looks him up and down. "I'd say it would take about ten of you put together, to come close to that weight."

"Really? Cool." Gabe goes back to looking at the pictures.

"I want our son to know his grandmother," Grace says. "As you can see, they've hit it off."

"We have indeed," she says and Gabe points to another picture.

"Do you know your mother lives in a room over Sears?" Grace asks.

"Yes. I'm the one who told you."

"A room no bigger than our laundry room, a room with no running water or bathroom. She uses a shared facility at the end of the hall."

"Oh, for heaven sake," my mother says. "I've lived in places that didn't have a facility at all. Having clean running water and an indoor toilet is a luxury most people in the world don't have."

"Then where do they poop?" Gabe asks and she sits him down on her knee and starts explaining.

Grace whispers out of the corner of her mouth that she smelled urine in the stairwell and saw rat droppings right outside the door to my mother's room – emphasis on the word mother. I whisper back that my mother chose to stay in town and she's free to leave whenever she wants.

"Grace told me you're involved with the mission's outreach." My mother is half looking up, half listening to Gabe's running commentary.

"That's right."

"Dad got beat up and went to jail, isn't that cool?"

"Getting arrested isn't cool," I say.

"I would venture to guess there's more to the story." She chuckles. "I remember a time when your dad was your age and Mr. King called saying Noah had been in a fight."

Gabe's eyes grow two sizes. "But Dad, you said Jesus never punched anyone and we shouldn't either."

"I meant it. I didn't punch anyone. It wasn't a real fight."

"If memory serves me," my mother says. "You stepped in as a peacemaker to stop a band of bullies who were beating up some scrawny kid."

"If memory serves me, I was the scrawny kid they were beating up."

She takes a moment to think about that. "Well, I remember one way and you remember another. That's the funny thing about memory, with each remembering it takes a twist or turn and comes out as a brand new memory. That seems to be the nature of memory, don't you agree?"

"I've never thought of it like that before," Grace says.

"My memories are quite clear," I say.

"Dad, Dad, did you know Grandma Libby built a school?" Gabe asks.

"I didn't do it by myself," she says. "That was several years ago, in Thailand."

"That's not all she did," Gabe says.

"I think we've talked enough about me." She starts sorting the pictures into piles. "You have such a lovely family, Noah. Thank you for having me over, Grace."

"Grandma Libby, you can stay for dinner and tell us more stories."

I shake my head. "She can't stay."

Gabe narrows his eyes. "Why not?"

"Because. Because, we have to eat fast and get back to Rolling River for evening services."

"We have time," Grace says. "Dinner's ready and there's plenty of it. All we have to do is set the table. I think it would be wonderful if you stayed, Libby."

"I should be going," she says and I agree.

"No," Gabe screeches. He's getting puffed up and red faced. "I don't want her to go."

"That's enough," I say, sharp enough that he stops, folds his arms and pouts.

"It just so happens that I have a previous dinner engagement and I do have to leave." She slips the poncho over her head and slings a big purse over her shoulder.

"Then come back after you're engaged," Gabe

says.

She chuckles. "You'll be sound asleep by then and I'll be back in my own room getting ready for bed."

"But there's rats in her room," Gabe says in a loud whisper. "Please, Dad, don't make her go back to the rats. You can stay with us, Grandma Libby. Coraline scares all our rats away."

Grace's face sours. "We don't have rats here."

"She can't stay with us. We don't have any room," I say.

"Yes we do," Gabe says. "We have a bedroom nobody uses."

"It's not a bedroom, it's full of boxes."

"There's a bed under the boxes, I've seen it. I'll move all the boxes out after school tomorrow and tonight, Grandma Libby can sleep on our couch, as long as you aren't sleeping on it, Dad."

"Don't be silly." Grace's voice is pinched. "We use the couch for sitting, not sleeping." Both she and I scowl at Gabe.

"But I've seen Dad sleeping on it."

"You know what, Gabe?" My mother lays her hands over his shoulders. "When your dad was a little boy, he was a problem solver just like you."

Chapter Nine

Grace wipes her hands on the seat of her pants. "I planted all the red here." She sweeps her hand over the dahlia beds the length of the fence line. White stakes mark each tuber. "Come late August, we'll have a lush carpet of reds, oranges, yellows, purples and whites."

"A showcase garden, people will be coming to our door asking to see it."

She breaks into smiles. "The reds are my favorite. This is called One Love." She squats next to a stake and shows me the picture on the tag. "The bloom is a true red."

"Uh-huh. I see."

"Your mom suggested planting blocks of color for a bold statement."

"My mother was over again?"

"Yes, your mother has been over several times. She has a fine aesthetic sense. In Peru, she worked with artisans from the poorest regions to bring them a fair living wage, did you know that?"

"No I did not know that. Apparently her world adventures weren't anything to phone home about."

She frowns, rights one of the stakes and pats the dirt around it. "Gabe's crazy about her and she's crazy about him. I think it took a lot of courage to come back and reconnect with a family who is bitter and unforgiving."

"You don't know her."

"Neither do you." She picks up the gloves she left on the fence and shoves them into her back pocket. "Did you know she received an eviction notice yesterday and has less than a week to move?" She picks up the shovel and starts walking toward the shed.

"Does this mean she's going back to wherever she came from?"

Grace glances over her shoulder and scowls. "She doesn't have a permanent residence to go home to and you know it."

"Does she want to move in with us?"

"She didn't ask."

"Good." I catch up and hold the shed door open. "Then why are you telling me?"

"Because you're her son." She pushes past me and heads toward the house.

"Oh come on, Grace, we've been through this."

"I thought I married a man who had a compassionate and loving heart."

The backdoor flies open and Gabe marches out. "Are you fighting again?"

"We aren't fighting," Grace says. "And Noah, we aren't finished discussing your mother, who will be homeless soon." She shoves me and Gabe aside and goes in.

"Dad, Dad, why is Mom always mad at you?"

"She isn't."

"James said when he's in his backyard, he hears you fighting with Mom."

"James?"

"He lives over there." Gabe points across the yard.

"That's just great."

I find Grace in the kitchen scrubbing her hands up to her elbows. She doesn't look up. "I'm going to invite your mom to stay in our spare room."

"Yippee!" Gabe says. "Grandma Libby's moving in."

"No she's not," I say.

"But Mom said," Gabe whines.

"Go play video games while I talk to Mom," I say.

"I can't."

"Why not?"

"Because the Lord of the Undead ripped out my heart and hurled it into outer space. It was epic. Then an evil monkey swooped in and ate it. I didn't have any lives left so I quit."

"What are you doing playing a violent game like that?" I ask.

Grace is drying her hands. "Is it the game you borrowed from James?" Gabe nods. "You told me it was about the Lord and about angels and prayer."

"It is. I wasn't lying. In the game you pray and if you give the angel your gold she will protect you and then the Lord of the Undead –"

"All right, that's enough." I throw up my hands. "Give the game back to James and no more borrowing."

"Mom said it was okay."

"Well it isn't. Grace, he's only eight years old. You're his mother, you should have reviewed it."

She chucks the towel down on the counter and comes over and stabs me in the chest with her finger. "You're his father. You could have reviewed it."

"Can Grandma Libby stay, Mom, can she, huh?"

"Go to your room," Grace and I say in unison.

"That's no fair. I didn't do anything." Gabe bursts into tears and stomps up the stairs. He stops at the top and peers down. "I hate you! I hate you both! I'm gonna run away and live with Grandma Libby in South Carolina. She's nice and fun and she never yells at me for no reason." His door slams and my bones rattle. Grace and I look at each other.

"South Carolina?" I ask and Grace shrugs.

"As I was saying, I'm going to invite –"

"No you're not."

"You're a hypocrite." She stabs me with her finger again. "What about grace? What about unconditional love and helping the homeless? It's all talk, isn't it? You'd deny your own mom shelter. Honor thy mother, Pastor Noah." She whirls around and stomps up the stairs, stops at the top and peers down. "I'm inviting her, whether you like it or not, because it's the right thing to do."

Gabe lugs a box out of the spare bedroom and Grace follows with the vacuum. She rolls it into the laundry room where Hercules is napping and when he wakes up barking at her, she yells at him to shut it.

Gabe sees he has caught my eye and he clomps

over to the dining room table where I've been reading for an hour.

"This is the last box." Gabe's sporting a grin as big as his face.

"So there was a bed under all those boxes," I say and Gabe nods and giggles. For the last week, he and Grace have been cleaning out the room. My mother is in it now unpacking.

"There are pictures of you in here." Gabe points with his head to the words on the side of the box and I see, in Grace's pretty handwriting – Noah's Pictures.

"I hope they aren't embarrassing baby pictures," I say and Gabe laughs.

"Noah's dog sleeps in the laundry room." Grace is standing in the doorway of the spare room telling my mother. "He's a surly little dog." Grace goes inside and now I can't hear what they're saying. I imagine my mother telling Grace a story about the time she trained dogs in the circus. She and Grace have been non-stop talking since Grace arrived with her and her belongings an hour ago.

"Mom said me and Grandma Libby can look at the pictures while Mom finishes dinner. Come on Dad. You can look at them too."

"I'm studying."

His smile disappears. "Okay." He trudges into the living room.

Coraline hops on the table and head-butts me on the chin. I shut my Bible. So it's not exactly true that I'm studying. When I open my Bible I hear Grace calling me a hypocrite. I shut it and I can still hear her.

I shoo Coraline off the table and notice a pink

scrap of paper stuck to my sleeve. I pick off one of those construction paper hearts I keep finding from when I preached on Valentine's Day. I turn it over in my hand – the way of love is the way of Christ.

Dad says my mother has forsaken Christ's love and now she's back with her smiles and her sensibilities and charitable works, but she belongs to the devil, the conniving beast. It's too late for her. Dad warned me. If I'm not watchful, she will drag me and my family down to hell. In hell you never stop drowning. Dad keeps telling me. Don't go near the river.

Grace peeks into a pot on the back burner. "Your mom's going to be out any minute now." She wags her finger. "You be nice."

Love is in everyone. There are no exceptions. My words, but the thing is, when I look my mother in the face, I don't feel love, not in her and not in me. I don't feel anything nice.

"Did you hear me?" Grace asks.

"Yes."

"Dinner smells wonderful." My mother walks in smiling and offers to help.

"You make yourself at home tonight," Grace says and stirs whatever is in the pot. "Gabe's in the living room with a box of family pictures he wants you to see. You and Noah have time to look at them while I finish dinner."

My mother's face lights up.

I open my Bible. Every verse is fuzzy. I squint, but it doesn't help.

"We're so happy you agreed to stay with us, aren't we Noah?" I look over my Bible and there Grace is, hands folded, eyebrows peaked and her head moving up and down. Up and down.

I look at my mother, a bright colored blouse, a ring on every finger, a smile as big as her face.

"Grandma Libby!" Gabe, minus the rain boots, runs into the kitchen sock-footed and slides to a stop. "I've been waiting a jillion billion hours for you."

"Oh my, that's a long time to wait."

"Uh-huh." He grabs her hand and pulls. "Come on. First we'll look at pictures, then we'll eat dinner and you can sit next to me, of course, and after dinner you can tell me another story."

"Don't be bossing your grandma, young man," Grace says.

"He's excited," my mother says and chuckles. "To tell you the truth, so am I."

"After the story," Gabe continues, "I have to go to bed and you get to tuck me in, Grandma Libby."

"No, I do that," I say with a force that surprises me.

Grace bangs a lid down on the stovetop. "What is the matter with you?" She sounds like she's scolding Gabe, but she's looking directly at me.

What I said isn't even true. I could count on one hand the number of times I've tucked Gabe in. It's what Grace does.

"We have a bedtime routine. We can't just change it."

She cocks her head and plants her hands on her hips.

"Tell you what, Gabe," my mother says. "I'll tell you a story, but I'll leave it to your dad to tuck you in."

"No, I want you to put me to bed." Gabe folds his

hands. "Just this once, Dad, please, please, please let Grandma Libby do it."

I remember her putting me to bed. It was her, never Dad. She tucked me in. Told the story, pulled the covers up to my neck, kissed me and turned off the light. Said goodnight and see you in the morning.

"Just this once –" Grace is saying.

The night before my mother left was no different. The light, the kiss, the see you in the morning, except she knew she wouldn't.

"Just this once won't hurt." Grace is holding onto my wrist. "Don't you think?"

"Does it matter what I think?" I turn to my mother. "For someone who didn't want a family, you have certainly won over mine."

"No-ah!" Grace says.

"It's all right," my mother says. "You feel how you feel, don't you? As soon as I find another place to stay, I'll leave."

"Nooo!" Gabe screeches. "You can't go now, Grandma Libby. I just got to know you."

I toss the ball into the basket and Henry trots over to Grace and sits at her feet panting. I hang my coat. "Fog's so thick I couldn't see over the fence." I blow into my hands and rub them together.

She doesn't look up from the salad she's making. "She's your mother." She chops fast and furious. "Gabe's grandmother."

"I know who she is. Why don't you give me a break, I needed to get out."

"What you need is to deal with this."

"You put me in a bad spot."

"I would appreciate it if you'd tell them dinner will be ready in five."

I find them sitting cross-legged on the floor in front of the fireplace, a fire my mother must have built. They're looking at pictures, laughing and chatting, their movements relaxed and their faces shiny. They don't see me come in.

"Is this Dad?" Gabe asks and my mother leans over and checks out the picture.

"Yes, this is Noah and Charlee's 8th birthday. See the banner on the wall?" She lays her hand on Gabe's head. "Oh my, you look just like your dad did."

"But Dad said you left when he was a kid. How do you know about the picture?"

"I was still here when this was taken. That's how I know. See, Gabe, I left like he said, but not until he was ten."

"Is that when you stopped loving Dad?"

"Oh, honey." She shakes her head. "I never stopped loving him."

"Then why did you leave?"

"Your Grandpa Paul and I didn't see eye-to-eye on most things. He wasn't happy. I wasn't and our unhappiness made Noah and Anthony unhappy too. So I left."

"Was Dad happy after that?"

She touches the picture and sighs. "I don't think so."

"Dad still isn't happy."

"He isn't?"

Gabe shakes his head.

Watching his head shake brings tears to my eyes. I squeeze them shut.

"Are you crying, Grandma Libby?"

I open my eyes and see Gabe craning his neck trying to get an up close look at her face.

"Oh no. I got the fire too hot." She swipes her palms over her eyes and smiles. "Let's scoot back a bit." She moves and drags the box with her.

"Dinner's in five." My voice is gravelly. I clear my throat as they're turning.

Gabe's face lights up and he waves the picture over his head. "Come see what we found."

I hesitate, but Gabe's arm waving with such passion gets my legs moving. I walk around the couch and squat beside him.

"Grandma Libby says you look just like me. Is it true?"

I study the picture. The walls of the house I grew up in, the banner my mother made, my family, their faces, Charlee and me. I look into my son's face and see my eight year old toothy grin, my wide open eyes. "She's right about that; you do."

He stabs my picture face with his finger. "Why are you smiling?"

"Uh – because it's my birthday?"

"But Grandma Libby said you were unhappy and people who are unhappy don't smile."

"I don't remember being unhappy," I say to my mother and Gabe shoves a different picture into my hands.

"Look. Somebody got cut out of this one." He holds it up to his eyeball and peers through the hole. "Did you cut somebody out, Dad?"

"No."

It's my mother, who has been removed, thanks to Twila's chop job, a ragged cutout and my mother's all gone, except for the shoes in this one. "Let's put these away. It's dinner time."

"Look." Gabe is studying the picture. "Everyone is here, except for Grandma Libby." He pokes his finger through the hole. "Grandma Libby, did the shoes in this picture belong to you?"

She takes his wrist and levers his hand with the picture ring on it closer. "Oh, yes, I believe they were mine."

"Did you cut Grandma Libby out because you were unhappy, Dad?"

"No. I mean, I didn't cut her out. I wasn't unhappy. Can we just go to dinner?" I stand. "Please?"

"Yes, of course, we don't want dinner getting cold." She unfolds out of her cross-legged position and I offer my hand.

She takes it and rises. "Oh my, your hands are much larger than I remember." She giggles.

"This is so cool." Gabe is pulling a book out of the picture box.

"What do you have there?" I ask.

He springs to his feet laughing and plummets backwards into the couch cushions, the book hugged tight to his chest. "I can't wait to show this to my class." He holds it high over his head for us to see.

On the cover is a sketch of Bigfoot I drew when I was his age. Charlee printed Top Secret across Bigfoot's belly. I reach for the book and Gabe opens it and starts reading.

– Bigfoot Hunter's Journal, property of Charlee

Radcliff and Noah Cathcart, Bigfoot Hunters.

"Bigfoot Hunters? Really? Dad, that's so cool. You never said you and Aunt Charlee-Ms. Radcliff were Bigfoot Hunters."

"We weren't, we were just kids."

He turns the page and reads.

– Bigfoot Hunters Forever

"It says right here that you and Ms. Radcliff-Aunt Charlee are real Bigfoot Hunters. Can I be a Bigfoot Hunter too?"

"No." My face is heating up.

"Please, pretty please, I want to be a Bigfoot Hunter too."

"We aren't Bigfoot Hunters. Now hand over the book." He doesn't.

He gasps. "Listen to this."

– Bigfoot Hunter's Code: Number 1

He looks up at me, his mouth gaping open. "You had a top secret code, that's so so cool." He goes back to reading.

–Number 1: Only the Pure in Heart Will See Bigfoot

"Did you see Bigfoot?"

"No," I say.

"You must not have been pure in your heart or you would have seen him, it says so right here." He points. "What's pure in your heart mean?"

My mother laughs. "I remember you and Charlee asking me the same question, Noah."

"Did you know they're Bigfoot Hunters?" Gabe asks.

"No, I believe this is their secret." She takes the journal out of Gabe's hands and gives it to me.

I tell Gabe the journal is private. It isn't his to look at. I tell him and my mother to go to dinner and I'll be right there. I turn the book over in my hands. The red is fading. The picture is smeary. I haven't seen this thing since we were kids. I flip a few pages.

"Noah, what are you doing? Dinner's getting cold," Grace calls.

"I'm coming." I slip our journal back in the box, under the pictures and put the lid on.

Gabe talked about Bigfoot all through dinner. Grace told him Charlee and I were kids pretending, but we grew up and we know Bigfoot isn't real.

After dinner, Gabe drags my mother to the couch. "Now it's time for the story." He plops beside her and she wraps her arm around him.

"Isn't this nice, spending the evening with family?" Grace interlocks her fingers with mine and walks me over to the loveseat. "We don't do enough of it these days, do we?"

I look at her. The expectant eyes, the words playing on her lips – Noah, you have to deal with this.

"We do enough," I say.

Grace frowns.

"Well, then, you asked what pure in heart means, Gabe," my mother says. "I'm going to tell you the story I told your Dad and Charlee when they asked."

"You can remember that long ago?" Gabe asks.

"It wasn't that long ago," I say.

My mother chuckles. "The story I'm thinking of happened a long, long time ago, in ancient Egypt, there was a goddess named Ma'at."

"Was she God's wife?" Gabe asks.

"God wasn't married," Grace says. "And He tells

us all we need to know about the pure in heart in the Bible – Blessed are the pure in heart: for they shall see God. Matthew 5."

"Your mom's right," my mother says. "The Bible does indeed say that. In the story, however, the goddess, Ma'at was married to Thoth, the God of wisdom and learning. You see, the Egyptians believed in a whole pantheon of gods, not just one."

"You understand your grandma is telling a story, a myth that's not real," Grace says, her voice is in a knot. "There's only one God."

"Lighten up," I say, "and let her tell the story."

Grace scowls.

"Oh my, Paul had a fit every time I told you kids a story that wasn't in the Bible." My mother chuckles.

"I remember," I say.

What I remember is Dad's eyes. I remember turning away so I didn't have to see them. I remember the way he talked to her – if your eye keeps you from seeing God, gouge it out, because it's better to have one eye than go to hell. I worried that someday I might have to choose between gouging out my eye or drowning for all time and eternity.

"Ma'at was the goddess of justice and truth," my mother is saying. "She wore an ostrich feather in her hair."

Gabe giggles. "Did she have a pet ostrich?"

"I don't know, perhaps. Ma'at provided her people a code to live by, a list of sorts, of actions they should avoid. Like dishonesty, laziness, jealousy, cheating, lying and so on."

"Would that god lady's people see Bigfoot if they didn't do that bad stuff?" Gabe asks.

"Seeing Bigfoot wasn't important to them. What they were most concerned about was their afterlife. That's where the pure heart comes in. They believed having one was the only way to an existence after death. You see, to them the heart was a vessel for the soul and all of your deeds, whether they were good or bad, were stowed away in your heart."

"Is that where my good and bad deeds go?"

She lays her hand over Gabe's heart. "Yes, I believe they do."

"What happened if they had good and bad in their heart?"

"When someone died, their heart was taken to The Hall of Two Truths. There Ma'at weighed it on a scale, the heart on one side and on the other, her ostrich feather, as a counterbalance to see which weighed the most."

"But hearts weigh more than feathers," Gabe says. "Everybody knows that."

"Not in this story. Only if the heart was filled with bad deeds, would it tip the scale. But if the heart was filled with compassion and love, the feather would tip the scale and the deceased would go on to an afterlife where they'd exist forever."

"What happened to all the heavy hearted guys? Did they go to hell?"

"Well. While Ma'at weighed the heart, the goddess Ammit laid in wait under the scale," my mother says.

"What was she waiting for?" Gabe asks.

"Ammit, the Devourer of Souls," I say and Grace's eyes narrow. My mother nods and tells me to go on.

"If I remember correctly," I say, "if the heart

weighed more than the feather, Ammit would pop out from under the scale and gobble up the heart and the person would cease to exist."

"Really?" Gabe asks, all wide eyed.

"No, of course not," Grace says. "That's not a true story. Now he's going to have nightmares, Noah."

"It's a story, a myth like you said, to scare people into being good," I say.

Chapter Ten

Ellie and I carry in the last of the hymnbooks and stack them on the desk with the others.

"Do you think I should apply?" she asks.

"You gave me all the reasons you should, so why not?"

"Because I don't have a chance in hell of getting hired, I mean, can you really see me working in a hospital gift shop selling exotic dark chocolate truffles, dragonfly broaches and life-sized stuffed ponies?"

"Life-sized?"

She bursts out laughing. "Yes, life-sized." Then she scowls. "The things cost more than I'd make in a week."

"You have a good chance of getting hired. You're talented, hard working. Look what you've done for River Street. Soliciting food donations isn't easy. I'll put in a good word, if you want the job. I know the manager."

She tips back her head and grins. "I do want it. Thanks for your help. No one has ever believed in me the way you do."

"Let me know when you get hired."

"Okay, I will."

She wore a dress today and took out her piercings, except for one silver stud in the side of her nose. Before church I told her she looked pretty. I meant nice. She looks nice.

Out front, Amelia starts squealing and Hercules skitters out from under the desk yapping and flies down the hall.

"Justice always gets those two worked up," Ellie says.

"Help us, Ellie, help us." Amelia skids into the office with Hercules on her heels and Justice chasing them with the push broom.

"Look at the rug-rats I swept out of the corner." Justice props the broom in the corner where he left his guitar.

Amelia plants her hands on her hips. "We're not rats, Brother Justice. I'm a girl and Hercules is a Chew-wow-wow."

Justice's friend, Raleigh, like North Carolina, guffaws. "Hey, kid, that Chew-wow-wow of yours looks like a rat to me."

Amelia covers Hercules' ears. "You don't look like a rat." She turns to Raleigh. "Hey guy. Hercules is Pastor Noah's dog and my best friend, next to Dolly, and God loves him no matter what he looks like. Pastor Noah says."

This makes me smile. Justice said Raleigh only came for the food, but we ate and Raleigh stayed for the service and he's still here. River Street is growing. It's heartening to see folks spreading the word and reaching out to each other when so many have so little.

"Me and Raleigh were just joking with you," Justice says. "We can all be buddies, right Little Miss Amelia?"

"Brother Anthony and Brother Mark are my buddies." Amelia sticks out her tongue.

"Did they head off to the beach without saying goodbye?" I ask.

"I dunno." Justice sticks his tongue out at Amelia, reaches for his guitar and sits down with it and strums. "We rocked today, don't you think, Pastor Noah's Ark?"

"We rocked, all right, thanks to you on guitar," I say and he grins and teeters on the two back legs of his chair.

"It helped to have the words." Ellie lays her hand on the stack of hymnbooks.

"Finn's the man," Justice says. "He bought those songbooks on pink tag Tuesday, did he tell you?"

"Three times." Ellie chuckles. "He's the king of thrift store deals."

"He's a good man," I say.

Finn donated the books and wouldn't let me reimburse him. He said it was nothing, but it was.

I say a quick, silent prayer. Finn is working a second job now. It's not fair. Neither pays a living wage. He's old and he served our country and deserves a good retirement.

Ellie lays her hand over my shoulder. "Are you all right?"

"I'm fine," I say. "I was just thinking." Her hand slips off my shoulder.

"I know why he looks sad. He's sad because he's an old man," Amelia says.

"Amelia!" Ellie says and Justice starts laughing.

"That wasn't nice to say," Ellie says. "And it's not true either. You apologize."

"I believe I am the oldest here," I say.

"He is. Brother Anthony said," Amelia says.

"What did Brother Anthony say?" Anthony asks. He and Mark stroll in.

"That I'm an old man."

"I told her your birthday's coming up in a few weeks." Anthony tries not to smile. "That's all. She construed the old man part."

"Yeah right. I thought you two went to the beach."

Mark gives me a wrinkled piece of notebook paper. "We got all the way to the car before I remembered I had this. It's the signup sheet I passed around for painting River Street next Saturday."

I scan the list. The Nurse's name is on it. I saw her a few days ago waving a sign – give generously – at passersby on the main road out of town. I gave her all my change that afternoon, along with an invite to River Street. I didn't think she'd come. Oh ye of little faith. She didn't stay for the service, but she stayed for lunch and long enough to sign this.

"Awesome, with all these volunteers, we'll finish painting before noon," I say.

"Speaking of awesome," Anthony says, "Mark and I booked our honeymoon trip."

"Where are you lovey-dove birds going?" Justice asks.

"I happen to have a couple of brochures on me." Anthony grins and pulls them out of his coat and gives one to me and Ellie and the other to Justice.

"I want one too." Amelia tries to pry it out of Justice's hands.

"You can look on with me and Raleigh."

She scrambles up on Justice's knee. Takes one look at the brochure and squeals. "They're going to the zoo."

Justice hoots. "They're going to the rainforest, missy, not the zoo."

"But the rainforest is in the zoo, mister, next to the Polar Bears. Daddy took me, right, Ellie?"

Ellie sighs and looks up. "Yes. He took you to the zoo, but Anthony and Mark are going to the real rainforest on their honeymoon, not the zoo rainforest."

"Did Daddy honeymoon you in the real rainforest?" Amelia asks.

"No."

"Why not?"

"Not everyone can go to the rainforest. Some don't go on a honeymoon at all. Now no more questions."

Amelia sticks out her bottom lip and turns to Raleigh. "My daddy's in jail." He offers her a sympathetic look.

I glance at Ellie. She's holding her side of the brochure frowning.

"If it wasn't for Libby, Anthony and I wouldn't be going on a trip like this," Mark says. "She hooked us up with a guide who leads excursions. He owed her a favor and gave us a sweet deal."

"That's nice. I suppose," I say.

"Give Mom a break, why don't you?" Anthony asks.

"It says here it's a week-long honeymoon of hiking and camping and scaling cliffs." Ellie is leaning over me reading my side. "Isn't jungle trekking for the physically fit?"

"Yeah and your point?" Anthony asks.

Justice breaks out laughing. "Dude, her point is your skinny-ass legs."

"Anthony's up for the trip." Mark winks at him. "Those skinny legs of his are pure muscle."

"Then I recommend honeymooning on the French Rivera," Justice says. "I'm telling you, it's where all the beautiful people go. Clothes are optional, you know, and the most physical exertion is applying suntan lotion."

Anthony snorts and we all get to laughing.

"Pastor Noah's Ark," Amelia shouts. "Look. It's the lady who came to see us at Grandma's."

Charlee is leaning against the doorjamb, her arms folded. The teacher bag hanging over her shoulder.

I let go of the brochure thinking Ellie's holding it, but she isn't, and it hits the floor.

"How long have you been standing there?" I ask and she doesn't answer. "Come on in." I introduce her around.

Ellie picked up the brochure and is tapping the corner of it in her palm.

I turn to Charlee. "You missed my sermon."

"I meant to."

Ellie is the last to leave. She's trying to put Amelia's sweater on her and Amelia is objecting. "Come on,

Munchkin, I have to get ready for work." She gives up on the sweater. "Noah, I'll come early on Saturday and help tape and lay tarp."

She gives me a hug and looks around me. "You really should come hear Noah speak, Charlee. He's the best."

"You sure know how to clear a room fast," I say after Ellie's gone. I smile. Charlee doesn't. "Why don't you sit down and tell me what's the matter."

"I don't want to sit down."

"Okay."

She slips the bag off her shoulder. "Ellie has a crush on you."

"Don't be ridiculous. I'm her pastor."

"She calls you Noah, not Pastor Noah."

"That doesn't mean anything."

"The way she looks at you does."

"You're seeing things. How about you stop worrying about something that's totally innocent and stick to worrying about Michael?"

She frowns and reaches in her bag. "I didn't come here to talk about Michael." She pulls out a red book. "I came to talk about this."

The Bigfoot Hunter's Journal.

"How'd you get that thing?" I reach for it and she won't give it to me.

"Why did you let Gabe take it to school?"

"I didn't."

"I thought you hid it from him."

"After he found it last week, I sat him down and told him it wasn't his to read. I told him to never open it again and I put it away."

"He never does what you tell him."

"I know. I'll talk to him."

"It was so embarrassing. Friday was show and tell. When it was Gabe's turn, he pulled out our journal and announced to the class that you and I are Bigfoot Hunters."

"That's just great."

I think of the last show and tell conversation I had with Charlee about Grace's Golden Bullet. The Bigfoot journal wanes in comparison, but I don't say so.

"Yeah, just great." She glares at the drawing of Bigfoot. "By the end of the school day, I'd been asked by every student if they could be a Bigfoot Hunter too."

"I'm –"

"The teachers got into it. You got a date with Bigfoot this weekend? Do you keep him in a cage in your basement? Or maybe in your freezer?"

I chuckle. "Not funny. I'm sorry. The journal's full of our innermost childish thoughts and my son opened them to the world."

"Not exactly the world. I know what we wrote is kid stuff, but it's special, you know, between you and me and nobody else."

"I know. I'll find a better hiding place for it."

"All right." She gives me the book and I open it. On the first page is a snapshot of us, our cheeks pressed together.

"Gabe also said that you're unhappy," she says.

"He told you?"

"He told the whole class."

I shake my head, sigh.

"Did he also mention that I sleep on the couch? That the neighbors hear Grace and I fighting every day?"

"No. It was more of a general comment. My dad's not happy. Something like that."

"Why would he say something like that to his class?"

"You'd be surprised what kids his age are willing to share in a public forum. Sooner or later, they learn to filter."

"I hope with Gabe it's sooner than later."

"I'm sorry," she says. "I thought you should know."

"Do you tell other parents the humiliating things their kids say?"

"No, of course not. They aren't Bigfoot Hunters." We chuckle.

In the picture, Charlee and I are grinning, all gums, our eyes crinkled, noses flared, and her lopsided glasses.

"Why does everyone think I'm unhappy? I'm not. I wasn't. Look." I hold out the book and she takes it. "See, there in the picture, look at my face. There's a smile, right? I'm smiling. I'm not unhappy."

She sits on the desk and studies it.

"Scoot over." I push the hymnbooks out of the way and sit next to her. The night Gabe found the journal rushes back. I hear my mother. We were one big unhappy family.

"You're right, you look happy here," Charlee says without looking up from the book.

"Yes, I do, see what I told you?"

"Uh-huh. Most everybody smiles when they get their picture taken, so I'm not sure if this is real proof."

"I remember that day. I was happy."

"You remember?" I nod. "What was the occasion?"

"Uh. No occasion."

She punches me in the arm. "You do not remember."

"Our birthday?"

"Nope."

"Well, I don't remember being unhappy."

She shrugs. "Speaking of birthdays. You're hosting our birthday party this year?"

"Yep, the party's at my house."

"Okay, cool." She looks down at the book. "Do you remember this?" She points to a rusty stain and our names scrawled underneath.

"How could I forget?"

We compare thumbs. Unless you know what you're looking for, you'd miss the pinch of discolored skin. Grace doesn't know it exists.

"Your dad's razor was sharper than we thought," Charlee says.

"We got plenty of blood out of our thumbs to make our oath."

We look down at the journal page we bled all over and she chuckles. "We're truly blood brothers."

"Yep. Who came up with the blood oath anyway?"

"We got it from one of your mom's stories, a legend about some battle, remember?"

"Uh –"

What I remember now is my mother, one arm wrapped around me and the other around Charlee. We were always asking her for stories.

"Yeah, yeah, there was a Norwegian warrior," Charlee says, "and he sailed to Sweden and they battled and… Her voice trails off.

"Didn't the fight end in a draw?"

"Oh yes, that's right. They fought a fair fight and afterwards they swore a blood oath as a sign that they were equals. And they were loyal friends for the rest of their days. Like us." We chuckle and press our thumbs together. "Your dad was so angry with your mom for telling us that story."

"He was angry with her most of the time," I say and she nods. "She left us because she and Dad made us unhappy. That's what she told Gabe, like she did our family a favor."

"Is that how she lived with herself all those years?"

"Who knows? She told Gabe she never stopped loving me. She's a storyteller. She even teared up with that one."

I don't understand why I'm tearing up. I squeeze my eyes shut for a minute and Charlee rubs her hand up and down my back.

"You could ask her to leave." She turns several pages and stops on Bigfoot Hunter's Code Number 5. The code is written in giant block letters in red felt-tip pen on two facing pages.

– Bigfoot Hunters Never Lie

"I remember when we added number 5," she says.

"After I found my mother's note in Dad's Bible. He knew she wasn't coming back. She knew she was leaving. They lied to us."

"Maybe they thought a lie would be kinder than the truth."

"They were only thinking about themselves."

"You're right. But what about now? Do you think your mom was lying when she told Gabe she never stopped loving you?"

"Yes. No." I shake my head. "I don't know. How

can a parent stop loving a child? I've been thinking about it. No matter what happens between me and Grace, I'll always love Gabe."

"Of course you will."

"Not that anything's wrong between me and Grace."

"Oh, sure, it was only an illustration."

"I can't tell my mother to leave."

"Because she's not as bad as you thought or because Grace would flip out?"

"A little of both, I guess."

She nods. "I should get going."

"We didn't make it to the end of the book."

She starts turning pages. I stop her when she gets to number 6.

– Bigfoot Hunters Don't Keep Secrets

"I'd forgotten that we wrote our secrets down," she says. "Look, you wrote this one."

– Elizabeth kissed me. She tasted like Sweet Tarts and I liked it.

Charlee bursts out laughing.

"Hey, let me see that."

"I never liked that girl," Charlee says.

"You didn't like any girl I liked. Read one of your secrets."

She's quiet for a moment. "Okay." She closes the book. "Your mom told me she saw Michael in the Oceanside Motel's parking lot with a woman."

"Oh. I'm sorry."

I wish I could take back my earlier comment about Michael.

"Do you think your mom was lying to me?" Charlee asks.

"Why would she?"

"Because she's a liar, I don't know." Charlee pulls off her glasses and chucks them in her bag. "Maybe she was mistaken. Lots of men look like Michael. From far away, you know? It could have been anyone, right?"

She looks at me, all hopeful, and I say it could have been anyone.

We hear sirens and see lights flashing. She cranes her neck trying to see out the window. "That's coming from the alley."

"Sirens are a common occurrence on River Street."

We hear bam-bam-bam on the back door and we shoot off the desk. Hercules comes out from under it barking. I chase him down the hall.

"Is it the cops?" Charlee asks. She's right behind me. I say I don't know, but my gut says it is. I scoop Hercules off the floor the same time the door flies open and bangs against the wall, revealing two police officers.

"How can I help you, Officers?" I know I sound scared to death. Charlee is standing beside me, her hands clamped onto my arm.

"This is a church?" one asks.

"Yes, this is River Street, an outreach of the 51st Street Mission. We use the building on Sunday afternoons."

He raises an eyebrow. "Are you the minister?"

"I'm Pastor Noah Cathcart. This is Charlee Radcliff."

The cop looks me up and down. I'm wearing ripped jeans, flannel over a t-shirt. Grace told me on my way out today, as she does every Sunday, that I ought to dress like a pastor when I come here to preach, not one of the homeless.

"Let's see some ID from both of you." He sends the other officer over for it and continues. "We found a Justice Worthington and a Raleigh Jones in the alley. They say they attend church here. Do you know them?"

"Justice attends church here," I say. "Raleigh came for the first time today. Why, is there a problem?"

The other officer collects my license and after Charlee finally finds hers in the bottomless pit of her bag, he takes it and goes outside.

"We've had several complaints over the last couple of months that your people are selling drugs out of your church," the officer says. "Do you know anything about this, Pastor?"

"Is that what you think Justice and Raleigh were doing?"

"Answer my question. Do you know anything about this?"

"No."

A few minutes ago, Justice was chasing Amelia with the push broom. He's been homeless and in and out of drugs since he was in middle school. Clean for the last six months. That's what he told me and I believed him.

"We have a search warrant." He takes it out.

"The only thing you'll find in here is the love of our Savior, Jesus Christ, Officer."

"Save it, Pastor," he says and a new officer leading

an athletic silver-grey dog comes in. Hercules yips and shoves his nose under my armpit.

Charlee and I are escorted to the office where I'm instructed to tie Hercules to the desk and give him a short lead. I try to reassure him. The officer's breathing down my neck. When I finish, Charlee and I are told to sit in the folding chairs and stay put.

I lean into my hands and pray for Justice and Raleigh. And God – please give Pastor Green an understanding heart when he hears about this and please give him the wherewithal to convince the 51st Street Mission board that what we're doing here at River Street is an important work, not a cover for illicit drug dealing.

The officer with our IDs comes back and announces that I have an arrest on my record and would I please stand and put my hands flat on the desk.

"You can't do that to him," Charlee blurts out and stands and the officer tells her to remain in her seat and be silent. "But the arrest shouldn't be on his record. He wasn't charged with a crime. He hasn't done anything wrong. He's a law abiding citizen. He has rights."

I ask her to please be quiet and I put my hands on the desk like he said and he starts patting me down.

I'm trembling the way I was the day they arrested me. I think how easy it was for the police to bring me down. I think of the knee pressed into the nape of my neck. In my head I hear Grace – don't ruin it Noah.

Chapter Eleven

We painted the office walls bright green. Ellie is laughing about it. She has me laughing. "This is glaring," she says and pulls the white plastic heart-shaped sunglasses off the top of her head and puts them on her face. "Oh much better."

"Hey, the green was your idea."

"Green will grow on you." She giggles. "You've got to admit, it's better than white. Besides, the white ran out before we finished painting the meeting room."

"I'm not sure about the yellow we used on the last wall out there. I hope it doesn't distract from the worship service."

She pulls the glasses down her nose. "If it does, we'll pass sunglasses out to the congregation." She chuckles. "Stop worrying. It's only one wall and come on, sunshine yellow is a happy color and being happy is what Jesus is all about, right?" She removes the sunglasses and hooks them over the front of her shirt. "Right?"

"Yeah, you're right about that."

She stoops over and takes the paint sticks out of the can.

"Don't bother cleaning up," I say and she reaches for the lid. "You've done enough." There's a splotch of sunshine yellow on her rear, a trail of drips down her thigh. "Uh –" I turn and look out the window. "Take the afternoon off. Enjoy this summer weather while it lasts."

"No way am I bombing out on the crew." She hands me the paint sticks and stretches her back.

A nice breeze is coming inside. It won't be summer for a couple more weeks, but it feels like summer. Ellie came wearing a hoodie over the little shorts and tank top this morning, but now the sun is full-on shining and the hoodie is hanging in the closet.

I toss the sticks into the trash bag. "You were hard at work an hour before anyone else arrived. You have Amelia to get back to."

"When I was a kiddo, if me and my brothers left a chore before it was done, we'd get a whipping." I hold the trash open while she shoves a wadded up plastic drop cloth in. "Taught me work ethic. So you're stuck with me. When I left, Sister Margaret and Munchkin were making bread. They won't miss me. After clean up, I'll treat you to ice cream over at Lawrence's. I owe you. I got my first paycheck from the gift shop."

"Congratulations and you don't owe me anything. Take Amelia out instead. Let's get busy. I promised my son an afternoon at the beach."

"Oh. Well, it's a great day for the beach. Next time we'll get ice cream." She comes over and lays her hand on my shoulder and steps in so close I can smell her sweet fruity fragrance. I step back and she laughs.

"You have paint on your face, silly. Come here, let me get it."

"Thanks. I mean no thanks. I'll get it when I wash up."

"It's in a hard to reach spot. Hold still." She plants one hand firmly on the back of my neck.

Her nails are long and painted black. The heart-shaped sunglasses press into my neck.

"So sorry to interrupt you two." Annabelle strolls in grinning and Ellie and I step apart.

"You didn't interrupt anything," I say.

"Do you have any paint left over?" Annabelle asks.

Ellie picks up the bucket of green and Annabelle looks inside. "This will do the job. Mel's out there wanting to spruce up Headquarters, why don't you give him a hand, Ellie?"

"Sure thing." Ellie looks over the office. "We did a great job. We work well together, don't you think, Noah?"

I nod. "Yeah, thanks for helping."

Ellie flashes me a big smile and leaves.

"Well, well, Pastor, maybe you're more like your old man than I gave you credit."

"I don't know what you're talking about." I pick up a paint stick we missed.

"Yes you do. What's your story?"

"My story is I'm not my dad."

"Oh come on, you and Ellie looked awfully friendly when I walked in on you."

"You didn't walk in on anything." I shove the last of the plastic into the trash.

"It's your business who you're banging. I'm simply making an observation."

"I'm not doing that, that thing, with her or anyone else."

I walk over to the window. There's no breeze now. What I said is true. I'm not even doing that thing with my wife. I can't think of the last time Grace and I did it.

"Maybe nothing is going on for you, but that girl has the hots for you."

"She doesn't. She's married. I'm married and I'm her pastor and a good ten years older."

"Look kid, I'm telling you, Ellie wants you. You're probably the first guy who ever respected her. You're good looking and kind hearted. You provide for her."

"I don't provide for her."

"No? You found her a place to live. She told me. You're the reason she has three jobs. All she has to do is come to you and you take care of her."

"I helped out, that's all, because I'm her pastor."

"No, you're her knight in shining armor."

"Knight in shining armor?" The Nurse walks in. "If you have some time left for shining, Pastor, I could use some help. The cops are back to harassing me."

"I'm sorry," I say. "Come see me after our service tomorrow and we'll talk and pray about it."

"I'll pass. God never did me any favors. Reason I came in was to let you know Mel's on that water-bottle-phone of his trying to contact the Commander. That's you, isn't it?"

"Yes."

Seems I've taken Anthony's commander job away. I tried to give it back, but he says he's fine with me being in charge, since I'm the elder brother and a pastor.

"I fashioned Mel an antenna out of coat hangers to attach to his headquarters for the purpose of talking to aliens." The Nurse chuckles.

"Thank you. God does care about you."

She makes a dismissive snort and Annabelle and I follow her out.

"I brought snacks for the weary painters." Annabelle picks up a case of soda she left in the hall.

"I'll get that," I say and she won't give it to me.

"I'm no weakling woman. Grab the chips, will ya?"

She lumbers out. Starts giving away sodas and tells Finn to pass the chips around.

"Sure thing, Ms. Annabelle." He waves Dorothy over to help and she glowers. He rips open the chips. "Women. You can't live without them. Or is it with them? You can't live with them? Either way, she's a jealous one. You know how tough it is keeping her and those little Muppet-dogs of hers happy?"

"It's a two-way street, isn't it?" I ask and the wrinkles between his brows peak. "A give and take, I mean in a relationship."

"I'm not up on street directions or relationships like you young folks are these days. You know, the yellow wall kind of grows on you." He stares in that direction. Whether he's pondering the wall or Dorothy who pales next to it, I don't know. Aside from that, the yellow isn't too glaring and it stirs up some good feelings. I think how far this little community has come in a few short months. Ellie looks up from painting and smiles and I smile back.

"Pastor Noah's Ark, I was afraid I missed you."

Justice sticks a paper in my hand. "I need this signed, you know, for the community service hours?"

"Sure, no problem."

Finn offers Justice the bag of chips and he wolfs a handful and then another. Finn tells him to pass it on after he's had his fill.

"Are you okay?" I ask. Justice guffaws and says he has never been better. "Have you found a place to stay?"

"Oh sure. You've heard of couch surfing, right?"

"I've heard of it."

I found him under the bridge rolling up a ratty sleeping bag the other day, not couch surfing.

"If you stick around, I'll take you to lunch," I say.

"No can do, I have a prior engagement."

"All right." While I'm signing his paper, he slips the bag of chips into his backpack.

"Commander Cathcart! Is that you?" Mel's standing next to his cardboard-box office yelling into his phone.

"You better take that call," Justice says and snatches the paper out of my hand. "See ya."

"If you change your mind about lunch –" He doesn't hear me. He hurries down the hall toward the back door and I wonder why the back, why the alley. Pastor Green found out about the drug bust the day it happened.

"Commander Cathcart? Can you hear me?"

"Yes, I hear you." I glance down the hall. Justice is gone. "Can you hear me, Agent Mel?"

"Yes, Sir, Commander, I'm happy to report that I've secured a new office and the aliens no longer have access to my locality. This is top secret. Don't speak of it again, but the green paint Agent Ellie is applying can't be seen by alien eyes."

"Pretty amazing how far technology has come since your last office, don't you agree?"

He drops his phone and it slides a couple feet away. "Hang on, Commander, I think we may be having an earth tremor."

Ellie sets the paintbrush down and sidles up next to me. "I'm a secret agent now," she whispers.

"It's dangerous work," I whisper.

"I'm up for it." She salutes and I salute back and she goes back to painting.

"Are you still there, Commander?" Mel's holding his phone to his ear.

"Yes, any damage on your end?" I ask.

"Not a scratch. There's a tsunami watch in effect."

"Thanks for the warning."

"You're welcome. As soon as the paint dries on my secret agent office, I'll be moving outside to an undisclosed location where I can better monitor the situation."

"How will I find you?"

"Look for the red pillar."

"Area 51?"

"Yes Sir."

"I think we ought to work on finding a new secret location, Agent Mel. I can help."

He bangs the water bottle against his hand. "I'm losing you, Commander."

"I'll go with you to Social Services. I'll help fill out the papers. There's a group home I heard about."

He smacks the bottle against his knee. "Our connection has been breached. I repeat, our connection has been breached. It's the aliens, Commander. Don't say one more word or it will be the end of the universe as we know it."

Mel puts the water bottle on the floor and stomps on it.

"Like I told you, he always goes back to his Area 51," The Nurse says.

The bell jangles and the front door opens.

"Hit the deck." Mel flops onto his belly.

"I'll take care of Mel," The Nurse says. "You get the visitor. He doesn't look very happy."

The visitor is Pastor Green and The Nurse is right, he doesn't look very happy. I fear the worst, but I manage to greet him with a hearty handshake.

He scans the room and stops on the yellow wall.

"What do you think?" I ask. "I know yellow is –"

"A bit unorthodox for a place of worship."

"Actually, no, the color is Sunshine Yellow and it reminds us that Jesus wants every one of His children to be happy and loved which is an important message for those who come to River Street."

"Ah, I see."

"A big crew of volunteers showed up to paint. They were more than happy to pitch in and make the space their own. It takes time, but we're making headway, building camaraderie and hope."

"I'm aware of the work you do; you mention it every time I see you."

"It's God, not me. Serving here has been a humbling experience."

"It certainly has." He drops his head and my stomach clenches.

"Will you join us? We're having a little celebration."

Pastor Green puts his hand over my shoulder. "Let's you and me go for a walk."

"I can't just leave."

"We need to have a talk. I won't keep you long." He slips his arm around my shoulders. "The wife wants me to pick up fudge for the grandkids over at the candy store. I'll buy you a coffee."

Lawrence's is packed. We get the last table on the patio, a white one rusted around the edges. Pastor Green orders a pound of fudge to-go and a drip coffee. I ask for water.

"I'll be direct," he says. "A drug bust looks bad on the Mission."

"Yes, I know, but –"

A kid screeches and I glance over and see a scoop of pink ice cream on the ground, an empty cone in her fist.

"There was nothing illegal going on during services or in the building." I lean forward and our table wobbles. "Justice had a little marijuana on him, that's all. They gave him 20 hours of community service and he has to go to a class."

"I read the police report. The board read it." The waiter brings out the order and Pastor Green tops off his coffee with cream. "The other boy is facing some serious charges."

"No one else at River Street was involved. I can't control what goes on in the alley after church."

"The board wasn't happy to learn the building

owner is affiliated with the strip club across the street."

"You're the one who –" I stop myself.

"Yes, I am the one and I'm in a bit of hot water myself. And then there's your arrest record, which unfortunately, was also mentioned in the police report."

"But wait, I don't have a record." I bump the table leg and his coffee slops out. "I'm sorry." I start sopping it up with my napkin. "I wasn't charged with a crime. The arrest shouldn't be on my record. It's a mistake. Did you tell the board?"

"They're worried about perception more than facts."

"This isn't fair."

"I know. This isn't about what's fair. It's about money."

I shake my head. This conversation is the same one I had with Dad after I got arrested.

"It isn't about money," I say. "River Street is about individuals who need support and hope, compassion and a place to go."

"You realize the mission exists on donations and grants. A thing like a drug bust jeopardizes their funding. You must understand their predicament. They've already suffered cutbacks. The board unanimously agreed they no longer need your services and River Street is closed, effective now. I'm sorry."

"No. Let me talk to the board. Please. I can make them understand."

"No, it's been decided."

"What will happen to the people? Where will they go? Who will help them? Who will love them?"

Chapter Twelve

I pull up to the curb in front of the nun's house, a Victorian like Grace has always wanted with a wraparound porch and ivy growing into the dormers. Ellie points to the attic window where she and Amelia are staying. "Munchkin made friends with a little bat who lives in our room."

"I'm glad she's making friends," I say and she chuckles. I leave the car running and set the brake. "Thanks for sticking around and helping me pack."

"I wasn't about to leave you alone after the bad news." She reaches for her hoodie in the backseat.

Now I have to go home and give Grace the news. I got fired from my volunteer job.

"It sucks what they did to you." Ellie stabs her arm into a sleeve.

"It sucks for the people I was called to serve." I reach over and hold the hoodie for her while she puts the other arm in. "I failed them."

"It's not your fault. The mission isn't being fair. They act as if our church is full of criminals when it was only Justice and his friend who committed a crime."

"Fair or not, it's been decided." The streetlights flicker on and off.

"Maybe we can change their minds."

I shake my head. "I already tried. I have to go home now. It's too late for the beach. I let my son down, again. I didn't call my wife."

She reaches for my hand. "Are you okay?"

"Yeah."

"If you feel like talking, call me."

"Thanks."

She looks in the backseat at the mishmash of items we found at the church. "I know who some of this belongs to." She grabs a large silver pan. "The Chowder House. I'll return it tomorrow. When you're ready to sort the rest of this stuff, give me a call." I nod and she squeezes my hand. "I mean it. You shouldn't do it alone. You have my number, right?"

"Uh –"

She reaches in her bag, pulls out a pink pen and writes her number on the back of my hand.

I find Grace in the dining room sitting adjacent a man, her face lit by his laptop and they're having an animated conversation. I flip on the overhead light and Grace looks over.

"Home already?" She reaches for a red sweater that's on the floor.

"It looks like I've interrupted."

"Oh no," they say in unison.

"You've met Joshua Barrett, haven't you, Noah?" Grace drapes the sweater over her bare shoulders.

"No."

He half stands, introduces himself as Josh, and extends his hand.

I shake it.

"We've been working on the renovation project all afternoon," she says.

"Time has gotten away, hasn't it?" Barrett chuckles and shuts his laptop. "I'm glad you phoned. We got more done in an afternoon here, than we could in a day at my office." He picks up a briefcase. "Your wife has proven invaluable to our committee. Her plan for a sustainable landscape rivals those of any city. Well, I'll let you two get on with your evening. It was a pleasure to finally meet you."

Grace walks him to the door. He's a large man, older, a gold watch, a grip. The Mercedes I saw parked on the street must belong to him. Grace comes back putting on the sweater.

"What are you doing inviting him into our home?" I ask and she ignores me. I follow her to the kitchen. "Well?"

"I told you. We worked all afternoon. Now, if you'll get out of my way, I'll start dinner."

"He sure knows how to load on the praise."

"I'm deserving of his praise." She puts her hands on her hips. "I'm an important part of the renovation project." She flips her pony tail and takes a box of macaroni and cheese out of the cupboard.

I told Finn a relationship is a two-way street, a give and take. Look at me and Grace. Who am I to give advice?

"I don't want to fight," I say.

She's glaring at the box, thrumming her fingers on the counter. "Then don't." She goes to the refrigerator and takes out a bag of salad.

"Want some help?"

She shakes her head.

"Okay."

I let the dogs inside and Hercules runs upstairs after Henry to annoy him.

"Hey Gabe," I call up to his room. "Let Hercules in to play."

"Gabe's not home," Grace says.

"Where is he?"

"Your mother took him to the beach for the afternoon."

"Oh." My mother covered for me. That's just great. I walk over to the window. It's completely dark now. "They've been gone all afternoon?"

"That's what I said."

"You invited Barrett over when you were here alone?"

"The proposal's due in a couple days." She brushes a strand of hair out of her eyes. "We worked in the dining room the entire time."

"What were you thinking? You're a married woman."

She pulls open the drawer under the stove and the pots rattle. "I was thinking about business. What were you thinking when you promised Gabe you'd take him to the beach and you not only didn't show, you didn't have the decency to call."

I pull out a chair and sit at the table. What was I thinking? When I could have come home and taken

Gabe to the beach, I stayed with Ellie and packed up River Street.

"I wasn't thinking," I say. Grace eyes me for a moment. "I screwed up and let Gabe down."

Grace sets a pot on the stove. "Yes, you did."

"I got fired."

"You got what?" She shuts the drawer with her foot.

I clear my throat. "Fired. The mission shut River Street down and they don't want me back."

She folds her arms and leans her back against the counter. "Why?"

"Pastor Green from the mission came by River Street to tell me. We were finishing up painting. We had a great turnout, far more than I expected, and we finished early. You should have seen what we did. One of the walls was bright yellow. It was –" My voice cracks.

"I guess the news came as a surprise."

I shake my head. "I should have seen it coming."

"Was it because those boys got arrested last week?" I nod. "I see."

"I don't get it. I felt called to serve the River Street people. We've come so far since it opened. God was on our side. Or I thought He was."

"Maybe this is a sign."

"What kind of sign?"

"Satan is trying his hardest to bring us down. His power abounds in environments like River Street."

"They're individuals, not an environment."

"Satan is in those people and he'll work through them to get to you."

"Those people are becoming a family."

"Your family is Rolling River. Rejoice not in iniquity, but rejoice in truth. You're making those street people family when you should be calling them to their knees. Being exposed to their vices and immorality week in and week out, makes you vulnerable. You're walking on the edge of deep waters. One slip is all it takes."

A shiver goes up my spine. "Ministering to the downtrodden is not walking on the edge. Jesus loved those who others hated."

"Now Jesus has given you a sign to bring you back to the path." She pulls a chair around and reaches for my hand. Ellie's phone number is glaring, the size of it, the sparkly pink.

Grace squeezes my hand between hers. "You are Rolling Rivers' miracle. Listen to me. God has a plan."

I pull away. "I know the plan."

"Don't lose sight of it. God is telling you. It's time for you to step up and lead Rolling River."

The back door flies open. "We're home!" Gabe shouts and Grace goes over to greet him. "Oh my goodness, look at you, you're all sunburnt."

"It doesn't hurt one bit. Grandma Libby put green slime on it. Look, we brought home pepperoni pizzas for dinner. I'm starved. Let's eat."

My mother, decked out in a straw hat and flip-flops, carries in two boxes. The greasy smell of pizza fills the kitchen. "You have the night off, my dear," she says to Grace and sets the pizzas on the table. "Sit down. I'll grab the paper towels."

"You didn't have to do this." Grace sits across the table from me and smiles.

"Grandma Libby's the best." Gabe plops down in

the chair next to mine. "We had a blast at the beach."

"Hey buddy, I'm real sorry I didn't get home in time to take you. I got tied up at River Street and –"

"Grandma Libby let me go in the ocean all the way up to my knees."

"Was it scary?" Grace asks.

"No. We held hands and when the waves came we jumped. At first we were freezing." He wraps his arms around himself to demonstrate how hard he shivered. "Brrrr, but then our legs got numb and we weren't cold anymore."

"I forgot just how cold the Pacific is," my mother says and chuckles.

"We had so much fun," Gabe says. "We got a little wet, okay, a lot wet, but we're dry now."

"We had a wonderful time," my mother says.

"Me and Grandma Libby built a sandcastle that was big enough for a giant." Gabe leans back and laughs. "Our castle was surrounded by a moat a sea serpent lived in. We had a drawbridge and turrets, a thousand soldiers, and a King and a Queen. Then the tide came in and they all drowned except for the sea serpent, of course."

"That's too bad," Grace says. "They should have prepared, knowing a flood was coming."

"It's just a story, not Noah's Ark." He takes off a tennis shoe and pours sand out of it.

"Hey, not in the house," I say.

Grace comes around the table and grabs him by the arm. "We're going to take the sand outside where it belongs."

"But there won't be any pizza left," Gabe says as Grace leads him to the back door.

"You go on, we won't start without you." My mother is washing her hands in the kitchen sink. When she finishes, she dries them on a paper towel and tosses it in the trash. "I hear you and Gabe go to the beach all the time."

"That's a bit of a stretch."

"He told me all about it. How you and he gather driftwood, like Lewis and Clark did." She chuckles. "You build a blazing fire when it's pitch-dark, eat hot dogs on sticks and S'mores for dessert and tell stories about Bigfoot."

"We've done that once in his whole life."

"Quantity isn't what matters to children, don't you agree?" She puts the box of macaroni and cheese back in the cupboard.

"I don't spend enough time with my son. I failed him today and today's not the first time." I shut my eyes for a moment or two.

"Children can be very forgiving. You look like you've had a long day. We don't have to talk."

"Okay."

She finds a pitcher and fills it with water, brings over glasses. She folds four paper towels into napkins.

"Did you ever believe I was Rolling River's miracle?" I ask.

"Oh, honey." She places a napkin in each of our places. "You and your brother are miracles without your Dad's come-to-Jesus conversion story."

"I wasn't talking about the miracle of birth."

"Neither was I." She sits at the table and leans back in the chair. Her face is sunburnt, white rings around her eyes, sunglasses propped on top of her head. She's smiling.

"You didn't answer my question."

"I didn't, did I? Well, as often as I heard Paul tell his miracle story, you'd think I'd believe it. I thought I could. I mean, his experience, whatever it was, turned him into a faithful husband. Talk about miracles." She laughs and waves herself off. "Paul believes God sent you to be his successor as part of some grand plan, while I believe the future is filled with options and Paul and I, not God, made you happen."

Gabe pounces on the bed. "Dad, Dad, wake up Dad." He's shaking me and bouncing on his knees.

I open one eye. Check the time and groan. "Come back in 45 minutes." I reach for Grace and find the covers thrown back, a cold sheet. She mentioned getting up early to go to an all-day committee meeting.

Gabe pulls on my arm trying to get me to roll over. "Don't you know what today is?"

"Hmm, let me see."

All week he's been talking non-stop about breakfast at the Little Bigfoot Café, the museum after and a hike in Bigfoot country.

I hear rain bouncing off the window. I turn onto my back and he plunks down on my stomach. "Oomph. Hey, watch it, you aren't little anymore." He says he's sorry. His face is beaming. He's dressed, jeans and a sweatshirt, hiking boots. "Of course I know what today is, it's clean the garage day."

"Nu-uh."

"Oh, am I confused? Because we don't get up this early on Saturdays unless it's clean the garage day.

Right, Gabe?" I start tickling him and he giggles and writhes. "Right?"

"Stop, stop. It's Bigfoot day, not garage day." I tickle him some more. "Okay, Dad, Dad, stop." He's laughing and breathless. "Stop, stop. Please. You can sleep longer."

I hug him tight. "I'm wide awake now. I have to get dressed and I want a cup of coffee, then we can go. Is Mom in the kitchen?"

"Nope."

"Did she leave already?"

"Uh-huh. She went with Mr. Barrett."

"He picked her up?"

"Yeah, his car is really cool, have you been in it?"

"No."

"Mom's lucky. She's been in it lots of times. She said it talks to Mr. Barrett and calls him Josh. Isn't that the coolest?"

"He gives her a ride often?"

"Sometimes. Can we get a car like Mr. Barrett's?"

Hearing Barrett's name irritates me, especially when it's associated with my wife.

"Dad, Dad? Mom and I would love a car like Mr. —"

"We don't waste money on extravagances. Our cars are just fine. You should be grateful for what we have."

"Why are you mad at me?"

I sound mad? What am I doing? He's asking innocent questions and I sound mad. I'm not going to let Barrett or anything else spoil our day.

"Sorry, buddy. I'm not mad. I need a cup of coffee. So tell me, how hungry are you?"

"I dunno."

"Hungry enough to finish off the Bigfoot Platter?"

"Really?" I nod and his face brightens. "I can order the platter?"

"Sure, if you think you're up to it. I hear no one in Bigfoot country has ever been able to finish it."

"Not even you and Aunt Charlee."

"That's right. We shared one and couldn't finish it off."

"I can, I know I can. Come on, get up." He hops off the bed. "This is going to be the best day ever."

Gabe jogs downstairs. "Dad, Dad, what do you get for eating the whole Bigfoot platter?"

I finish off the last gulp of coffee. "A stomach ache?"

He stops on the forth stair from the bottom and jumps. "No, I mean a prize, like if you finish, you get a million bucks or something like that."

"In your dreams Gabe. Put on your raincoat."

I'm counting on the rain to stop by the time we finish our meal and wander through the museum. In our morning prayers, Gabe prayed it would stop. Who knows if it will?

He grabs his coat. "I think they'll take my picture and put it on the front page of the newspaper and I'll be a celebrity like you were when your picture was in the paper."

"I wasn't a celebrity."

My cell phone rings.

"Don't answer it," he cries and runs toward me,

one arm in a sleeve and the rest of the coat dragging.

I think about letting the call go to voice mail, but what if it's an emergency. I reach in my pocket and Gabe tackles me.

"No," he screeches.

"Hey, what if it's your mom or what if Uncle Anthony and Grandma Libby broke down on their way to P-Town and need our help?"

Gabe backs off and sticks out his lip. "This always happens."

It's Ellie. Probably about the stuff from River Street that's still in my backseat. I let the call go and stick the phone in my pocket. "No emergency." I smile and Gabe smiles. I hold his coat for him and he punches his fist into the sleeve. "What do you say we hit the road?"

The phone rings again. It's Ellie. Gabe's eyes narrow. "No worries," I say, but she calls right back.

Gabe folds his hands and pleads. "Please Dad, don't answer it."

"We're taking Mom's car. You go on and get in. I'll take care of this and be right there."

He slams the door on his way out and the dishes rattle in the cupboard.

The nun inspects my business card while I stand on the porch in the sideways rain. "I'm Ellie's pastor. She called and asked me to come. Her daughter's not well."

Ellie was crying. Amelia is sick. The rest I couldn't understand, except for I'm freaking out and need you to come over.

The sister gives me back my card and invites me in. "Wait here."

The smell of bread baking is strong here in the entryway. I hear water running, pans rattling and women's voices, laughter.

Gabe was pretty mad when I left him. I don't blame him. He didn't believe I'd be back in an hour max, like I said. Grace will be mad too when she finds out I left him with people we don't know. Well, they are the next-door neighbors and Gabe knows their boy from school and they hear all our arguments, so we aren't exactly strangers.

"I'm so glad you're here." Ellie, dressed in tennis shoes and pajamas, is hurrying down the stairs carrying Amelia bundled up in a blanket. "I'm so worried."

I meet her on the stairs and take Amelia. I feel heat coming off her. "Feeling pretty yucky, huh?" I ask and she coughs and wraps her arms around my neck.

"Can you pray for her?" Ellie's face is tear-streaked.

"Sure, I'd be happy to."

Ellie leads me into a sparsely furnished room and turns on an antique floor lamp. Amelia whimpers when I try to lay her on the couch. I sit with her on my lap instead. Her glands are swollen, her cheeks ruddy.

Ellie sits beside me and lays her hand on Amelia's forehead. "She's been sick all week, with a cold, it wasn't much, but this morning she woke up with a fever. I didn't know what to do. She's never been this sick."

"I think we should get her to a doctor. It's probably an infection. The ER is the best place to go this time of the morning. I'll drive you."

"I don't know what we'd do without you." Ellie's eyes are filling with tears.

"I'm glad you called. I'm sure Amelia's going to be fine." I wrap my arm around Ellie. "Let's have a prayer before we go."

Amelia's sprawled in my lap under the blanket and Ellie's flipping through a magazine she isn't looking at. "I'm glad we saw a doctor," she says. "She said strep gets worse without antibiotics." I nod. "All this waiting, we've been here for hours. What's taking the pharmacy so long? We need to put her to bed. How could they make a sick child wait so long?"

Rain pelts against the skylights. "I don't know. Understaffed maybe?" I've lost the feeling in my arm. I reposition Amelia and stretch it out. I check my watch. It's well after noon. While she was seeing the doctor, I called the neighbor woman to let her know I was running later than I thought I would. It will be okay. Gabe and I will still have our day, lunch instead of breakfast, the museum and a hike in the late afternoon. The weather will clear up by then.

Ellie directs me to park around back. We'll use the stairs the servants used when the house belonged to a rich guy and the nuns don't use. She reaches for the groceries. "Thanks for taking us to the store. There's nothing a can of chicken noodle soup won't cure, right?"

"Grace swears by it."

"Oh, your wife." I nod. "Munchkin and I couldn't have gotten through this ordeal without you. I mean it, thank you."

"That's what pastors do, right?" I take off my raincoat and lay it over Amelia, who's snoring in Ellie's lap. "It's a drencher out there. I'll come around for her. You carry the bags and we'll make a run for it."

"Ready whenever you are, Commander." Ellie grins and salutes.

"On three, Agent Ellie –"

I'm a bit out of breath when I get up to the third floor. Ellie is already in her apartment. She left the door open and she's bent over straightening the covers on a hideaway bed. Her pajama bottoms are thin and soaked through.

"Come in," she says. "Munchkin is dead weight when she's asleep. Look at you Noah. You're as soaked as me. Let's get her to bed and then we'll dry off." Ellie takes my coat off Amelia and hangs it over the back of a wooden chair.

Amelia's eyes pop open. "I don't want to go to bed. I'm not asleep." She starts squirming.

"In that case," Ellie says, "you can give Noah a quick tour of your room."

"I can?" Amelia asks.

"Show me the way," I say.

I carry her into an adjacent room and she tells me to stop next to the rollaway bed. "This is where I sleep. And over there." She points to a dresser. "Is where I put my clothes and on top is where I keep my favorite lamp. Ellie lets me sleep with it on because the Boogieman is very scared of the light." She coughs. "See up there?" She points into the rafters and I nod. "My bat, Tommie, lives up there. Tommie where are you?"

"Tommie's a day sleeper, remember?" Ellie says and pulls back the covers. "You can look for Tommie in Dreamland."

"I like Dreamland," she says.

"Me too." I lay her down and Ellie and I tuck her in.

Amelia pats her blanket. "Sister Margaret gave this to me. See, it has pictures of dogs all over it. Do you like it?"

"It's very nice," I say.

"Hercules would like it. Look, here is a Chew-Wow-Wow just like him and here's a weenie dog and a Great Dame."

Ellie laughs. "That's Dane, a Great Dane."

"That's what I said." Amelia coughs. "Ellie says we'll get a real dog someday when we have a real house and a real yard with a real fence. Ellie told me you live in a real house with a real yard."

"Ellie's right about that." She's standing on the other side of the bed smiling.

"Can me and Ellie come over to your house?"

"Munchkin!" Ellie says and her cheeks blush. "It's rude to invite yourself to someone's house. Now go to sleep." Ellie leans over and kisses her.

Ellie's pajama top is wet and clinging to her. It's practically see-through. I clear my throat. "I'll pray for Amelia before I go, if you'd like."

"I would like," Amelia says.

"Me too, Munchkin," Ellie says. "Can I pray with you?"

"Yes, of course you can."

I lay my hands on Amelia's head and Ellie places her hands over mine. She tells Amelia I'm going to make her all better.

Ellie tiptoes to the closet and glances over at Amelia curled up with Dolly in her arms. She takes two towels off a top shelf and gives one to me. "You can turn the heater up," she whispers and points toward the space heater in the other room. "You have to stand right in front of it to get warm. I'll be out in a sec."

She shuts the door behind me. I walk around Ellie's bed to get to the heater. I turn up the thermostat and start toweling my hair. Why am I still here? Amelia's in bed. I prayed. What I need to do is to go home, peel out of these clothes and put on dry ones. It's no longer raining. From the window, I can see the highway and bridge, the river black and choppy.

"Figures." Ellie comes out drying her hair. "Now that we're home, the rain stops. Did you get warmed up?" I nod. She changed into a short robe. "You prayed Munchkin right to sleep. Oh, that sounded wrong." She giggles and hangs the towel around her neck.

"That's all right, I know what you meant."

"I meant your prayer came straight from here." She lays her hand over my heart. "Amelia adores you."

She pulls me into a hug and I return it, because it's a thank-you hug, that's all it is, but it lasts longer than a thank-you hug. A shiver travels through my body.

"You didn't dry off very well." She uses her towel to dry the back of my head. She dries my neck and under my ear. Along my jaw. I feel her breath on my face. I hear it change.

I should go.

She kisses me. Her lips are soft and wet. I see down inside her robe. How her body curves. I see everything. I pull her into an embrace and lean into the kiss.

Gabe is confessing. He's red-eyed and so sorry. I know what he did. Charlee filled me in when I arrived and then she called for him and while he trudged up the stairs, she got all over my case about where the hell had I been? She'd left a dozen messages on my phone. I told her the hospital.

She sent Gabe to her family room a couple hours ago, after she found him in the candy aisle at the grocery store while she was shopping. She brought him over to her place, the wall sized TV he loves to watch – turned off, with orders to sit quietly and think about what he did.

"Dad, Dad, please don't be mad." Gabe's hands are clasped. "I didn't mean to."

"You didn't mean to?" Charlee's sitting beside me on the arm of the chair looking over the top of her glasses scowling.

Gabe shrugs and toes the hardwood floor with

his sock foot.

"Why would you do such a thing?" I ask. "You know right from wrong."

A long drawn out sigh and he doesn't look up.

After I left Ellie's, I headed home, thinking about a hot shower and changing into clean clothes. I wanted to salvage what was left of the day with my son.

"Dad, Dad." He's looking at me now, the pleading eyes. "You got to believe me, James gave me the candy."

Charlee called when I was a block from home. I pulled the phone out of my coat pocket and noticed the dozen notifications of her previous calls and knew something was wrong.

"James told me to put the candy in my pocket. He said it was okay, no one would know."

"It was not okay." I spring out of the chair and he steps back. "Good Lord, Gabe, if James told you to follow him off a cliff, would you?"

"No. I don't want to fall off a cliff."

"See, you have a head, Gabe; you can think and act for yourself. No one can make you do something you don't want to do."

I think about Ellie and the kiss and backing up to her bed.

"You should have said no." I pace back and forth in front of him and by his wide open eyes; I can tell I'm scaring him. "You should have walked away. Did you even think of the consequences? Did you, Gabe?"

I try pushing Ellie out of my head. I did a stupid thing. I didn't think about consequences until after.

Tears are rolling down his cheeks. "It was just one little bag of Skittles, that's all I took. I'm not lying.

Honest. James stuffed candy in all of his pockets and he told me to, but I didn't." He sniffs and wipes his nose on the back of his hand.

He didn't, he's telling the truth. Charlee found him slipping the Skittles into his pocket. She saw him refuse more. She patted the boys down, made them put the candy back and gave them a good talking-to. Then she marched them straight to the manager, a guy we knew from high school, who had a giant crush on her, and made the boys own up. He gave them a scare and they promised to never shoplift again.

I slip my arm around Gabe's shoulders. "I know you're not lying, but what you did is wrong, do you understand?"

"I know. I won't ever do it again, I promise. I learned my lesson. You aren't going to tell Mom are you?"

Am I going to tell Mom? I sit on the oversized ottoman that's pushed up to the couch and lean into my hands. Today wasn't supposed to turn out this way. I look up and there Gabe is, his hands clasped and his begging fist extended. The right thing would be to confess.

"What do you think you should do?" I ask and his hands fall to his sides. "Well?"

"Well. Mom will get really, really mad and scream at me and when I try to tell her I only took one and no more, she won't listen and she'll send me to my room like forever. While I'm in there, you and her will have a big screaming fight and I'll hear it with my door closed. Not telling isn't lying, right, Dad?"

If I hadn't left him with that James kid, none of this would have happened.

"Right, Dad?"

He got the fear of God put in him today. He feels bad enough. "I think you've learned your lesson. No need to burden Mom with it."

Charlee shoots me a narrow eyed glance and turns to Gabe. "Go back to the family room while I talk to your dad." She sits beside me.

"Thanks Dad."

"To the family room," Charlee says, "and this time you can watch TV."

"Really?"

"Yes, really."

He jets down the hall to the stairs and she pulls up her legs and sits cross-legged on the ottoman facing me.

"I think he understands how serious this is, don't you?" I ask.

"He was pretty shaken by the whole thing."

"Then why the look?"

"No look."

"Technically, not telling isn't lying."

"I'm not at all sure Grace would agree." She shrugs. "But that's between you and her. So tell me what was it you were doing while your son was shoplifting?"

"I told you." I run my hand through my hair. It's dry now. "I was at the hospital on River Street business."

"But River Street's shut down, isn't it?"

"Yes. Amelia woke up with a high fever this morning. Ellie doesn't have a car so I drove them."

"Why did she call you? The nuns drive, don't they?"

"She needed me. She needed help and called me."

"And driving her to the hospital took most of the day?"

"Why are you grilling me?"

"I bailed out your son. I deserve an explanation."

"Thank you for doing that." She looks at me. "Ellie was scared. I stayed with them. I still consider myself her pastor, okay?"

"Okay."

We sit without talking. The lights flicker and come back.

"I screwed up," I say.

"You sure did. Aside from the shoplifting issue, Gabe told me how excited he was about your Bigfoot plans. He said he was going to eat the whole Bigfoot platter and be a celebrity. Were you really going to let him order that?"

"Yeah." I shrug and she chuckles. "That wasn't my only screw-up."

"There's another one?"

"Yes, bigger."

"Bigger?" She seems surprised.

I nod. "If I tell you what I did will you listen?"

"Well, yeah."

"I mean listen without judging and try to understand where I'm coming from."

"What the hell did you do?"

"Uh. I took Ellie home and –"

"And?"

"I, I mean, I carried Amelia upstairs to their apartment, they live on the third floor. Ellie asked me to come inside and put Amelia in bed so I did and then afterwards, uh, I uh and Ellie –"

"Oh my God." Charlee comes up on her knees

and clutches me by the arms. "Did you have sex with that girl?"

"No, oh no, that's not what I did."

"Please tell me you're not a cheating husband."

"I'm not." I hold up my hands and she lets go of me. "I didn't, we didn't."

"Then what did you do?"

"She kissed me. I didn't ask for it. She just did it."

"That's the big screw-up? She kissed you?"

"Isn't it big enough?" I ask and she looks at me. "You were right. She has feelings for me."

Charlee smirks. "You should have listened to me."

"I know."

I never meant to tell Charlee this much.

"Is there more?" she asks.

I don't answer and she slumps back on her heels.

When I think about what happened, it isn't me who did it, it's a stranger. He liked how Ellie made him feel. He wanted it.

I returned the kiss is what I tell Charlee. I keep the details to myself.

She shakes her head. "Didn't the fact that you're married cross your mind?"

It didn't actually, not in the moment, but I don't say so.

Lord. Forgive me. I learned my lesson. I won't go anywhere near her apartment again. I won't let it happen again.

"I didn't go inside to have sex with her," I say. "I wanted to help her. I was trying to be her pastor."

Charlee is twisting her wedding ring around and around. She's probably thinking about Michael.

"Maybe you aren't the right one to help her," she

says without looking up.

I tell myself what happened today didn't mean anything. "I'll keep my boundaries from now on."

"Are you going to tell Grace?"

I imagine confessing, asking her forgiveness and the fight that would follow. The kind of screaming, not listening, not hearing kind of fight Gabe knows so well.

"Confess to Grace?" I ask. "Are you out of your mind?"

Chapter Thirteen

Grace hugs my neck and sings "Happy birthday." She kisses me all over my face.

"I thought you wanted me to set up the table." I unfold a chair and place it at the head.

She takes a breath and sings. "Thank you, dear husband. The table looks grand."

"You're welcome." I dodge a kiss and reach for the ninth chair. "Last one. You're in high spirits tonight."

"We're having a party." She licks my ear.

"Hey," I say and she does it again.

"Come on, it's your birthday," she says. "And you don't look a day older than you did the first time I laid eyes on you and –"

"Maybe it's time you made an appointment with the eye doctor." I chuckle and push the chair up to the table.

"There's nothing wrong with my eyes." She squeezes my cheeks. "Now if I may finish what I was saying?" She makes my head nod up and down. "Good – the first time I laid eyes on you and God witnessed to my heart that you were the man for me."

"I'm not the same man."

"I'm not the same woman." She breaks into the birthday song again. "Happy birthday to Noah –" She draws out the last note and twirls.

She's wearing the new blue and white polka-dot skirt she modeled last night and a low cut blouse. I grab her around the waist, dip her back and kiss her. "You are one sexy pastor's wife." I kiss a line down to the first button and she moans.

"We're home." Gabe clad in baggy shorts and the bright green rain boots, skips in and Grace comes out of my arms straightening her blouse.

"Me and Grandma Libby picked up the cake. Can we show it to Dad?"

"I don't see why not." My mother sets a pink box on the counter.

"Thanks for picking up the cake last minute," Grace says. "I've been running behind all day."

"Not a problem." My mother starts picking the tape off the box.

Hercules yips and tears down the stairs, Henry on his tail and they both hit linoleum and skid into my mother. She bends down and scratches their ears. "The kitchen is off limits to you boys tonight." She sends them back upstairs and they actually go. She watches until they reach the top stair and then she opens the cake box.

The cake and decorations are the same every year, since me and Charlee were kids. Only the age changes, this year, Happy 35th Birthday Noah and Charlee is scrawled in red.

"Can I have a lick?" Gabe asks.

"No way." I latch onto his wrist as he goes in for one. "This cake's off limits to sneaky fingers." He giggles.

I remember the birthday Charlee and I turned Gabe's age. We sneaked into the kitchen to steal a lick and found an undecorated cake and a bowl, brimful with fluffy yellow. I remember sitting behind the willow tree, the bowl between us, and Charlee drawing a finger line down the middle, my side – your side, and sticking our fingers down, down, until they touched ceramic. I remember our frosting hands, velvety and sweet. We licked the bowl clean. Then I puked all over Charlee's new hot-pink Jellies, the shoes, an early birthday present from my mother. I chuckle.

"What's funny?" my mother asks.

"I was thinking about another birthday."

"Let me see, could it be the year of the frosting fiasco and the hot-pink Jellies?"

"Yep." We break out laughing.

"The frosting what?" Gabe asks. "What are Jellies?"

Grace looks at me. She doesn't know the story.

Gabe tugs on my arm. "Dad, Dad, what are –"

"You know what?" I ask and he shakes his head. "The cake is perfect. So what's everyone else going to eat?"

"He can't eat the whole cake, right Mom?"

Grace is checking the salmon. "Almost done, and Gabe, Dad will be so full of salmon; he'll only have room for one, maybe two, pieces of cake, so you have nothing to worry about."

"Really, Dad?"

"I don't know about that, I'm pretty hungry."

Gabe punches me in the gut and I start tickling him. He screeches and the doorbell rings.

"We have a party to put on," Grace says and races Gabe to the door.

"I'd like to show you something." My mother reaches in her pocket and takes out her wallet and flips through a half dozen pictures. "Here it is." She leaves it in the sleeve. "This is you on your birth day, 35 years ago, taken a couple hours after you were born."

I don't remember this picture. In it, she's holding a baby wrapped in blue. He has a headful of hair. She has a wide open smile, but it wasn't for the camera.

"Me and you," she says, smiling like she did then and I nod. "One of the few pictures Twila didn't take the scissors to." She chuckles, closes the wallet and puts it back in her pocket. "Honey, the day you were born was one of the happiest days of my life." She hugs me and wishes me a happy birthday.

"What's keeping you two?" Grace calls from the living room where she's serving appetizers. "Everyone's here."

I hear laughter. Laughter is heartening, a good start, as I've been worrying about my mother and Dad and Mark at the same party.

"Coming," I say.

"We'd better join the guests," my mother says. "For what it's worth, the best thing I've ever done is come back home."

"I can't celebrate our birthdays without you." Charlee is standing at the edge of the dining room grinning. She runs into my arms and I lift her off the floor.

"Happy birthday," we say in unison.

The family is dishing up chips and dip and carrot sticks. When they see us, they pull out their cell phones and start taking pictures.

"All right, you got enough," I say.

"Say cheese." Anthony's phone sounds like a camera.

"No more," Charlee says and we dodge a few and they finally give up and start sending their pictures out to their internet friends.

Michael brings Charlee a plate and slaps me across the back. "Great party so far." I thank him and we exchange bits of small talk while he eats chips off Charlee's plate.

I notice my mother walking toward Dad. I jab Charlee in the side and she raises her eyebrows.

Michael is going on about his new ocean side housing development which is awaiting final approval and how he doesn't plan on selling the multi-million dollar model home, but is keeping it for short weekend getaways.

Charlee shoves the plate into his hands. "I thought we were still considering this, not that it's a done deal."

"Oh, sorry, baby, it's not. We'll talk more, I promise."

"Uh-huh, right," she says.

"If you two will excuse me," Michael says, "I'm going to see what Grace knows about the Sears building remodel."

While he's walking away, my mother reaches for Dad and hugs him. Charlee jabs me. Dad returns the hug, stiff-armed and a scowl on his face. My mother tells him how happy she is that they can put aside their differences and come together to celebrate an occasion they both agree is special. Charlee and I exchange glances and my mother slips her arm through Dad's and starts walking him over to the loveseat where Anthony and Mark are sitting.

"Let's not watch this," I whisper.

"No, let's do." Charlee snickers. "I think the family has exceeded the – anyone can be civil for a half hour – mark." We lean into each other laughing.

"Say Noah," Michael calls. He's bending over the coffee table filling up his plate. "You might want to check out your dog."

Henry is sniffing under the table for crumbs. I see a line of paw prints, a glob of yellow on his ear. I bolt into the kitchen with Grace on my heels. Find a crumpled pink box on the floor and Hercules standing knee deep in cake, grubbing around in it like a little pig. Grace is going to kill him. His head snaps out of the mess. He bats his frosting eyelashes and she doubles over laughing.

A whole roasted salmon, chrome bright, topped with lemon slices and smelling of dill is on a platter ready for me to cut into fillets. "You sit here, Dad," Gabe says and seats me at the cherry red, you-are-special, plate Grace bought three days ago to celebrate him passing third grade.

"Dinner looks delicious, Grace." Dad seats himself at the head of the table.

"Thank you. And a big thanks to Michael for providing the salmon." Grace sweeps her hand over the table. "All right, everyone, sit where you want."

"No, Mom," Gabe says. "Aunt Charlee Ms. Radcliff has to sit by Dad." Gabe pulls out the chair and pushes her into it. "And this is where I'm sitting." He plops down on the other side of me.

"Tell me, Michael, when did you find time to go fishing?" Dad asks.

"Unfortunately, I didn't. I got the salmon from a river guide friend. There's nothing better than fresh caught Spring Chinook pulled out of the Rogue."

"Hear, hear," Mark says and tells Michael he goes out once a year on a friend's jet boat custom made for Springer fishing.

Gabe gets up on his elbows and looks around me. "Aunt Charlee Ms. Radcliff, Dad will share his red plate with you, since you are special today too, and we only have one red plate."

"Oh, that's so nice of your dad."

I draw a finger line down the middle of the plate. "Your side, my side."

She nods. "Fair enough. Just so you know; these are my favorite shoes." We break out laughing.

Grace clears her throat. "Gabe, plates don't make people special. Dad and Charlee are special because it's their birthday. You don't have to call Aunt Charlee – Ms. Radcliff anymore, remember?"

Gabe smacks his forehead. "I keep forgetting she's not my teacher anymore."

I call on Dad to offer the blessing and when he finishes I ask if anyone is hungry. They cheer. "Then let's do this." I start cutting up the salmon.

"Hey, everybody," Gabe says. "Mom made brownies after Hercules ate all the birthday cake."

Anthony raises his water glass. "Here's to Grace."

"She's always a step ahead," my mother says.

"Thank you," Grace says. "The birthday brownies are in the oven and should be done by the time we finish dinner. There will be no more doggie shenanigans tonight. Hercules was sent to bed."

"Hercules didn't pull the cake off the counter," I say. "He had an accomplice." I slip a bite of salmon under the table to Henry who has been hiding under it since I put him and Hercules in the tub and sprayed them down. "Thanks for whipping up brownies," I say and Grace smiles and blows me a kiss.

Charlee whispers in my ear. "Did you slip Grace a happy pill?"

"She's in a celebratory mood." I eat a bite of salmon. "This is some good salmon."

"Grace cooked it just right. I don't remember her being this celebratory on any other holiday."

I look over at Grace. She's leaning on an elbow having an animated conversation with Anthony.

"Dad got pranked today. Tell them Dad." Gabe shoves a forkful of rice into his mouth.

"I went into my office this morning."

"His chair was all wrapped up in plastic wrap," Gabe says and starts laughing. "Isn't that hilarious? Show the picture."

I get out my cell phone, find the picture and give it to Charlee. "Take a look and pass it around. My chair wasn't all they wrapped up. They also –"

"They wrapped up his desk too, right, Dad?"

"Yes, that's exactly what they did. It took me an hour to cut through all the plastic wrap layers."

"The bow's a nice touch," my mother says and

giggles.

"A great prank," Mark says.

"It was a joint effort," I say, "between my youth group and GSA."

"Sweet," Anthony says and pours himself more water.

I don't mention the birthday card they left in my chair. Naomi and Brian's names weren't on it.

"How about more water over here?" Anthony passes me the empty pitcher.

Gabe leaps up. "I'll get it."

"No, it's the crystal pitcher and when it's full, it's too heavy for you to carry," Grace says.

"I'll get it," I say.

"No," Gabe says, "I'm strong. I'm a fourth grader now. I can do it. Give it." He reaches for the pitcher and my mother takes it out of my hands. "You and I will work together, Gabe." He slumps and starts objecting, but my mother's already in the kitchen. "Wait up, Grandma Libby."

He returns carrying the pitcher. "See, I told you, I am strong." He's holding it with both hands, straining a little, and pretending not to.

"It's too much for him," Grace says.

"He'll be fine, don't worry," my mother says.

He stops next to my chair and the water sloshes, but not enough to spill and he checks himself. "Would you like me to pour it, Dad?"

"No," Grace says.

"Yes, please do." I move my glass where he can easily reach it and he starts pouring.

Henry pops out from under the table and presses his cold damp nose on Gabe's elbow. "Henry!" Gabe squeals. "That tickles."

The pitcher tips too fast, too far and water gushes out over the rim. I can't speak, can't get out of the way fast enough. Water splashes into my lap, water heavy with ice.

I hang my pants over the shower curtain rod. I chuckle. This birthday rivals the frosting fiasco. I turn on the space heater, strip out of the rest of my wet clothes. While I towel off I'm reminded of the rain-soaked afternoon at Ellie's. Her robe came untied while we kissed. It all happened so fast. We backed up to her bed.

I open the dresser and find dry boxers, pick some jeans off the floor.

She unzipped my pants. The zipper is what jarred me back to my senses. Thank God. I sit on the edge of the bed and put on socks. Thank God, I stopped.

God told Grace I was the man for her. I think of our kiss in the dining room, the moan. We've been going through some rough spots. I'll take the moan as a sign of better days ahead.

I bend over to tie my shoes. See a glint under the bed, a piece of trash. I pick it up and aim for the garbage can and a word jumps off the wrapper, it is a wrapper, and the word is Trojan, a silver block of letters – Trojan. We haven't used condoms for years. I feel a pinch in my gut. This is a bad dream.

I'm dreaming. Of course, I am. I'm in our bedroom sitting on the edge of our bed holding a black shiny wrapper – real skin-to-skin intimacy – it says on it. The wrapper's ripped open and nothing's inside.

The bedroom door swings open and I close my hand over the wrapper. Thank God, this is it, the part in the dream where I wake up.

"Hey birthday boy, what's taking you so long?"

I see Grace – the polka-dot skirt, the blouse, the smile – she climbs on the bed and walks on her knees over to my side and wraps her arms around my neck.

I open my fist. "You didn't clean up very well."

She looks over my shoulder and into my hand. Her breath catches.

There has to be a logical explanation.

She's silent, her wide-open eyes fixed on the wrapper.

My hand begins to tremble. She comes around and sits beside me. "It isn't what you think."

I slap the wrapper into her hand. "This tells me it is." My feet come down heavy, the floorboards rattle. "Who is it? Barrett?" Her cheeks blush scarlet. "How long has this been going on, you and him?"

"Let me explain." She stands and tries to hold my hand.

I push her away. "You're having an affair."

"It's not an affair. Please, you have to believe me. I was overwhelmed in the moment today. I made a mistake."

"Today? No wonder you were running behind. You've sinned against me and your son and you have sinned against God." I lay my hands flat on the dresser and lean over it. I've broken into a sweat. My heart pounds in my ears. She pulls on my arm and I turn and see black tears rolling down her cheeks.

"I won't do it again."

"Why did you do it?"

She rubs her forehead with her fingertips.

"Now I know why we haven't had sex for months. You've been getting it from him all this time."

"No, I certainly have not." Like I've insulted her.

"I'm not good enough for you?"

"It's not like that."

"What is it like? I don't drive a fancy car? Wear expensive suits? I don't live in a mansion?"

"I don't care about those things." She plants her hands on her hips. "I don't. What happened wasn't about you."

"How could it not be? I'm your husband. You're married to me."

"Try to understand. I love you."

"You love me? No, you betrayed me." I stab my finger in her face. "You wanted to be with him."

"I want to be with you. I won't do it again." She tries to hug my neck.

I step back. "Don't touch me."

"Don't be like that. I didn't mean for this to happen."

"You didn't mean to? Grace, you're a whore."

She pops me in the chest with her two flat hands. "God will smite you for saying that. How dare you."

"How dare I what? This isn't my sin."

"It is. You've been neglecting your work at Rolling River and you've neglected us at home. River Street shut down, but you drop everything and run to those people's aide whenever they call. You haven't been a father and you haven't been a husband, Pastor Noah."

An alarm goes off. The sound is deafening.

"The brownies," Grace shouts.

I bolt downstairs and she slams the door behind me.

Bad Route Road, the street Charlee I have called Bad Heart Road since I can remember, is steep. I walked the half mile to the top without a breather and now my side is splitting. I bend over and rest my hands on my knees. Sweat is pouring off me.

The image of my wife's face, at the moment she realized I knew, is as strong in my mind as it was before I walked. How can this be real? No one can walk up Bad Heart Road without stopping.

They heard the whole thing, the God awful mess Grace has made of our life. I tried to apologize to the family. I felt like I should and I started to, but I broke down before I got through it.

My breathing is beginning to even out. I stretch my back and lean against the wrecked pole the street sign, mangled and lying over there in the bushes, used to be attached to. I catch a whiff of burnt brownies.

Dad and the others opened the windows, cleared most of the smoke and my mother threw out the blackened pan, explaining there was no salvaging the brownies. Then Dad announced his intent to expel the devil from my home. My mother wagged one of the bright orange oven mitts she was wearing in his face and said he would do nothing of the sort. She came over and held me, patted my back with her mitts on and let me know that Gabe was all right, in her room watching the History channel and hadn't heard much of the fight. Charlee took me by the arm and walked me outside and said if I wanted to take a walk and clear my head, everyone would understand.

Grace said I was the man for her and had sex with another man. How am I supposed to clear that out of my head? She led him up to our room. Took off her clothes, laid down in our bed and he was ready with his sheepskin condom.

A horn beeps. A Jeep. It's Charlee. She powers down her window. Pulls her glasses down her nose and looks over them. "Get in." I shake my head. "You've been out here long enough. Come on, get in the car."

"No, I'd rather walk." I start down the hill and she turns the car around and drives down the wrong side of the street alongside me. "Go home," I say.

"No. I'm worried about you."

"I'm fine, really."

"Where are you going?"

"I don't know." My voice breaks and tears well in my eyes. "I want to be alone." The sidewalk dips and I stumble.

"You're going to hurt yourself."

"I don't feel like talking."

"Then don't." She reaches over and opens the door.

Chapter Fourteen

I try unlocking my office, but the key I was holding a second ago is no longer in my hand. I look on the floor. I don't see it. Hercules is standing on his hind legs scratching the door with his paw. "I'm fine. I'll find it and we'll go inside and start work like we do every morning."

"Good morning, Noah," Dad says and I look over my shoulder. He's escorting Grace out of his office, her face buried in his chest, his arm around her shoulders. She's a wrinkled mess in yesterday's skirt and blouse. "I'll see you now." Dad beckons with a nod.

"Not now."

He walks Grace toward the chapel, as if I said nothing at all, speaking to her in a soothing, kind voice and it angers me, hearing him talk to her like that. I start digging through my pockets for the key and see it on the floor, a dull gold and plain as day beside my foot.

Charlee said I looked like hell when she dropped

me off at home to change clothes and pick up my car. I thanked her and she reached for my hand and squeezed it. "My spare room is yours for as long as you need." She offered to come inside, but I declined, because I was fine and besides, she'd already done so much, taking me to her place and staying up all night, even though I was lousy company. She said I slept some, but I sure don't feel like it.

My office door swings open and Hercules trots in and sits the way I taught him waiting for his chicken treat, but I gave him the last one yesterday. "Sorry, buddy." I squat down and scratch him behind the ears.

I found the poor little guy staked in the back-yard this morning. Our house was cold, all the lights turned off and the blinds pulled, like we'd been on vacation. I thought the folded piece of notebook paper I found propped against the coffeemaker was a note from Grace. I opened it with shaky hands and discovered it was from my mother saying she and Anthony took Gabe and Henry hiking for the day. No mention of Grace and I wondered if she spent the night with her lover.

I sit at my desk for some time, doing nothing, but stare into my hands and go over what Grace did, starting with the realization she'd been caught to when I stalked out and back to the beginning: the Trojan, the realization. I'm ready to bash my head against the wall to stop the loop, when Joni opens my door and tells me Pastor Paul wants to see me now, right now.

A talk with Dad is inevitable and I decide now is as good a time as any to get it over with. I give Hercules his squeaky bone and shut him in my office.

Dad's door is wide open. I knock on it and he nods toward a chair.

"I'll stand."

He leans forward, folds his hands. "I understand how painful this is to talk about."

"We don't have to talk about it." I walk over to the window and stare out over the river, the same dismal gray as the sky, and slopping against the pylons. "I don't know what I'm going to do. Grace turned my life upside-down. I need time to think." A gull perches on a post, its beady eyes looking in. "I need space."

"I understand. You're in shock. You're angry and deeply hurt. You don't have to go through this alone. Come sit down." He pauses.

"I'm fine, Dad."

"I don't believe you are. No one makes it through a trauma of this intensity without counsel or without their family, which brings us to your wife. Grace was here when I arrived. We had a long and serious talk."

"What did she tell you?" I turn while he's taking off his glasses. "This wasn't her fault? I'm a lousy husband and a bad father?"

"We prayed together. In the end, I was impressed to admonish her to fast and pray with a contrite heart, to let go of her adulterous ways, and plead with God to find it in His heart to forgive her grievous sin." He sets his eyes upon me, his jaw clenched.

"And?"

"What do you think?"

"I can't see myself forgiving and forgetting if that's

what you're asking."

He sighs and leans back in his chair. "Your wife is a smart woman. She fully understands her sin and the eternal consequences. I believe she'll take this opportunity to get back on God's side."

"If I hadn't caught her, she'd still be living in sin."

"Listen to me. Your wife is in danger. She's hanging by a thread. Satan wants her. He wants her bad. He's lurking in the shallows, waiting with welcoming arms while he urges her on - come closer, come unto me."

A shiver goes up my spine. "Well, that's her problem, isn't it?" I think of the Trojan, our bed and her and Barrett having sex in it. "She took what she wanted with no regard to me and Gabe. She wrecked our marriage."

"An affair doesn't mean a marriage is over. Your wife needs you more than she's ever needed you before."

"She found someone else." I throw my hands up. "Whose side are you on?"

"I'm on God's side. Now sit down." He waits until I do. "Grace needs your love, she needs your prayers and support and as her husband, you're required to give her an outpouring of all those things."

"She committed adultery. I'm not required to give her anything."

"When you married her, you promised to stay through the best and the worst." Dad stands, lays his hands flat on the desk and leans across. "These are the worst times, are they not?"

"Yes. They are the worst."

He comes around and sits on the corner of his

desk. "For a moment, I want you to think past your own pain and consider Grace; she is in the darkest place she has ever been. When I laid my hands on her head to pray, I felt the power of the beast within her. She's sinking. She can't pull out by herself. She needs you. You can save her."

"Maybe I don't care."

"If she were standing in front of a train, you'd scoop her off the tracks, without one thought to how she wronged you, without a thought to your own safety." He grabs me by the shoulders. "Noah, my son, you're a good man. You're honest and above all, you're loyal."

"I don't know if I'm any of that." I shake him off. "All right, we've hashed over my personal business long enough. So, unless you have anything church related to discuss, I'll go back to work."

"This mess you're in isn't all personal. What happened between you and Grace has very much to do with Rolling River."

"My wrecked marriage is a private matter."

"Your wife had an affair with a prominent citizen of Rivers Edge. No matter how discreetly we handle this, people are bound to find out. As leaders in Rolling River, the way you and Grace conduct yourselves through this crisis will make or break the ministry I have worked the last 35 years to build."

"Oh, of course, we've been over this. Business before family."

"I'm very much concerned about you, Son. You are the head of your household. You are responsible for your wife. She is not alone in her sin. Somehow, whether it was through sin or neglect, you've allowed

Satan access to your home."

I spring out of the chair. "I'm not responsible for Grace's actions."

"Satan has attacked your beautiful wife and led her astray. She partook of the forbidden fruit. Like Eve, she's weak."

"Grace isn't weak. She chose to have an affair."

He smacks his hand down on the desk. "You've been called to take up the cross. You have a long, arduous journey ahead." He pauses and his face softens a bit. "Oh Son. Do not despair. I promise you, when you let go of your pride and turn your heart completely over to Jesus, you will lead your wife and son back to the fold. You will stand as a shining example to the faithful and faithless that Jesus heals the heartbroken, that Jesus overcomes all and Jesus redeems every sinner who sincerely repents. Rolling River is counting on you. Your family is. Be brave. You have a great work to do."

I remember. When I was little and Dad in the middle of his preaching would leap into the congregation. Scoop me off the bench and taking the stairs two at a time, he'd carry me on stage, to the edge where the white lights come out of the floor and burn holes in your eyes if you stare at them. I remember looking out over a river of people and Dad telling them I was Rolling River's miracle, a sign that hope shines bright in a dark and disappointing world. We live in the dark end days, he'd say. Believe you me. God's sword is whet and drawn! But don't you worry; He's on the side of the righteous. His plan will not be thwarted. In the end, good will overcome evil and Noah will lead the good and faithful back to Jesus. Dad kissed my face and lowered his voice talking only to me. You are the chosen one. Be brave, Son, and the windows of Heaven will be opened unto you. Dad put me down; raised his hands up to Jesus and shouted – Thus saith the Lord. The mighty river crashed against the pylons, I remember. The floorboards shook, the building reeled and I grabbed onto Dad's leg and hung on for my life.

Dad's hand clamps over my shoulder and I look up and see Grace coming in. Dad pulls a chair around and tells her to take a seat. She crosses her ankles and folds her hands in her lap.

"Restoration is God's way," Dad says. "Restoration is the only way. We have much work to do and as long as you are both agreeable, we may as well get started."

Grace looks over at me and says she's ready.

Gabe clomps out of the house. "Dad, Dad, I'm really, really, really sorry about the water. I won't ever pour it on you again, I promise. I mean it, I'll be more careful. Will you forgive me?"

"There's nothing to forgive. It was an accident. How was the hike?"

"It's so not fair. After the hike, Grandma Libby and Uncle Anthony were meeting Uncle Mark at the Chowder House for dinner and Mom wouldn't let me go." He folds his arms, blows air out of his nose. "She knows how much I like clam chowder."

"Sorry about that, but Mom and I want the family around the table for dinner tonight."

"Grandma Libby's the grandma of our family and

Mom didn't make her stay home."

"Your grandma's an adult. Come on, let's go inside."

I let Hercules off the leash and he disappears. I'm home early, 15 minutes before the time Grace and I agreed on this morning. I smell dinner cooking. The aroma doesn't make my stomach growl or mouth water, like it used to when I came home.

Gabe tugs on my hand. "Are you still mad about the water?"

"No, I'm not mad, I never was."

"Okay." Gabe hangs his head.

I slip my arm around his shoulders and walk him to the living room, sit him down on the couch and squat in front of him. "Listen, Gabe, Mom and I are going through some rough times." He nods. "Our troubles are not your fault. Getting a lapful of ice water was a bit of a shocker." I chuckle and he giggles. "But it was an accident like I said. I assure you the water didn't start or have anything to do with what's going on between me and Mom."

He fiddles with his fingers. "What's going on with you and Mom?"

"It's a complex matter that's not for your ears." I sigh. "What's important is Mom and I love you and no matter what's going on between us, we'll never stop loving you."

"Do you love Mom?"

"Uh."

I pause. After what she did to me? Do I love her? "Dad, Dad?"

I look in his eyes all filled with hope. "Sure, buddy, sure I do."

"You're home early." Grace comes around the couch.

"A little bit." I stand and try to gauge by her expression how much she heard, but I can't. She has changed into tight jeans and her hair is down.

She hugs me. Over her shoulder, I see Gabe watching. I hug her back.

"All right." She pulls away. "Before dinner –" She looks at me, raises her eyebrows and pauses.

"Before dinner we'll read a passage from the Bible and say family prayers." I sound like a robot, repeating Dad's instructions, but it's a start, I guess.

"I'll get your Bible." Gabe runs off.

"How was the rest of your day?" Grace sits on one side of the love seat.

I want to tell her today was another heart wrenching day, thanks to her, but it wouldn't be in keeping with the spirit of rebuilding a relationship, so I say fine, my day was just fine, and I sit in the chair across the room, not beside her. Her lip trembles.

After Dad finished counseling us this morning, I walked to Area 51. Per the agreement I made with Grace as a step toward reconciliation, I called Mel on a water bottle phone I found on the way over and smashed before I gave him the news that I was stepping down as commander.

"If you're wondering," I say, "I recruited someone to watch over the River Street folks, like I said I would."

"Thank you."

Finn was reluctant to step in for me, but finally agreed saying God would send me back. I let him think it. He said he'd watch over Mel. He was worried about Justice. Together, we went to see him. Found him living in a lean-to with a guy Finn thought he recognized as the one who provides drugs in exchange for favors from young men.

I lean into my hands.

"I forwarded you the email I sent resigning from my committee," Grace says, a lift in her voice. I look up and see her nodding. "I also made a list of all my passwords. Gave you access to my calendar, my computer and cell phone, like I said I would. Feel free to check on me any time you want."

"Thank you."

"You talked to Anthony and Mark?"

"No."

"But you will, right?"

"Yes."

"It's part of the agreement."

"I know, I know it is," I shout and she flinches. "I know what we agreed on."

She looks wounded. Replace anger with forgiveness was Dad's counsel and he stood by her side while she formally asked me to forgive her.

I didn't forgive her.

"Dad, Dad, I found your Bible under a pile of grocery bags." Gabe rushes in, holding it over his head.

"I have a passage." Grace says and reaches for it. She flips pages. "Here it is. Psalm 147:3. He healeth the broken in heart, and bindeth up their wounds." She smiles. "Isn't this a beautiful promise?"

"Did your heart get broke?" Gabe asks and Grace's smile disappears.

"Yes, it did," she says, "and Dad's did too." She closes the Bible and gives me a sideways glance.

"How can you stay alive if your heart is broke?" Gabe asks a little panicked.

"Our hearts aren't broken like that," I say. "Heartbroken is a way of saying a person is sad."

"You've been sad for a really long time," Gabe says.

"Maybe a little," I say.

Grace clears her throat. "The good news is God will heal our hearts and in the end, we'll have brand new shiny hearts that are stronger and nicer than the old ones."

"When's God going to heal you?" Gabe asks.

"Soon," Grace says the same time I say – "Hearts take a long time to heal."

Grace served one of my favorite meals, roast beef with mashed potatoes and gravy. Eating dinner together was awkward at first and every bite tasted the same. Then Gabe started talking about the hike. How Grandma Libby pointed out different kinds of mushrooms along the trail. How Uncle Anthony swung on a tree branch that broke and landed in the mud on his butt. This got us laughing and the rest of dinner felt kind of normal. Grace is so pretty when she laughs.

She's pretty now, bending over kissing Gabe goodnight. I turn off his light and we shut the door. In the hall, Grace embraces and kisses me. I don't want to kiss her, but we haven't kissed like this for a long time and I don't want to stop. We kiss into the bedroom and she shuts the door with her foot, unbuckles my belt while I unbutton her blouse and kiss her neck and throat. She's beautiful. The blouse slips off her shoulders and I stop.

I stop because I've remembered the day at Ellie's. Her untied robe slipped off one shoulder. The other side came off easy. I came so close to doing what Grace did with Barrett. But I stopped. I stopped. Grace didn't.

She steps back. "What's the matter?"

"Why did you bring him up here?" I try to buckle my belt. "You said you weakened in the moment. How does that work? You walked him up the stairs. You had all that time to think. You could have stopped it."

She doesn't answer. She follows me downstairs buttoning her blouse. "Paul said God hasn't forsaken me. This is our trial and God wants us to learn from this."

"I heard what Dad said." I grab a jacket.

"Where are you going?"

"I'll be at Charlee's."

"But you agreed we'd reconcile."

"Did I say I wasn't reconciling?" She shakes her head. "I don't want to sleep with you."

"It's part of reconciling. We can put this tragedy behind us. You have to try."

"I can't put it behind. You and Barrett having sex is all I think about. How am I supposed to trust you again? This is going to take time."

"Are you getting a divorce?" Gabe shouts. He's standing at the top of the stairs.

Chapter Fifteen

Ellie glances over her shoulder and grins. I smile and say hi and sit at the counter. The customer at the drive-through adds a pizza bagel to his coffee order and Ellie pops one in the toaster oven.

I'm still smiling. She makes me feel like smiling which is the reason I started coming here for coffee two months ago. That and the easygoing chit-chat back and forth and for a half-hour my life feels normal. Two months ago, Grace betrayed me.

Thankfully, Ellie's still at work. I thought I'd miss her, since I got stuck watching Gabe and Grace was late picking him up, an hour late from a meeting and when she finally did arrive she was flushed and not sorry.

Ellie leans out the window and gives her customer his iced coffee and the bagel along with a warning that it's hot out of the oven. Her little shirt is riding up her back. She's wearing short shorts.

I eye her longer than I should. If the easygoing chit-chat I come here for turns serious, which it does on occasion, I try to lighten it up. Like the day Ellie asked if I was divorcing my wife. I remember the bite in the way she said – your wife. I changed the subject to something that didn't matter, I don't recall what, but then on and off for the remainder of the day, I wondered what life would be like without Grace in it.

The customer drives away leaving a cloud of exhaust rich in fuel. "My shift was over a half hour ago." Ellie swipes her arm across her forehead. "If Deb wasn't running late, I would have missed you." She sticks out her bottom lip. She has a big coffee stain in the middle of her shirt. "Don't tell, but I'm glad she's late."

"Our secret."

She giggles and starts my coffee. She knows what I want.

When the idea of divorce enters my mind, thoughts of Gabe follow, and the night he asked if we were getting one and my stomach ties in knots. Of course I'm not divorcing Grace. Divorce is wrong, especially for a pastor. When I told Ellie, she said I deserved a wife who loved me with all her heart and mind and soul. I thought Grace was a wife like that. How many of Dad's twice a week marriage counseling sessions will it take before Grace starts loving me with all her heart and mind and soul. Or will she ever?

Grace talks to me in Bible verses now. Colossians 3. I forgive as the Lord forgave you. Isaiah 43. God blots out our transgressions and remembers them no more.

"Noah?" I look up. Ellie's scooping ice into a plastic cup. "I was just saying that Finn's taking his role with River Street to heart. He arrives at Area 51 promptly at eight every morning, along with Dorothy and the dogs, for prayers and fellowship with anyone who wants to join in. Me and Munchkin went a couple times. He has a following, can you believe it?" We chuckle. "Even Mel comes out of his cardboard box. I mean headquarters. He calls you on his secret agent phone and Finn tells him you can't pick up because you're away on a secret mission, but you're coming back."

"I'm not."

"So that means you're not my pastor, doesn't it?" She cocks her head. Her dark eyes sparkle.

"I guess."

The day I went to her apartment comes to mind. I've been asking God to take these lustful thoughts out of my head. The sex drive, a mighty gift from God, Dad says, can corrupt your soul and Grace must learn to control hers. Dad and Grace don't know about Ellie.

I clear my throat. "God chose Finn to lead River Street. He will be there for you and the others."

"I don't want him." She picks up the can of whipped cream and shakes the heck out of it.

"Please give Finn a chance."

She squirts whip on top of my coffee.

Grace accuses me of not putting my heart into reconciling. I left River Street, didn't I? I'm trying to trust again. Not once, have I checked up on Grace, who claims she's an open book now, although the idea flashed through my mind this morning when she was so late. Per agreement, I go home for breakfast and devotional in the mornings and eat and pray there every night. She says we can't expect our marriage to heal if I don't come back to her bed, if I don't pull out of my gay brother's wedding. I lean into my hands.

"I made you a triple." Ellie sets my coffee on the counter. "You look like you could use a boost." I thank her and pay, tell her to keep the change.

She brings over a straw and peels off the paper. I stick it in my drink and the chocolate coated coffee beans rattle on top of the plastic lid.

She leans over the counter and whispers. "I don't give just anyone two coffee beans."

I think of the day I kissed her. I didn't want to stop kissing her. Her lips are close enough to kiss now. Is that what she wants? A shiver goes through my body and a customer pulls up to the window.

Charlee left a magazine next to the coffeemaker open to an article – Ten Things Not to Do after Your Wife Cheats on You. In neon yellow, she highlighted #4 – Revenge Sex Hurts You More than Her.

I don't intend to have sex with Ellie, revenge or otherwise. She's someone else's wife. I'm Grace's husband.

Grace was setting two long tapers out on the dining room table last night when I went home for dinner. She beamed when she saw me. Threw her arms around my neck and kissed me. We're dining alone tonight she said and rattled off where my mother went and who Gabe was spending the night with. I tried to be excited, but she could tell I wasn't.

I finish the last of my coffee drink. Wipe the counter off with a napkin. Ellie's busy toasting bagels. I'll leave as soon as she finishes with this customer.

Dinner was nice, candlelight and all. Grace and

I didn't have much to say, until we started reminiscing, our first Christmas, family barbeques, the day we moved into our house. The night Gabe was born.

Grace wanted to go upstairs to the bedroom after dinner, of course. For a surprise, she said and led me up there, flung open the door and went inside. I stopped in the hall and peered in.

The dresser was where the bed used to be and the bed was in the corner positioned at an angle and covered with a white comforter, instead of the blue.

"Well, don't just stand out there," she said. "Come in." I hesitated and her lip trembled. "Don't you like it?"

"Sure, I'm just surprised."

"Gabe helped move the furniture. It didn't cost much. I bought the Bed-in-a-Bag from Target on clearance." She forced a smile. "Now our bedroom is all new."

She stood next to the bed. She was beautiful, her hair down, face flushed. It had been so long since we made love. I went inside. I said the room looked nice and a real smile replaced the forced one and she said she loved me. I didn't say anything.

The coffee shop door flings open and the other barista bursts in, breathless and praising Ellie for covering, and she jumps in to help with the order.

Our bedroom was not all new like Grace said. The pictures on the dresser weren't new, the hole in the wall wasn't, not the stain on the carpet. I tried not to think about the bedroom at all. I focused on my wife's lips, her neck. She pushed me down on the bed. I pulled her on top of me and we sunk into the new comforter. I pulled her shirt over her head. She unbuttoned mine. She kicked off her shoes. One banged against the garbage can and knocked it over.

The garbage can was not new. It's in the same place it has always been. It made me remember the trash I found under the bed. When I aimed at the trash can and didn't let go. I remembered. The ripped open condom wrapper, silky smooth lubricant it said on the backside.

Grace rolled off me and set the garbage can upright. I buttoned my shirt and she put on hers. I said I was sorry. She said it was all right. Her face said it wasn't.

I stayed for dessert. She asked me to. She brought two chocolate lava cakes into the living room, along with coffee, and we ate quietly like two people who didn't know each other very well. We prayed after that and I kissed her goodnight. The kiss goodnight turned into a long kiss, a deep and frantic kiss and I made love to her on the couch.

She expected me to stay after that, like sex righted everything that was wrong with us. I didn't stay. As I was leaving, she folded her arms, narrowed her eyes. She had one thing to say. Genesis 2. Cleave unto your wife.

"I'm ready to go." Ellie tosses my cup in the trash.

"I'll give you a lift to the hospital." But today is her day off at the gift shop and I end up taking her home. I pull around back.

"Come up with me," she says.

My body says yes and my mind conjures up her hideaway bed, the metal workings of it, thin mattress and bare skin. "No, I can't."

"You can." She smiles and nods. "The nuns are in

Portland all day and Munchkin's gone on a play date. We can."

We could go up to her apartment right now. Start where we left off. She wants to. I want to. The sex drive is a gift from God. It has the power to corrupt your soul.

"We can't. Like we talked about before, I'm a pastor –"

"Things have changed. You said so. You aren't my pastor, Finn is, and you don't live with your wife. She cheated on you. I'd never hurt you like that." She scrambles to her knees and clamps onto my shoulders. "Noah Cathcart, I love you. I love you with all my heart and mind and soul." She presses into me and plants her lips on mine and gives me one long wet kiss.

I pull away and knock the back of my head against the window. "This is wrong." I sit up straighter and she goes back to the other side of the emergency brake. "My life is a mess right now. I can't start a new relationship. I'm still married to Grace and I'm a pastor, not yours, but Rolling River's. I have obligations there."

"I understand." She smiles and a wave of relief washes over me. "You have moral obligations."

I nod, thankful she's taking this well.

"Making love wouldn't be proper since we aren't married. You're right. It will be hard, but I'm willing to wait until you get your life straightened out."

I look at her – the coffee stain, big eyes, big smile – and tell her I don't feel the same way about her.

❁

I unclamp my hands from the steering wheel and stretch my fingers. I'm feeling a bit uneasy about seeing Ellie again. A week has gone by since the misunderstanding. It was a misunderstanding.

Hercules comes out the backseat and licks my chin. I've been waiting in the coffee shop parking lot hoping to catch Ellie at the end of her shift so we can talk privately. I've waited 45 minutes and feel like a stalker.

Last week, she gave me her schedule the way she does every week. She told me not to be a stranger. She called what happened a misunderstanding. Still, hearing the words, I love you Noah Cathcart, coming from someone who wasn't my wife, shook me up. Did she think I loved her back?

I peer in the coffee shop window, but the sun is at an angle that makes seeing inside impossible. I'll give her ten more minutes. Then I'm going in.

I've come to tell her I won't be taking any more coffee breaks here. I'll tell her I have God's work to do. He has a plan for me and Satan is working overtime to thwart it. Dad's been telling me all along. I can't straighten out my life until I get Satan out of it. Ellie will understand.

Ten minutes is up. I take Hercules with me. Inside, the barista from last week is sitting at the counter playing a game on her phone. Ellie isn't here.

"Woot, gotcha, sucker," the barista says and drops her phone in her purse. "Can I start you a drink?" She looks up and notices Hercules. "No dogs allowed."

"I'm looking for Ellie. Did I miss her?"

"You sure did. She quit a few days ago."

I stand dumbfounded for a moment. "Why did

she quit?"

"She moved away."

"Away?"

"Yes, away, as in relocated in another town."

"Did she go back to Portland?"

"I don't know."

"Did she leave a forwarding number?"

The barista cocks her head and scrunches up her face. "You think I'd give it to you if she did? You could be a stalker for all I know."

I open the door to leave and a light wind off the water comes inside. "I'm Pastor Noah Cathcart, not a stalker, thanks anyway."

"Did you say Noah?"

I nod. "Noah Cathcart."

"In that case." She starts going through her purse. "She left something for you, if I can find it in this mess."

She must have left a note and a way to get in touch.

"Here it is." The barista pulls out an envelope and gives it to me. "A grandma of Ellie's husband passed a while ago, and Ellie and her kid moved into her house. Nice place I guess, but Ellie didn't tell me where it is."

I turn the envelope over in my hands and wonder if she left because of me.

"Sure I can't get you a drink?"

I tell her no and go back to the car. I rip open the envelope and pull out a piece of notebook paper. It's a letter from Amelia.

Hercules licks my chin and lays his head on my chest while I read.

– deer bastr noa.

I chuckle.

– we ar moovn too a butiflu hows. i luv yu an her-
coolees. cum ce us sune. Yr Frein, Amelia Sue Rawlins. ovr –

On the back is a drawing of a tree, a picket fence
and a tall skinny house. The point of the roof touches a smiling sun. Two stick figure girls are standing
in front holding stick hands along with a dog, a dog
with pointed ears and three stick legs.

I sigh.

The little girl has a banana smile, a balloon head
and perched on top is Sammy the bat and Dolly.

The girl wearing a triangle dress has a sparkling
stud in her nose. She has Ellie's big dark eyes.

The garage door is open and Gabe, his hands
full of shopping bags, is trying to shut the trunk. I
remember now, Grace mentioned back-to-school
shopping and how much she dreaded it.

"Let me get the trunk," I say as I climb out of my
car. Hercules leaps over me and speeds into the garage. Gabe drops the bags to pet him.

Grace is still in her car looking at her phone. I
knock on a window and she waves her fingers and
opens her door. I watch her legs swing out, bare legs,
a sundress.

"Dad, Dad, we bought school supplies." Gabe
holds a Target bag as high as his arm will reach. He's
beaming. "You have to see all my stuff –"

"Okay," I say and look around the car. Grace is
bending over reaching into the backseat. "How'd the
shopping go?"

"At least I don't have to cook tonight." She comes out with a large pizza box and I take it.

Gabe tugs on my shirt. "Dad, you're not listening. All 4th graders have to buy a soprano recorder for school. It says so on the 4th grade list. Can you believe it? I get to be in the Soprano Recorder Band this year, isn't that the coolest?"

"Yeah, the coolest." I try to shake Amelia and Ellie out of my head and smile.

"I already know how to play it. I'll show you." Gabe reaches in the bag.

"Leave that thing in the bag," Grace says. "You can show Dad later."

Gabe's lip goes out, then in, and he pats his leg and calls Hercules. He skitters out from under the car. "Come on, boy." They pound up the steps.

Grace comes around and picks up the bags Gabe dumped on the ground and shuts the trunk.

"He played that recorder all the way home. This is going to be a long year."

I press the garage door button. The door groans and starts inching down. "It already has been a long year. Looks like you found some school clothes."

"The stores were packed. It was an exhausting day." She pecks my cheek. "You had a long day too?"

"Yeah."

She studies my face for a moment. "You'll feel better after you eat."

I doubt pizza will take away this sinking sensation that washed over me after I read Amelia's letter. I follow Grace inside. Coraline is sitting atop her pillow yowling and Gabe, his cheeks puffed out and ruddy, is following my mother around the table while she pours milk, playing his recorder. Henry and Hercules are prancing behind him.

My mother asks me and Grace, and she has to shout over the commotion, how our days went and we groan. I set the pizza in the middle of the table. Grace puts the bags on the counter and kicks off her shoes. "Noah, there's a Caesar salad kit in one of those Target bags." Gabe's recorder squawks and she winces.

I look through a few bags before I find the salad. Grace sidles up to me. Her toenails are painted red. "Let's conveniently misplace the recorder until school starts, before it drives me insane."

"Uh-huh."

Grace cocks her head. "Want to tell me, what's the matter?"

"Nothing's the matter."

I can't get Amelia's picture out of my head. Ellie in the triangle dress, the three legged dog, the house.

"All right, mister," Grace says to Gabe. "Parade's over." She takes the recorder out of his hands and in spite of his protests, sticks it on top of the refrigerator.

After we dish up, Grace starts talking about her day, the long lines, pushy women.

I try not to think about Ellie, about no goodbyes, about her abusive husband who went to jail.

"Dad, Dad!" Gabe's leaning on his elbows. "Dad?"

Grace is explaining how much Gabe has grown since last year and how hard it was to find pants that fit at the waist and aren't too short.

"Dad?" Gabe shouts. "Dad, can you hear me?"

I start to shush him, but his troubled expression stops me. I lean across the table and whisper. "What is it?"

"How come you look so sad?" he blurts out and Grace stops talking and she and my mother turn and look at me.

"I uh –"

I remember the day Ellie took out her piercings, all but the silver stud in her nose, and she wore a dress to church and I said she looked pretty. I remember when Amelia was sick and Ellie and I tucked her in and prayed together.

Grace lays her hand over mine. "We told you, Gabe. A heart takes time to heal."

No one talks much after that. Gabe finishes off the pizza and Grace starts clearing the table.

Gabe is eyeing the refrigerator. "No way," Grace says. "No more recorder playing tonight. You got that?" He folds his arms and pouts. "Why don't you and Grandma go in the living room? As soon as Dad and I finish cleaning up, we'll come in for Bible study."

In the living room we find Gabe kneeling beside the coffee table. He has turned it into a showcase for the school supplies. Grace grumbles. "I told you not to take everything out of the wrappers. School doesn't start for a couple weeks."

"He's excited," I say. "Charlee and I used to do that."

"Humph." Grace sits on the couch. "Sit by me." She pats the space next to her. I sit and we fall into silence.

Grace never met Ellie, I never mentioned her name. I wonder if she's all right, if she plans on reconciling with her husband or visiting him in jail.

Grace pushes a pile of spiral notebooks out of the

way and puts her feet on the table.

Gabe gasps. "Mom, you ruined it." He pushes her feet off. "My supplies were in order. See, the notebooks go here." He starts putting things back the way he had them.

Grace rubs her foot. "Is Grandma going to join us?"

"She went to bed," he says.

Grace finds the Bible under a package of wide-ruled notebook paper. She offers to read and starts turning pages. It isn't long before she stops on a verse. She clears her throat. "James 4. Submit yourselves therefore to God. Resist the devil and he will flee from you."

"Does the devil have fleas?" Gabe chuckles.

"I guess the devil's called ol' Scratch for a reason," I say.

"Come on you two." Grace scrunches up her face. "This is serious." She explains flea verses flee and Gabe moves a box of crayons next to 12 pencils he already sharpened.

"Do you understand the passage?" she asks Gabe.

He nods and turns the pink eraser over and over in his hand.

"I'll tell you what the passage means," she says. "Give God control of your life. He knows your path and what's best for you, and He will never lead you astray." She shoots me a this-is-for-you look and continues. "Much like when you ride the school bus – the driver knows where he's going and how to get there. All you have to do is stay in your seat, obey the rules, and let him do his job and if you do all that, you won't have to worry about getting into trouble and you'll arrive at school safe and happy and on time."

"Good analogy," I say and Gabe asks what an analogy is. "An analogy is Mom likening God to your bus driver."

"My bus driver can't be God, she's a lady."

"That's a topic for another day," Grace says. "It's past your bedtime."

I start to get off the couch to put Gabe to bed and Grace lays her hand on my leg. "Gabe, you go brush your teeth and put on your pajamas and we'll come up and tuck you in."

"Promise?" Gabe asks and she promises. "Dad too?"

"Promise," I say.

I feel pressure from Grace's hand. See the plain gold band on her finger.

"Don't move my school stuff," Gabe says.

"Go." Grace points.

"Please, please, don't touch my school supplies. I haven't finished looking at them."

"I won't touch them. Will you please just go to bed?"

"Okay, okay, come on Henry." Henry raises an eyebrow and doesn't budge. He and Hercules have been asleep. Hercules is running in his dream.

Grace's eyes narrow and Gabe whirls around and runs. She sighs deeply.

"Want to tell me what this is about?" I ask.

"I'm concerned." Her hand slips off my leg. "You seem so sad. Gabe's noticed, your mom. People at church have been asking."

"I see. People are talking." I pause, wondering just how many people at church, or for that matter, community, know all the details about what happened between us. "Rest assured. I'm working on putting my wrecked life back in some semblance of order as fast as I can. Sorry if I haven't been happy fast enough. It's harder than you think."

"You are making it hard. There's a clear path, one that will make your life easier and happier, but you think you know best and you're steering clear of it."

"Easy for you to say, you don't know what it's like after you've been betrayed by your spouse." I get up and glare at her. "Your spouse never betrayed you."

"If you'd just listen to your dad –" Grace says.

"I'm sick and tired of you and Dad telling me what to do."

"Maybe you've forgotten that your dad speaks for God. God has mapped your road to happiness. God has, Pastor Noah, and you're not going to be happy until you shake off your pride and start obeying Him. I'm telling you. You've pushed God out of the driver's seat. You've taken control of the bus and you're speeding down a rickety wooden dock toward deep brackish waters where sea lions dwell and Satan lies in wait, anxious to drag you down to his frigid bottomless sea."

I find Charlee sitting in the dark at the breakfast bar. She waves me over. "Grab a spoon."

I flip on the lights. She's eating pie, a whole pie in a tin along with a quart of vanilla ice cream. "I already ate," I say and sit on the stool beside her and Hercules trots over to his bed in the corner of her dining room. "You okay?"

Charlee frowns. "Sure. I'm eating dessert. Why are you all sweaty?"

I look down at my shirt, the big wet spots. "Bad Heart Road."

"Dinner didn't go well?"

"Dinner went fine. Is that peach?"

She nods and I go to the kitchen and bring back a spoon. I eat a generous spoonful. "This is good."

"Don't talk with your mouth full." She gives me the ice cream off her spoon to go with it.

"The text you sent me didn't sound like you were okay. I came as fast as I could. Want to talk about it?"

"I was going to broil steaks for dinner."

"But Michael didn't show."

"I bought a pie for dessert. Peach. Peach is his favorite." She scowls at what's left.

"He didn't call."

"He did call. Are you sure you aren't hungry? I'll broil you a steak."

"No thanks."

"I hate to see them go to waste. Michael said he had to work late, but I know he isn't working."

"How do you know?"

"I read a text message on his phone earlier."

"You read his messages?"

"He was in the bathroom when it came. He stopped taking his phone in there after he dropped one in the toilet. He set the damn thing on the table right next to my eyes."

"Well, in that case, what did the text say?"

"It confirmed a meet-up with his ex at the new beach house tonight."

"I'm sorry."

"He's a big fat liar." She folds her arms and breathes out her nose. "I'm so tired of getting lied to. You know what? I don't care what he does anymore and when he comes back in the morning, if he comes back, he won't be staying long."

I want to say she'll be better off without him, but instead I give her a bite of pie and pull her into a hug.

Grace got a phone call at dinner tonight. I think back. She let it go to voice mail, but not before she broke her own no-phone-at-the-table rule and checked the incoming number. I was surprised she did. Gabe started ranting about Mom being a rule breaker and she simply said she was expecting an important call, but didn't say from whom, and at the time, I didn't think much about it. Now I wonder who. Who was she expecting a call from? Who is important? Barrett?

Charlee buries her face in my shoulder and I rub my hand up and down her back. "You okay?" I ask and she nods and a few moments later she comes out of my arms. I brush a crumb off her cheek.

"Thanks," she says. "You need a shower."

"Yeah, I do."

She shovels pie into her mouth. "Tell me why you walked up Bad Heart Road."

I prayed when I got to the top of the road. I asked God if Grace was right. I think about the events leading up to the walk – aside from Ellie leaving, the whole talk about driving the bus, how quiet we were after. What we did say was short and edgy. She didn't kiss me goodnight. She said – Proverbs 19. The foolishness of man perverteth his way: and his heart fretteth against the Lord.

I've been the foolish man. That was what God told me when I got to the top of Bad Heart Road or I think He did, if I heard right, I was breathing loud and heavy.

I stretch my back. "I'm probably going to regret the walk."

"Probably."

"After family dinner, Grace read out of the Bible." I quote it.

Charlee licks ice cream off the side of her hand. "Let go – let God?"

"Basically."

"So?"

"It got me thinking."

"About?"

"For starters, I tried to be Ellie's pastor, but I made her life worse."

"How did you do that?"

I pull Amelia's letter out of my back pocket.

Charlee reads it. Studies the drawing and gives it back. "She moved into a house?"

"She's gone. She moved out of town."

"She didn't talk to you before she left?"

I shake my head. I haven't told Charlee about El-lie falling in love with me. Now I do. I tell her how messed up that was. How guilty I feel.

Charlee drops her spoon into the ice cream car-ton. "You think she left because of you."

"I led her on. I didn't mean to. But I kept going back to the coffee shop on the days she worked. She made me feel good. I liked her company. She gave me a break from all my problems at home, but I didn't love her. She left after I told her."

"I see. You've been a stupid man, but Ellie makes her life better or worse, not you."

"That's not all I've screwed up. I wasn't a good pastor for River Street. And look at my marriage."

"That's ridiculous. You didn't make Grace cheat on you. Everyone is accountable for their own choices. The only thing you can really screw up is your own life."

"That's what I've done. I walked up Bad Heart Road to figure out what to do about it and I came to the conclusion that Grace is right. I'm driving the bus and I shouldn't be. I'm going to drive it into the river."

She scrunches up her face. "You're driving a bus into the river? What the hell are you talking about?"

"I hadn't turned my life completely over to God. That's why it's a mess. It's why I cause others unhappiness and why my marriage is falling apart. Man is an enemy to God. I have been. God wants me to fix my marriage. He outlined the way, but I haven't done all He asked me to do."

"You wanted to stay on as River Street's pastor, but your dad – God – whoever, told you to give up River Street, in order to save your marriage. You didn't want to, but you did. Was it saved? No. You felt worse, not better."

"How I feel doesn't matter. God doesn't guarantee happiness, at least not in this life. Sometimes He asks us to do hard things we don't understand or agree with, like give up on the idea of a River Street ministry. Like tell Anthony I won't marry him and Mark."

"Are you actually thinking of bailing out of their wedding?"

"No. I'm not thinking about it. After Bad Heart Road, I went to their apartment and told them." I start tearing up.

Charlee shakes her head. She doesn't understand. Anthony didn't. He wanted to know how I could flip after teaching inclusiveness. After teaching love and not judging. My explanation fell short. I started crying and left.

"Now God's driving the bus," I say.

"I get it."

"You do?"

"Yes. You're unhappy. Your life isn't working out the way you imagined. It's hard. So you've decided to hide behind your dad's dogma. You're taking the coward's way out."

I roll over and my hand bangs the coffee table knocking off another school supply, a pen, something, I don't know, it's still dark. I sit up on the edge of the couch and groan. Yesterday's walk up Bad Heart Road settled in my back and thighs. Hercules is curled on the other end of the couch snoring. We arrived in the middle of the night. The house was dark and quiet. I didn't call ahead. I left the lights off and felt my way to the couch. I shouldn't have done that. I rub my leg where I rammed it into the corner of the table last night.

I need coffee. I turn on the lamp and see the mess I made of Gabe's meticulously ordered school supplies. I try putting them back the way they were, but I don't know where the ruler or pink erasers go. I don't know which direction the pencils were lined up. I decide vertical. There's one on the floor over by my suitcase. I set it on the table in line with the others and grab yesterday's clothes off the back of the couch. Button my shirt wrong twice and leave it unbuttoned. I'm fine; really, just tired. I find my Bible stuffed between the couch cushions. I fell asleep last night in the middle of praying for Charlee. God – forgive me. Please help Charlee through her terrible trials with Michael.

While the coffee's brewing, I lean against the counter and imagine Grace coming down in her robe, bare footed and sleepy-eyed, and a beautiful bright smile emerging when she sees I came home. I'll meet her at the bottom of the stairs, pick her up and kiss her long and hard.

I open the blinds. The dahlias Grace planted are in full bloom, the red blazing in the sun. The red, Grace's favorite, I remember her saying so, and I wonder which is called One Love, the dahlia that blooms a true red. One love, a true red. How can One Love be Grace's favorite?

I pour my coffee. I made enough for Grace and my mother, but no one is stirring. Except Coraline, who races me to the table and jumps in my chair. I shoo her off. Now I've done everything I agreed to do. Dad ought to be happy. Grace will be. I draw in a breath and let it go. I'll move back to our bedroom tonight. Or I'll try.

I read the Bible while I wait for my family. Stop on Isaiah 43. Remember not the former things, nor consider the things of old. Behold, I am doing a new thing; now it springs forth, do you not perceive it? I will make a way in the wilderness and rivers in the desert.

God. Charlee's wrong. I'm not a coward. I'm doing it right now. You're in charge. Faith is all I need. No questions. Go ahead and drive me back to the bedroom.

God will get me through this. He has to. I'm on my second cup of coffee when Gabe pads down the stairs. He gets to the bottom before he notices me. "Dad, Dad!"

"Gabe. Gabe." I hold out my arms and he rushes into them.

"Are you home?"

"Yeah, I'm home." I hug him tight.

"Forever?"

"Yeah, buddy, forever."

In one of our marriage counseling sessions, Dad said stop looking at reasons to break up and start looking for reasons to stay married. Gabe is a good reason to stay married.

He pulls back and places his warm sticky hands on my cheeks. "Are you happy now?"

"Of course I'm happy. I missed you."

"And you missed Mom?"

I nod. "Sure."

"Mom told Grandma Libby you weren't ever coming home. I knew Mom was wrong. I'll go get her."

"No, let her sleep. Are you sure Mom said I wasn't coming home?"

"I'm sure."

My stomach clenches.

Gabe rushes over to greet Hercules who's wide awake and running top-speed toward Coraline,

Coraline who has transformed into a hissing mountain of fur. He skids into her, yips and runs the other way. Coraline goes after him, Gabe on their heels.

Grace will be glad to see me. This is what she wanted. I'll take the day off. With temperatures predicted in the 70s, it's a perfect day for a family picnic. We'll drive to Bigfoot country where it's cool and moist, go on a leisurely hike. We'll have fun. I try to think of the last time the three of us spent the day together having fun and I can't.

Gabe hollers from the living room. He must have noticed his school supplies aren't the way he left them.

The bedroom door opens and closes. Grace is awake. Maybe we can be happy. We will be happy. She starts downstairs. She's dressed up, a sundress and she's carrying high heels.

She stops and peers down. "What are you doing here?"

"I came home."

She steps off the last stair and I pull her into an embrace and kiss her. She smells nice, a new perfume. She feels nice.

She pulls out of my arms. "Why didn't you tell me you were coming home?"

"I live here. I thought you'd be happy."

"Oh. I am happy." She glances at her watch. "Just surprised."

"I thought I'd take the day off. Let's pack a picnic. Go hiking –"

"I can't. I have an all-day meeting."

"I don't remember you mentioning an all-day church meeting."

"Uh, no, I didn't, because the activity is a Master Gardener's planning session. For next year, I must have told you."

"You dress up for that?"

"I didn't say I was spending the day in the garden."

"No, you didn't. Well, you look pretty."

"Thanks. If I knew you were coming, I could have skipped out of it."

"Gabe said you didn't think I was ever coming back."

Her eyes narrow. "I didn't expect you home today. That's all. Sorry, honey. Take Gabe hiking. He'll love it."

"Yeah. I'll pour you coffee before you go."

"No time."

I pick up my Bible. "We can make time for the Lord." I call Gabe in and look for a passage.

"Good morning." My mother shuffles into the kitchen yawning. "You're here awfully early."

"I moved home. Come join us for Bible study."

She opens the cupboard and finds a mug. "Welcome home, honey. Go on without me." She pours herself coffee and goes back to her room.

"Dad, Dad, get in here," Gabe calls from the living room.

"No, you get in here like I asked. We're having family devotion before Mom leaves."

"Hurry up Noah." Grace is putting on one of the heels. "I'm running late."

"We have time," I say and she scowls.

"Somebody moved my school supplies." Gabe stomps in, stopping at the edge of the dining room.

"And they messed them all up."

"Spiritual matters first and then we'll talk about your stuff," I say.

Gabe grumbles, leans back against the wall and folds his arms.

I feel my face heating up. "You do what you're told and get your behind over here."

"Just read, will you? We're listening." Grace lays a hand on my shoulder and balances while she puts on the other heel.

I shut the Bible. "Joshua 24. As for me and my house, we will serve the Lord."

Chapter Sixteen

A dog yips and my head snaps over to the pew Gabe is sitting in, thinking he finally succeeded in smuggling Hercules into Sunday morning worship service. He gestures, feigning innocence. I don't see Hercules.

My time is about up. I come out from behind the pulpit. "Satan is waging an all-out war on the faithful. The beast wants you. You don't want to be on his side. In hell, you never stop drowning." I pause for a moment to let that sink in. "It's time to put on the full armor of God. Take up the sword and rise ye up to do battle for the right. God will lead you on to victory. I promise you. Let's hear Amen!"

The amen isn't the amen Dad gets when he preaches, but it's something. I look out over Rolling River's faces, there are so many. Sister Monk. She's pleased. Grateful I came to my senses and she gave Naomi and Brian permission to come back to my youth group meetings. I'm grateful for that. In the back of the chapel, behind the Benson brothers, I catch a glimpse of Dorothy and her bag of dogs, which explains the yip I thought I heard, and Finn slouched beside her. I haven't seen Finn since he agreed to minister to River Street folks. I can't imagine why he'd come here.

I give Grace the cue and she starts playing the piano softly.

"If you haven't joined God in the battle for good, it's not too late. I invite you to come up and kneel at the altar. Leave your burdens here and Jesus will welcome you home. I know He will. He welcomed me home."

People rustle in their seats. I bow my head and wait.

I moved home and got myself on God's side a month and three days ago. Dad turned Sunday morning preaching over to me. I say what he says and he's happy. Every week gets a little easier, I guess. Preparing to take over the full operation of Rolling River has kept me busy and thankfully, hasn't given me time to think about the days before or after my life took an abrupt turn. This is our new normal, Grace says.

A few are making their way up to the altar. "God loves you. He died that you might live. Come forward. Admit you're a vile sinner, we all are, and beg God's forgiveness and He will wash you clean in His blood. I promise you. All you have to do is repent. Repent and your sins will be forgiven. Repent and God will remember them no more."

I remember. The first night I preached at the 51st Street Mission and Finn was sitting on the edge of his seat, waiting for the altar call, waiting so he could tell God how vile a sinner he was. I remember the fear in his eyes. I don't see it now. He isn't rushing up to repent now.

After the closing prayer, Grace comes over and takes my hand. We walk together to open the chapel doors. She's beaming. "You've made me a happy woman, Pastor Noah. I prayed that one day, you'd find it in your heart to not only forgive, but forget." She embraces me and I wonder if this is how happy feels in the new normal.

Grace and I shake hands with folks as they file out. It's a beautiful fall day, the river that blue-blue it gets. White-edged waves break on the pylons. I drape my suit jacket over Grace's shoulders and she pecks me on the cheek.

Finn and Dorothy slipped out before I had a chance to say hello. I see them now, standing out on the sidewalk, Finn, dressed in the kilt, socks pulled up to his knees, leaning against a parking meter and Dorothy having a smoke. I excuse myself, leaving Grace in an animated exchange with Sister Monk.

Finn clasps my hand and pulls me into a hug, slaps me across the back. "Long time, no see."

"I'm happy you and Dorothy came out to worship with us. Thank you both for coming." I reach for Dorothy's hand to shake and she stubs out her cigarette.

"Thank him." She tips her head toward Finn. "He wanted to come, not me." One of her dogs pops its head out of her bag, barks and she drops what's left of her cigarette in her shirt pocket.

I give my business card to Finn. "Our meeting

times are on the back. I hope you'll worship with us again."

Finn studies my card. Then he steps back and looks out over the church, the tip of the steeple obscured by a small unassuming cloud. "Hoo-boy. You're a big time pastor now." He gives the card to Dorothy and she drops it in the bag with the dogs.

"No, I'm not a big time pastor – that would be my dad."

"You will be soon, I guess," Finn says. "You're moving up the ladder. Good for you. Your sermon today got me to thinking."

"That's good."

"It put me in a conundrum, actually."

"Maybe I can help you figure out your conundrum?"

Finn scratches at a scab on his knee. "You can try. See, you taught me that I wasn't the God-awful sinner I thought I was. Well, I thought that was what you taught me, but you must not of, 'cause today I got from your preaching that I'm a vile old codger in need of repenting or else." He puts 'or else' in air quotes. "Seems all us poor folk out at River Street are bad news sinners destined for hell."

"I – uh –"

"You see what I mean about a conundrum. I got something to show you." He looks through his wallet. Dorothy relights the cigarette.

"Here it is." Finn pulls out a raggedy piece of paper. "My eyes aren't up to par today. Will you be so kind and read it for me?" He gives me the paper.

I remember this. The Bible verse he asked me to jot down that night at the mission. Ephesians 2. I start reading and he nods. "For by grace are ye saved through faith and that not of yourselves. Grace is the gift of God."

"Thank you, Pastor. Now help me understand. First you said all us dirty rotten sinners are saved like it says in the Bible verse, and now in your fancy church, you say God doesn't like us sinners and unless we repent, we're going to drown in hell forever and ever. What I'd like to know is what happens if you go and die suddenly, before you get a chance to –" His voice gives out and big tears roll down his cheeks into his beard. "Sorry. If you would just enlighten me to why God is so confused, I'd be grateful."

"Are you all right?" I ask.

He nods and tells me to go on.

"All right. You are saved by grace, like it says in Ephesians, and you must repent also, like it tells us in the verse I read in the book of Revelation today – repent or I will come quickly and fight against you with the sword of my mouth."

He cocks his head, puzzled eyes, and the tears.

"There are times when God asks us to accept things we don't understand," I say. "Like now. Have faith, Brother Finn. God isn't confused. He knows best."

"I don't know about that. But the part you said about coming quickly and killing us off makes some sense, 'cause that's what He did to Justice."

"What do you mean? What happened to Justice?"

"Well," he says and full-on cries.

Dorothy flicks her cigarette butt into the street and lays her hand over his shoulder. "Do you want me to tell him?"

"No. No, I will." He takes a breath. "Some county worker found Justice in that lean-to he built. Found the kid dead." He wipes his face with his palms. "Dead, they found him dead. Yep. He'd been dead a couple of days. He died all alone."

"Oh, Brother Finn –"

I think of the day I saw him folding up his sleeping bag under the bridge. He said he had a place to stay. I knew he didn't. I think of the day I told him I'd take him to lunch and he said no and left out the back. I should have gone after him. I should have tried harder to reach him.

"Let's go, Gordon," Dorothy says. "It's not good for you to get all worked up. You told the preacher what you came here to tell him. It's time for us to go home."

"Hold off, give me just one more second," Finn says. He pulls a handkerchief out of his shirt pocket and wipes his nose. "I believe I've figured out my own conundrum. I'm going to have faith like you said. I'm having faith that you were right the first time you preached and wrote down that Bible verse. I'm also going to have faith that our friend, Justice, is in heaven." He gazes into the sky. "The Paris part of heaven where that Moulin place is. Justice is there playing a golden accordion God made special. He wears a top hat made of silk now and a real live crow sits on his shoulder. Justice had some problems. But he was a good kid. God would never make him drown forever in Satan's frigid bottomless sea. God just wouldn't."

I lean against the parking meter and watch them walk away, in step and Finn's arm looped through hers. He left without his Bible verse. I start to go after them to give it back, but they've disappeared in the maze of Sunday Market shoppers.

Chapter Seventeen

Grace opens the drawer and picks through her clothes. "You didn't have to wait up." She pulls out flannel pajama pants. The lacy thing she wore once, on Valentine's Day, is stuck to them.

"I didn't. I couldn't fall asleep."

I close the Bible and pick my end of the quilt off the floor and drag it up to the bed. I didn't read. I thought about Justice. I couldn't stop thinking about him. The day he chased Amelia with the push broom, the last time I saw him in the lean-to and he asked me to come back and I didn't.

"How was Bible study?" I ask.

"Good." She shoves the lacy thing back in the drawer and pulls out an old t-shirt of mine.

"You must have had a lively discussion going, it's after 11."

"Not really, after Bible study, Sister Lonnie told us all about her trip to China." Grace takes her earrings out, steps out of her shoes. "Every detail of the two weeks she spent there." She walks into the bathroom, her pajamas wadded up in her arms. "She rode camels through the desert, walked on the Great Wall. How was the funeral?"

"No one from Justice's family came."

"Did he even have a family? He was homeless, you said. A drug addict." She shuts the door with her foot.

"He has a family," I say, but she doesn't hear.

He mentioned them once, an alcoholic dad, a sister living in France, but no one knew how to contact them. If they came to the funeral, they would have heard Finn's speech, an assurance that God loved Justice just the way he was. I start tearing up again.

"You know what they ate in China?" Grace shouts and I wipe my eyes. "Can you hear me?"

"Rice?"

"No." She pokes her head out, bare shoulders. "Pond snails and donkey meat sandwiches."

"Did she hand out recipes?"

"Ewe." She makes a face. "Did you get any dinner?" She shuts the door and turns on the shower.

My mother reheated the burger Grace fried before she left, even though I said I wasn't hungry. I didn't mention I walked up Bad Heart Road after the funeral. I didn't tell her my stomach cramped and my legs were already stiff. Or the walk didn't help this time. It didn't give me perspective. It didn't make what happened to Justice make sense.

There were only a handful of people at the funeral, Annabelle, The Nurse, Pastor Green, Dorothy and the dogs, of course. Finn said Justice died of an overdose, but not to worry, Jesus welcomed him into heaven, gall-durnit. He asked us to pardon his French and told us he was absolutely sure God didn't send

Justice to hell. He dropped Justice's mangy crow and top-hat in the grave and chuckled a little and I knew he was thinking about Justice playing his Paris music and a heavenly audience cheering him on.

After the funeral, I tried to give Finn back the Ephesians verse he forgot last week. He told me to keep it and refer to it as needed. I slipped it in my suit pocket and now it's on my nightstand.

Grace opens the bathroom door and steam pours out. She pads over to her side of the bed and climbs in, pecks me on the cheek. "Goodnight." She rolls over and turns off her light. "Well?"

"Well, what?"

She pulls the covers up to her neck. "Aren't you going to turn off your light?"

"I've been thinking."

"You know how late it is, don't you?" She puts her pillow over her head.

"Grace is a gift, it says so in Ephesians." I pick up Finn's paper. It's beginning to tear on the folds, the edges are fuzzy. I read the verse out loud and return it to the nightstand open, not folded.

"Can we do this in the morning? I'm tired. I have to get up early and so do you."

"I've been thinking about Justice. He was just a kid. How could a loving God let him drown in hell?"

She rolls onto her back and pushes the pillow off her face. "Because he was a druggie, and it's a shame, but he was the cause of his death. He died in his sins and now he has to pay the price."

"But Jesus already paid it."

"It's a mystery. Now go to sleep."

"That's what I told Finn. It's a mystery, I said, and

after I said it, I felt bad. Maybe the real mystery is why we, as God's children, can't accept a gift Jesus freely gave, grace plain and simple, without hell and trepidation, without the bad news sinners and the guilt." Her brow wrinkles. "I mean, God made us in His image and God's not a vile old codger, right?"

"What are you talking about?" She sits up. "Are you questioning God and His laws?"

"No. I don't know. I'm confused."

"You shouldn't be confused, you're a pastor. Asking questions opens the back door of your mind to Satan. Get on your knees. Hand your burdens over to God."

"I have."

"Then what's the problem? I thought we were on track again. Letting God drive the bus, remember? Your dad's retiring. The church is going to be ours."

"Thanks a lot for understanding." I get out of bed and find my pants.

"I do understand. God has a plan for you."

"Does He? I haven't had a miracle like Dad's."

"You are the miracle and you know it. Stay the course. Don't ruin it. Come back to bed."

I find a shirt on the floor and pull it over my head.

"What are you doing?"

"I'm going downstairs."

"You're going to wake up Gabe."

I whisper. "I'm going downstairs so you can go to sleep like you want." I open the bedroom door and there Gabe is, standing on the other side, rubbing sleep out of his eyes.

"Why are you fighting? I thought you started loving Mom again. I thought you were happy."

My mother rolls her suitcase into the living room. "Good morning." She sits in the recliner and Hercules jumps in her lap.

"Charlee texted that she's on her way," I say.

"I'm ready to go." She stifles a yawn. "Boy, it's early. Charlee wants to show me around her house and get me settled before she goes to work."

"Good thing, you could get lost in that place. I hope I didn't wake you up last night, I had trouble sleeping."

She waves it off. "No worries."

I lean back into the couch cushion. No worries is what I told Gabe when I put him back to bed – I am happy. I do love your mom. I came down here and went straight to my knees. I prayed for understanding. I asked God what to do. Don't ruin it was the answer I got and it came to me in Grace's voice. You are the chosen one came in Dad's. I was as mixed up after I prayed as I was before.

Hercules leaps into my lap and I scratch him behind the ears.

"Gabe and I had a talk," my mother says.

"How'd that go?" I see a red Jeep pulling up to the curb. "There's Charlee now."

My mother glances out the window. "Gabe's fine with me staying at her place to keep her company while Michael's gone."

"You didn't tell him they're –"

"Getting divorced? No, that's for you and Charlee to do."

"Uh-huh. Gabe was pretty upset with me and

Grace over you leaving."

Charlee lets herself in. "Do I smell coffee?"

"Grab a mug," I call, but she's already in the kitchen.

"Gabe understands it was my decision to go," my mother says. "I assured him I was coming back. Before I leave, I have something to show you." She reaches in her bag and pulls out a red book and sets it on the coffee table.

"Dear God," I say.

"Hey good morning all," Charlee says. "Oh, my God, is that what I think it is?" She sets her mug on the table and plops down on the couch beside me.

"I found it under my bed," my mother says, "when I was packing my suitcase. I had a chat with Gabe. Apparently, he stashed it there and was reading about your Bigfoot adventures when I wasn't around."

"That's just great."

"I thought you hid it better?" Charlee asks.

"I did."

"Gabe was trying to find out what he needed to do to become a Bigfoot Hunter," my mother says. Charlee and I frown. "He sees the special bond you and Charlee have and he wants in on it. You can't blame him."

"I'll get on Gabe about it, again," I say. "He doesn't seem to understand boundaries."

"I admit," my mother says, "I was a bit curious."

"You read it too?" Charlee and I ask in unison.

"I flipped through it a bit."

"What don't you get about – Top Secret?" I ask and point to the words on the cover.

"I apologize, really. I shouldn't have stuck my nose

in it. But I have to say, as kiddoes, you two figured out something most adults never get."

"What?" I ask.

"You don't know?"

Charlee and I look at each other.

"I'm ready to go, whenever you are," my mother says to Charlee.

"Wait," I say. "I want to ask you something and maybe it's not any of my business, but now you owe me." I tap my knuckles on the journal.

She cocks her head. "All right, fair enough, ask."

"Did you leave us because you were having an affair?"

She looks into her hands for a moment. "I'm not too sure if this question is comparable to reading your journal or not."

I wait for her to go on.

"No, I never cheated on your dad."

"Then tell Noah why you left," Charlee says, a spark of anger in her voice.

"There were many reasons."

"And they were?" I ask.

She fidgets for a few moments. "Contrary to popular belief, I didn't leave on a whim. I think of me leaving one piece at a time, beginning a couple of months into our marriage. When Paul went on his drinking binge and had numerous affairs, which you know intimately, since he includes them in his conversion story."

I nod. Every member of Rolling River knows them intimately.

"Well, that's neither here nor there. As I was saying, a piece of me left when Paul turned religious, another piece when he told me I'd end up in hell if I didn't embrace his beliefs. A piece left every time he spoke for me, thought for me, insisted on rules, the how-tos, and didn't listen to what I had to say. I was married to a pastor, not a husband. I had to pretend I was someone I wasn't to keep the peace. It wears on you. All those years of pretending, until one day, I realized there was only a speck of me left."

"Your speck abandoned the family," I say.

She sighs. "I believed there was no way in hell Paul would let me go and have my boys too. He would have fought me and I wasn't up for a fight. I thought I made the right decision at the time. But that was me then, a woman I didn't know or like or respect."

I lean into my hands and Charlee rubs hers up and down my back.

"For what it's worth," my mother says, "I deeply regret walking away from a relationship with you and your brother."

I look into my mother's face and see a genuineness I haven't seen or maybe I missed.

"The 'me' now," she says, "would make a different choice. I'd fight. I'd never stop fighting." She tears up. "I don't want your forgiveness. I don't want you to forget. That's not how life works. We can't learn if we don't remember the hurts or if we forget the mistakes we made."

I think how I forgave Grace. How I forgot what she did. Or said I forgot. But I still remember. I can't stop remembering.

After Charlee and my mother leave, I sit down with another cup of coffee. Pick up the Bigfoot Hunter's Journal and flip through it like my mother did and wonder what the thing Charlee and I figured out was. I stop on number 9 of the Bigfoot Hunter's Code. Be brave. I think of Dad, be brave Noah, when it's something he wants me to do. I turn a few more pages – Bigfoot Hunter's Code Number 10. Don't do it, unless it makes you happy and makes your heart feel good.

My heart doesn't feel so good right now. I shut the book. Kid stuff. I'm an adult and I can't always have what I want, can't always do what makes me happy. Be brave. I've got my life back on the path. If I steer off again, I could slip and fall into deep waters and I don't know how to swim.

Gabe is squirming and Grace is waiting at the hotel. My windshield wipers are working as hard as they can. I resist the urge to speed up. Grip the wheel with both hands and drive slower.

"Da – aad," Gabe says, "I have to pee."

"Hold it. This won't take long." I stop in front of the hotel in the three minute passenger pick-up zone. "Mom said she'd wait out front."

"Hurry, hurry, hurry."

"You should have peed at school."

"I didn't have time. Mom's not out there."

His wet clothes are causing the windows to steam up. I power his down and peer out. There's no sign of Grace under the eaves where she said she'd be. I groan. She said if she wasn't out yet, text, do not come inside. I pull out my phone and text – we're having an emergency out here. Where are you?

"Dad, Dad."

"Rather than jumping in every puddle between the school and car, you could have been in the boy's room taking care of your business."

"But Dad, it's raining inside the car. Can I shut the window?" Gabe points at the open window.

I power it up. "Why do you care if you get any wetter?" He pouts. "Mom's going to flip out when she sees your new shoes soaked through and muddy."

"I have to pee now." Gabe grabs his crotch.

"She'll be out in a second."

He's overdramatizing. Like this morning. After my mother left and he raced downstairs having a fit – why didn't you tell me she was leaving? You made her go. I hate you.

He hates me. I try not to take it personally. He's a kid. I said the same thing to my dad. I said it to my mother. I said it about my mother after she left. Still, hearing my son say it is disheartening.

A second is up. I phone Grace and my call goes to voice mail.

Gabe wriggles and kicks. "I can't wait one more second!"

"All right, all right," I say, unable to ascertain if I heard real urgency in his voice or just thought I did. "We'll use the hotel bathroom." We scramble out of the car and run inside.

The doorman points us to the restrooms. While I wait for Gabe, I watch for Grace, text her – in lobby crisis averted, and still, she doesn't reply. Across the lobby, the elevator beeps and opens. I glance over my shoulder. Gabe's still in the restroom.

When I look back, I see Grace coming out of the

elevator. Grace and Joshua Barrett and they're walking close, talking close, his hand moves to her shoulder and something powerful rises out of the spot inside me that has hurt every day since I found the Trojan wrapper on my bedroom floor, the wrapper that contained the fancy sheepskin Trojan Barrett used when he had sex with my wife. I charge across the lobby. I hear shouting. It's me shouting get your filthy hands off my wife. His hand slips off her shoulder and they step away from each other, surprised, and Grace looks at me like she has never seen me before.

"Your garden meeting, Grace?"

I feel the impact of my fist connect with Barrett's jaw. I watch him stagger backwards. Watch him fall on the floor. I hear my wife's voice. What do you think you're doing? Stop. Stop. Stop.

What am I doing? I should stop. Barrett sits up and blinks. I grab two handfuls of his expensive suit and yell in his face. "You bastard, don't ever go near my wife again."

"Dad, Dad, don't kill him." Gabe tackles me from behind and I release Barrett.

Grace bends over him. "Oh, Josh. You're bleeding."

"It's nothing." He dabs the corner of his mouth and checks his fingers.

She offers her hand to help him up. "I am so, so very sorry."

The doorman asks if he should call the police.

"Is Dad going to jail again?" Gabe shrieks and I feel the eyes of onlookers.

"Just a misunderstanding," Barrett says and takes

Grace's hand. He stands and straightens his jacket. "No police needed here." He looks over at me all smug. His lip looks fine.

"You're still seeing him, aren't you?" I ask Grace.

"I was attending a meeting," she screeches, grabs Gabe by the forearm and marches toward the exit

"You're a liar." I follow her. "You lied to me."

She glances over her shoulder. "Get away from us."

Her face is flushed, hair all flyaway, her coat draped over her arm, one sleeve dragging on the ground. People are milling around the lobby, watching this and pretending not to. I watch the doors slide open and she and Gabe are gone.

I rub my hand. It's starting to throb. She lied to me. She's been lying this whole time. She never quit Barrett's committee. She never quit Barrett.

I'm not surprised my car is no longer parked in the pick-up zone. Grace has a key. The doorman offers to call me a cab.

"No thanks, I'll walk."

"Are you sure about that? It's one of those dark and stormy nights."

I say I'm sure and he pats my shoulder. "We all have a bad day once in a while. You take care."

I give him what I would have spent on the cab and walk out into the drencher.

I arrive home soaked through and shivering and find Hercules on the front porch tied to the doorknob and a plastic grocery bag hanging from it. Hercules has a note from Grace pinned to his striped sweater.

I humiliated her in front of her colleagues and she doesn't want to talk to me. Or see me.

Inside the bag is my toothbrush, Bible, a change of underwear. I open my car and toss the bag in. Hercules springs into the backseat, shakes off the rain, and curls up on his blanket. I think about going back. This is my house. She locked the door. I have my house key. I think of the fight we'd have if I do. Starting with – you're a liar, moving on to who humiliated who.

The dining room light is on. I can't tell if she's in there or not. Gabe's light is on. He's standing in his window. I raise my hand and he leans his forehead against the glass.

Dad slams the morning paper down on my desk. Hercules growls and Dad eyes him for a moment. "You've made the news again. Care to explain?"

The paper is folded to the page where the article he's huffing about is located. I have no trouble finding it – Rebel Pastor at it Again.

"What? I punch Barrett in the face and it only makes page four?"

He glares. "You did what it says?"

"I did indeed." I stand and chuck the paper in the trash. "And I'd do it again. If you'd like to discuss it further, I suggest going to the source – Pastor's Adulteress Wife at it Again."

His eyes move to the trashcan and his shoulders slump. "You and Grace are on my calendar for counseling this afternoon. We'll discuss this matter then."

"I won't be there."

"No one said reconciliation would be easy. With

God on your side, you and Grace can do this."

"God drove my bus into the river." My fist comes down on the desk and Hercules scurries into the corner. "I trusted Him with the keys. I thought He knew how to drive."

Dad rubs his chin, thinking. "God hasn't forsaken you. He sent you here to lead His church."

"I don't know about that."

Dad seems genuinely shaken which surprises and pleases me. He puts his hand over my shoulder and I shrug it off. "Please leave me alone."

"All right, fine." He hesitates at the door. His hand slips off the knob and he turns. "Son, I suggest that you get on your knees and have a heart-to-heart talk with God. Ask, and it shall be given you, seek, and ye shall find, knock, and it shall be opened unto you. This is a minor setback. Stay the course. Plan on making it to counseling this afternoon and we'll pray together." He waits for an answer and when I don't give one, he leaves and shuts the door.

Rain pummels the window. I'll pick Gabe up at school this afternoon so he doesn't have to walk home in this. We'll talk about me and his mother then. I'll assure him that both Grace and I love him with all our heart, mind and soul.

I'll pack a suitcase while I'm home and go back to Charlee's. I'll tell her how tired I am of trying to hold my wrecked marriage together when I'm not at all sure if it's worth it, or if I want to.

I sit and look over my desk. The construction paper heart – we love you Pastor Noah – I taped to a tin can pencil holder Gabe made me one Father's Day.

I thunk my knuckles down on a notepad where

I sketched out this week's sermon. The thing doesn't resonate. I rip it off and throw it in the trash.

God – what do you want from me? The keys to the bus back? I don't think so.

Hercules is under the desk licking my shoe. "Up here, boy." I pat my lap and he jumps, lays his one paw on my shoulder and licks my face.

My cell phone rings. It's Grace's ringtone, *Amazing Grace*.

Hercules grumbles. I let her call go to voicemail and she calls right back. I turn off my phone. I have to get out. "Let's go for a walk, buddy."

Joni lets herself in while I'm putting the leash on Hercules. The expression on her face makes my heart skip several beats. "Grace is on the phone. It's urgent."

Chapter Eighteen

My son is missing. I can't turn the car off fast enough. I pound up the steps with Hercules scurrying after me. This can't be real. I keep telling myself. I heard wrong. Grace is overreacting. The front door flies open and Grace plows into me cry-talking.

I peel her off and walk her inside. Hold her by the arms and look into her red-rimmed eyes. "I don't understand. How can Gabe not be at school?"

She gulps and sniffs. "I don't know."

"Did he ride the bus?"

"No. He was dawdling around and missed it and I had to drive him." A gust of wind slams the door shut, startling both of us.

"Did you walk him inside?"

"No. I let him out at the drop-off zone."

"Did you see him go inside?"

"Yes. Where else would he go? He went inside and –" She whimpers. "And he didn't wave because I was mad at him for missing the bus again."

"Was anyone else around when you dropped him off?"

She glares at my hands clamped around her forearms and I let go.

"Other parents and their kids."

"You dropped him off, then what?"

"Then nothing, I drove home. The school called an hour later saying he wasn't in class." She rubs her hands up and down her arms. "Oh dear God, my baby's out in this downpour."

"We don't know that. He could be somewhere in the school, you know, dawdling around. Maybe he's in one of the restrooms."

"He's not. They checked all of them and the gym and playground too."

She breaks into tears and I pull her into my arms and stroke the back of her head.

"There has to be a logical explanation."

"There isn't." She pushes me away and wrings her hands. "He's not with your dad or your mother. He isn't with Anthony or Mark or Charlee."

"Did you call the police?"

"Yes. Yes, of course I did." She paces for a moment. "We'll need a picture." She runs upstairs to find one.

Anthony and I shed our raincoats and shoes. I told him to go back to my house without me and dry off and pick up a new supply of flyers, while I scoured more neighborhoods. He wouldn't have it, citing all the illnesses that start with a chill and develop out of a lowered immune system which is only exacerbated by stress.

I blow into my hands. A handful of people I don't know are in my kitchen, one eating pizza off a paper plate, another on a laptop, someone on a phone. Grace is talking to a police officer on the stairs. She sees me and I shake my head no. No. We didn't find Gabe. No clues. No signs. No nothing.

The officer taps her clipboard to get Grace's attention. The never-ending questions. Blood type, birth marks, pediatrician, cuts and scrapes and bruises, I didn't know all the answers. The places he plays, what he plays, and who with. Stress in the family? How do you and Mrs. Cathcart get along?

How do we get along? The details please. And the worst detail of all – last night. By the time I finished answering the question, I wondered if the police will give us back our child when they do find him.

"This will hit the spot, Bro." Anthony puts a steaming mug in my hands. "Drink up and then we'll hit the street again."

"Seven hours is a long time for a child to be –" The word missing catches in my throat. According to police, a missing child ten and younger is considered – endangered. "My son is endangered."

"No, no don't think like that." Anthony squeezes my shoulder. "I bet he's playing another trick on you. Like he did after he watched that old movie, E.T., with me and Mark and the next time you were in Sears, he hid in a bin of stuffed animals. Remember? You told me all about it. How you found him there with his head poking out like E.T.'s did in the movie." Anthony chuckles and tears up. "Remember?"

"This isn't the same."

"Maybe it is. He was okay then and he is now. They'll find him. Along with police, the Search and Rescue unit is looking. You know Mark's a volunteer. They've coordinated efforts on the waterfront and in the woods already. Mark will call the second they find Gabe."

"What if they don't find him?"

"We're going to think positive." My mother scrapes ground coffee out of the bottom of a bag and adds it to the coffeemaker. "Besides you and Anthony, a good sized group of volunteers are handing out flyers. They're checking playgrounds and ball fields. Then there's your dad who has taken to telling everyone around here what to do. He's good at that. He called out his church people. They've gone downtown asking around, tacking flyers on windows and doors. One fellow brought his redbone coonhounds. They're not trained at all, but very friendly."

"Where are the trained police dogs?" Anthony asks.

"They put a call out and expect some dogs later today." She takes clean mugs out of the dishwasher and sets them around the coffeepot. "Now go in the living room you two and warm up by the fire. And eat some pizza." She points her forehead at the boxes on the counter and calls Grace over. "You have to eat something, dear." She opens a box and slaps a slice down on a paper plate.

Grace stares at it and whimpers. "Pepperoni is Gabe's favorite." She looks over at me. Her eyes are swollen and there's a patch of bright red under her nose. She dabs at it with a wadded tissue. "Did we remember to tell the police pepperoni is his favorite?"

"I don't know," I say. "Why would they care?"

"If it's important, they'll ask," my mother says, pats Grace on the back and guides her over to the dining room table.

I add wood to the fire and it crackles. The sweet smell of pitch. Anthony pokes me in the arm with my plate and urges me to eat more than one bite of pizza. I push it away. "It's like cardboard."

"I'll eat it then."

"Go for it. Just make it fast."

"I'm a fast eater." He takes a big bite and chews. "I've been thinking for a while and I want to say how sorry I am for getting mad and snubbing you after you pulled out of our wedding." He picks off a pepperoni and drops it into his mouth.

"You don't –"

"I do. I've been acting like a child. You've had a whole lot of pressure from Dad and all you want is to make everything good between you and Grace and Gabe and move on with your life. I understand." He eats the last bite and gathers the napkins and paper plates. "You did what you felt was right in your heart, and while I don't agree, I respect you for that, Bro."

I pick up the empty mugs, working to hold back tears. "I don't know if my heart's been a part of my decision making lately."

"I trust you'll get it all figured out." He claps me across the back. "Know the invite to our wedding is still good, if you'd like to come and sit in the audience, or stand in the back, or wait in your car, whatever, you're welcome." He holds up his hand. "No pressure. With the wedding in two days, not that I don't think you'll find Gabe by then, but we'll postpone it, if it comes to it, until Gabe returns home."

"Don't postpone, please, not for me."

"Bro, it wouldn't be for you. We want our day to be happy and fun and it wouldn't be with our nephew unaccounted for. I'll ask Mark to pick up a pepperoni pizza tonight just for Gabe."

"He'd love that."

We stop in the driveway. Dark clouds hang heavy over our heads, the rain is unstoppable. Anthony adjusts the straps on his emergency pack. Flashlights, first aid supplies, emergency blanket. I pray we won't need any of it.

Pray? I haven't prayed about anything today. When Dad called on the family to pray this morning, I walked out. I remember his expression, a mix of fear and anguish.

"There's Charlee," Anthony says and I see her across the street driving up on the curb to park. I meet her in the middle of the road and we throw our arms around each other's necks.

"I'm so scared," I say.

"Me too," she says.

The three of us wait for the light to cross the highway. Charlee takes her hood off and shakes her hair out. She pulls my hood down when I don't. The weather turned from a drencher to an intermittent sprinkle and I'm grateful. Traffic zooms past, some with headlights on, some not yet, and they're hitting pockets of mucky rainwater and we step back to avoid getting splashed, except for Anthony, who's hitting the crosswalk button with a vengeance.

We knocked on all the doors, between my house and the highway, and found no one who had seen my son. Now we'll walk the length of the river path. People don't disappear into thin air, Gabe is somewhere.

After we cross, we take a shortcut through the Safeway lot and there's his smiling face, enclosed in 8 ½ by 11 plastic sheet protectors, duct taped to all the light poles. The picture is the one Grace found when she went upstairs to look. She was gone for a while. I heard her sobbing and between sobs, she prayed – please dear God, give me back my baby. I'll do anything.

Charlee loops her arm through mine. "You okay?"

"I did everything."

"You did everything?" she asks and I nod. "What do you mean?"

"I did everything God asked."

Charlee squeezes my arm. "I know you did."

Anthony gives me a flashlight. "Maybe that Rolling River God of yours isn't who you think He is, Bro."

He gives a flashlight to Charlee. She turns it on and sweeps the beam over the path ahead.

"You can see for miles with these babies," Anthony says. "All right, troops, let's go."

We call Gabe's name, over and over. Gabe, Gabriel, high and low, until our voices are ready to give out. We stick to the path, which is washed out in parts, shining our lights in nooks and crannies, where grass is tall and rocks are mossy slick. A foghorn blows and my heart skips a beat. I cannot allow myself to believe my son could be out there in those black roiling waters. Still, I force my eyes to follow the bright beam over to the water and out across the surface, frightened it will pick up the glint of a silver buckle, the color red, a tennis shoe.

The river path ends under the bridge at Area 51. We tramp through gravel around a construction site that's cordoned off to the public. End up on the sidewalk across the street in front of the Downtown Improvement Project sign explaining the three stages of development and a sketch of the outcome. In it, the green space Grace planned.

"Did I tell you that Mel parks his box in a remote spot further down the river now?" Anthony asks.

I think of Justice and dying alone. "No. I hope he's safe and all right."

"I saw him a week ago and he said he hadn't seen any aliens for a while. Finn keeps a close eye on him, makes sure he's eating and warm and dry."

"I'm glad."

A group with flashlights comes around the corner. "Ahoy, Pastor Noah," Finn says and he and Dorothy and her bag of dogs, The Nurse, Annabelle and others I don't know, gather around us and all of them say how sorry they are about my boy.

Finn clasps my hand. "You've been in our prayers today. And Ahoy to you Anthony and Charlee, long time, no see." They say ahoy.

"Anthony told me you formed a search party," I say. "I'm grateful to all of you."

I see searchlights. Hear Coast Guard boats near-by. All commonplace in Rivers Edge, but not tonight, tonight they're for my son. I shiver and blow into my hands. "We have to go."

"Wait," Finn says, "I'd like it if you'd stick around and join us while we pray for the weary searchers. It won't take me but a minute to call on the Big Guy." He bows his head before I answer. "Hello God. You said in the Bible for us to love one another, for love is of God. We hear You, Lord. Tonight, we're grateful for love." I open an eye to make sure the passionate voice I hear is Finn's. "I'm speaking in particular about our Pastor Noah's love. See, he loved us River Street folks just the way we are, and, as You know, we aren't so lovable to most. He taught us that we're worthwhile and as important as anyone else." I blink back tears and Charlee presses her face in my coat sleeve.

"I could go on," Finn says, "but I said I'd only take a minute. You get the drift. What I want to say is Pastor Noah loved me without a hitch and now my life is good and every day it gets a notch better than good. I believe others can attest to the same." Several hearty Amens, a bark, and Finn continues. "What we'd like to do, God, is give Noah back the love he gave us. But we need some help here. We've been looking for his boy all day and a clue to his whereabouts would be mighty helpful –"

"We are in need of a mighty miracle tonight, are we not?" a booming voice in the shadows and I turn and see Dad.

Finn salutes. I salute back and he and the others head for the wooded area to search under the bridge where the police are afraid to go, but Finn knows well. He suggested we search around the cannery, where it's pitch dark, and in the general vicinity. I shiver and zip my coat all the way.

Gabe has no body fat to keep him warm if he didn't think to layer before he left, first a t-shirt, over that a thermal, a stocking cap, extra socks.

Dad lays a hand over my shoulder. "Did you hear, Son, a miracle? I'm telling you, I feel a mighty one coming on."

He spotted us after he finished passing out flyers to a group of theater goers waiting in a line that wound around the block to get in the newest Spiderman movie. Dad held back, waited until Finn finished or came close to finishing his prayer, before revealing himself.

What Anthony said earlier comes to mind. Maybe my Rolling River God isn't who I think He is.

"I don't know about any mighty miracles. But if you'd like to join us, Dad, you're welcome."

"We'll split up then. Noah, you and I will take the cannery docks and Charlee and Anthony, go west on River Street. There are many places a child can hide." His voice cracks. "God help us, let's find my grandson."

The sign – Danger Sea Lions on Dock – hangs by a nail, same as the last time I was here looking for Mel. Dad shines his light on it. "The devil is here tonight."

My stomach clenches.

Dad reaches for heaven. "Almighty God, help us." He scrambles up the steps to the cannery pier and looks down on me. "Be brave. Fear is Satan's tool. Let's not keep Gabe waiting."

I follow Dad into a misty fog. We head toward the far end of the pier, calling for Gabe and sweeping the ground with our flashlight beams. We look in dumpsters, in shadowy corners, under soggy cardboard. We stop at a loading dock and peer down the ramp into a swirling cloud.

"Let's take a look," I say.

I tramp over weeds growing out of deep cracks. I call for Gabe. Slip on loose rock. At the bottom, I step into tall prickly grass and feel myself sinking into sodden ground.

"Over here," Dad says.

"Do you see something?" I crouch beside him on a chunk of concrete and we shine our lights under the pier into the shallows. There are a couple of good-sized rocks a boy could take shelter on, but there's no boy on them.

I shake my head when I really feel like shaking my fist. "Where is my son, God?"

"You must keep the faith."

"Keep the faith?" A wave rolls in and breaks on a barnacle encrusted pillar. "Help me understand faith.

My son disappears. My wife cheats on me. Lies to me. We're not happy. I drove a wedge between me and my brother. I preach fear on Sundays. And you say fear is the devil's tool? This makes no sense. My life makes no sense. It feels wrong. I feel wrong."

"God is giving you a wake-up call. Don't you see – this is your refiner's fire? You are the chosen one. To lead His church, you must be well-built and made of tempered metal. Endure your trials. Endure to the end." He stands, clasps my hand and pulls me to my feet.

"If I wasn't the chosen one and you were just my dad, would you give me the same advice?"

"I would indeed. Any father who loves his son as much as I love you would."

I walk ahead of Dad up the ramp. He falls in beside me and we commence searching. We don't say much.

Then I see something. "Dad, look, over there." I shine the flashlight. At the farthest end of the cannery behind a stack of crab pots, I see a figure, squatting and hunched over, hugging his knees. "Gabe?" My heart leaps and I run. "Gabe, it's me."

I can't run fast enough. I imagine Gabe in my arms, his weight, legs swinging, the sweaty boy smell. Dad – Dad, he'll say. I scramble around the crab pots ready to scoop him off the ground.

He isn't here. A rusted out Safeway shopping cart tipped on its side is here. Fishing net is here, a busted lantern is here. The hunched over figure is here, but it isn't a figure. It's a wadded up tarp. In the light it doesn't look anything like a boy. "You are a cruel God," I shout and kick the life out of the tarp.

"Do not despair." Dad wraps me in his arms. "God has not forsaken you or your son."

"I think He has."

Dad points with the flashlight. "See, out there at the end of the pier?"

"I don't see anything."

"The dock," he says. "The dock where I had my miracle. There's a moored vessel, see it? Gabe may have found shelter there."

I see it. I follow Dad. I want to believe Gabe's there. But I ready myself for another letdown. Dad strides out to the end of the pier and pounds down a plank.

I clutch a weathered handrail, what's left of it. Gabe is more like his granddad, than me. He would speed down the plank the way Dad did. He wouldn't use the rail. I stop midway and look in the water. The river is too deep to stand up in. If Gabe took a tumble and fell, no one would have heard his cry for help.

We should have let him take swim lessons. He begged us. All of his friends know how to swim.

"Watch out for the missing board," Dad says as I come off the plank onto a dock that's rotting and one person wide. Fog rolls off the pea-soup river and swirls around Dad's legs. He sweeps his light over an old fishing boat. Its name, bold and blocky, has chipped away over the years, leaving an impression of a name, the initials E.T. I feel a twinge of hope.

Dad knocks his flashlight against the hull. "Gabe? It's Granddad, are you in there?"

No answer, not a sound or the slightest movement. I remember how mad I was when I found Gabe in the bin of stuffed animals. I grounded him, took away video game privileges and everything else I could think of.

"I'm not mad," I shout. "I promise you're not grounded. Please, please tell us where you are."

The boat groans and rocks and the dock rocks with it. I grab for a railing to steady myself, but there are no railings.

"Let's take a closer look." Dad waves me over with his flashlight and clambers up and over the side of the boat and offers a hand.

The boat isn't big. The roof's rusted through. A life preserver is hanging crooked on a nail. We walk around crab pots, step over faded fishing floats. Shine our lights in broken windows and call Gabe's name. He doesn't answer.

"If we find my son in the river," I say, "I won't be able to live with myself, knowing I could have agreed to swim lessons and didn't because of some fantastical story about a sea lion and hell and the devil in the water." I pound my fist on the life preserver, the nail falls out and the ring hits the deck.

"Are you questioning my miracle?"

"I just wish Gabe knew how to swim. That's all."

We climb out of the boat and Dad slips his arm around my shoulders. "Son, I believe we're going to have a miracle tonight."

I shake my head. "No we're not. Let's go."

"Jesus didn't name his church after mighty miracles for nothing."

"Save your breath."

"You listen to me. My miracle was real. It happened right here on this dock. After the sea lion slapped me into the river, I expected to hit bottom and never return. Your mother would have been freed from the bondage of an unhappy marriage. But, alas, that wasn't God's intention. Don't you see, God's plan isn't always clear, or pleasant or easy or what we want or think we want."

"Maybe what you think is God's plan – isn't."

"If not for my miraculous event, you wouldn't be alive. I testify that God's will was done on the night of my miracle. He allowed the devil to drag me through the watery corridors of hell to the depths of his frigid bottomless sea. If that's not a wake-up call, nothing is."

"I know the story. I'm going back to find Charlee and Anthony."

Dad grabs my wrist. "I witnessed the giant blue beast back-stroking with his mouth opened wide, ready to slurp me up. Hell is real. Satan resides there and he wants you, as much as he wanted me. Trust me."

"I don't know if I can."

"Oh, Son. Satan has led you astray. Open your eyes. He's making you an unhappy man. He's ruining you and your family and your future. You allowed him access and now you must cleanse your heart and mind and kick him out for good. It's a hard road, but you can, I know you can. With Jesus, you can do anything."

I lay my hand over my heart. "Satan isn't here."

On the far end of the dock, we hear barking and see a sea lion rear up and slap its chest and my heart tries to crawl right out of mine. I stumble back a few steps and find myself teetering on the edge of the dock, my heels no longer planted on solid ground.

Dad grabs me in a bear hug and walks me forward. Leaves me trembling and marches toward the sea lion, his arm raised to a square. "Get thee behind me, Satan."

The sea lion points its whiskered snout up to the heavens and that's all it does.

"Did a sea lion really push you in the river on the night of your miracle?" I ask and another sea lion squirts out of the river and flops on the dock at Dad's feet and trumpets. The dock creaks and shakes and takes on water and Dad stumbles back. He raises his arms. It trumpets again. "I rebuke you, Satan. I rebuke you, in the name of Jesus."

I feel a nudge and I stumble and fall backwards into frigid brackish water and go under like I'm made out of metal. I swallow the river and sink into outer space. It's dinner time there. I go home and find my family starting without me. I smell salmon. I pull my chair out, but someone smarter and richer and better looking is sitting in it. Grace sets a platter of fresh-caught salmon in front of him. Gabe asks if he'll drive him to swim lessons after dinner. The imposter says, "Whatever you want, kiddo."

My head comes out of the water and I gasp for air. "Dad, Dad, help me." My arms make waves and I take on more water and cough and sputter.

"Take my hand," Dad says from a gauzy far away world.

I don't see a hand to take. I see a light. A brilliant white light and it hurts my eyes to look at it. The light says, "You're washed clean."

A tsunami washes over me and I sink. I'm washed clean. Under water, the idea is funny almost. Funny, like a sea lion praying. Funny, like having a bat for a friend. Like drowning in hell and hair turning white. Like a condom made out of a sheep, a golden bullet, a pig eating a birthday cake. It's funny almost. Like saying yes when I mean no.

Chapter Nineteen

I wake up gasping and sputtering, grabbing for Dad's hand. For the dock, a life preserver ring. There's no air left to breathe.

But there is. I'm not soaking wet cold to the bone. I've grabbed handfuls of sheet and comforter. I'm home. The river was last night. I'm lying in my bed looking up at my ceiling and I'm breathing. Breathing and unable to recall how I ended up in the river.

Grace's side of the bed is still made. The last time I saw her was yesterday afternoon. When she assured me she only slept with Barrett once and lied about the committee because she had to. She had to.

Rain pelts the window. I roll over and look at the clock. Gabe has been gone 24 hours.

While I shower, I rack my brain trying to think of a place where we haven't thought to look. My body aches all over. Twenty-four hours. I think to pray, but dismiss the thought and try harder to think of a place Gabe might be.

Downstairs, the dogs plow into me and Charlee

walks in the back door with my mother and one of the police officers from yesterday.

"Have you found any leads?"

"I'm afraid not." The officer puts a notebook on the table and hangs her wet coat over the back of the chair.

"I'll make you some breakfast, honey," my mother says.

"I'm not hungry."

"You look a hell of a lot better than you did last night." Charlee embraces me.

I'm tearing up. I lean into her and she holds me tighter.

"He's been gone a day and a night," I say. "What if something bad –" I stop myself from finishing the thought and step out of her arms.

"Saying what you're afraid of won't make it come true."

"I'm afraid my son isn't coming home," I shout and walk through the kitchen and dining room flipping on lights. Fighting back tears. I pull open the blinds. I can't see the river for the rain. I try to imagine Gabe hunkered down in a safe dry place waiting for me to find him and I remember the tarp I thought was my boy that wasn't a boy at all.

"Excuse me, Mr. Cathcart," the officer says. "We can get started with the briefing as soon as Mrs. Cathcart joins us."

"Go ahead and start. I don't know where she is."

"Isn't she upstairs?" my mother asks.

"No. Why don't you call her at her boyfriend's?"

"I put her to bed in Gabe's room last night," my mother says. The toast pops up and she starts buttering it. "She insisted on sleeping there, remember?"

"No." I shake my head. I do remember shivering. I remember they got me out of the wet clothes and wrapped me in warm blankets and I still shivered. I thought I'd never stop. I remember panicked faces. Grace's wasn't one of them.

"I'm sure she'll be along soon," the officer says and tells us to sit around the table. My mother puts mugs and the coffeepot in the middle and sets the toast in front of me.

"I said I wasn't hungry." I shove the plate away.

"Let's begin, shall we? My name is Officer Walker and I've been assigned as the family's primary law enforcement contact. All the agencies and volunteers involved in the search effort report to me and I report to you. I'll conduct daily briefings. Here's a stack of my cards." She sets a pile in the middle of the table. "My main number and alternates are here. If you think of something that might give us a clue to Gabe's whereabouts, anything, even the most insignificant seeming, please don't hesitate to call any time day or night."

I close my eyes and rub my forehead. The river last night, the briefings, my family missing is like a television drama, not a real life.

"I'd like to begin by encouraging you, Mr. Cathcart, may I call you Noah?"

"Yes." I open my eyes and she's still here, this police officer who said she was our partner yesterday and then asked if I'd be willing to submit to a polygraph test if needed.

"Taking care of yourself, Noah, is essential and this goes for all of you. Having the family strong and alert will aid in the search effort. Force yourselves to eat and sleep. If you need help, call your physician." She eyes the toast. "Now I'd like to go through today's search effort and answer your questions."

"I have a question," I say. "I want to know why the hell you haven't found my son."

"Do not despair." Dad strides in smiling. "Miracles will never cease."

I shake my head. "This is my dad."

"We met yesterday," Officer Walker says, offering Dad a pointed look. "Pastor, you're in time for the briefing. Please join us. And I assure you, Noah, we're doing everything possible to find Gabe."

"God is on our side," Dad says and pulls up a chair. "Last night was a miracle. You were washed clean, Son, and today, thank you Jesus, God is bringing Gabe home."

"My only miracle is that I didn't drown." I smack the tabletop.

"You went head to head with the devil," Dad says, "and came out the victor."

"I'm no victor. My son is still missing." I push away from the table and start pacing. "How are you going to find Gabe?" I ask Officer Walker.

"The plan is to meet at Rolling River at ten this morning for a prayer service," Dad says. "Expect Miracles, is what I'm calling it." Charlee rolls her eyes. "I've called on our flock. They'll be there. You'll come, Noah. There will be a miracle. Believe you me."

"I'll be on the street looking for my son at ten."

"Attendance is of the utmost importance. Where's Grace?"

"I don't know."

"You see to it that she comes. Together we'll pray as a united body of Christ, sending our heartfelt desires aloft and God will send Gabe home. Expect a miracle, Son."

My mother blows air out of her nose. "Paul, you're interrupting. Please go on Officer."

"Libby, let's be clear about this," Dad says. "You have no say in family matters. You gave that up years ago when you abandoned your family and signed on with the devil."

"Will you just stop?" I ask. "We're here to find Gabe, not rehash your dysfunctional marriage."

"Times like these are stressful on families," Officer Walker says. "It's normal. We've found if the family is abreast of what's happening, the child is often found sooner than if not. My job is to brief you. Sit Noah. Sit Pastor Cathcart. And Libby, around my table, everyone has a voice. Now, the Coast Guard has sent out units from other parts of the state to aid in today's search. They'll be out in force combing the river."

"Is that where you think Gabe is?" I ask.

"No, not at all. We cover all the bases. We received a couple of dogs from a Portland Search and Rescue unit last night. We'll continue searching in the woods and along the waterfront. The family can pass out more flyers, talk to people and the media. The more who know, the better our chances are of finding Gabe."

"This is precisely why our Expect Miracles Prayer Service is imperative in the plan to bring our boy home," Dad says. "I've contacted my congregation, Officer, and believe you me, we have 1000 plus followers from all over the county. I've been talking to the ministerial association as well, who is calling on 1000 more. Praise God, Noah, today your son is coming home."

Downtown is deserted. We run to JC Penney, the closest store to where Charlee parked and take cover under the awning. Rain pummels overhead.

She divides the pile of flyers in half. "Change of plans. We'll give these out to all the customers inside. I'll take the women's department and shoes and you take the men's and automotive."

I don't see anyone in automotive, not even a sales clerk. I take a roll of tape out of my coat pocket and attach flyers to jigsaws and leaf blowers, tool chests. On my way to men's, I stop next to a mannequin, a little boy wearing a yellow rain slicker and matching boots. I tape a flyer to his hand.

"Can I help you find something?" a clerk asks, eyeing the flyer the boy is now holding.

"Yes." I give her a flyer. "My boy's missing."

She studies it. "I'm so sorry. I'll hang this at the register where everyone will see it."

"No one will see it because no one's in the store." She looks at me. "My son left home without his rain boots."

She folds the flyer in half. "I'm sure you'll find him."

"You can't be sure. No one can be sure. He has been gone a day and a night. It won't stop raining and your mannequin boy is wearing boots inside while my real flesh and blood son is wearing tennis shoes outside in this drencher."

The clerk steps back and Charlee comes up from behind. She loops her arm through mine. "It's not fair," I say.

"I know," she says and thanks the clerk.

The clerk seems upset. I tell her I'm sorry.

"You have nothing to be sorry about," Charlee says and we walk back to the main aisle. "I taped flyers in the maternity department after I finished in women's. Let's put up the rest."

"I'm losing it."

"No you're not."

"What's the point?" I hold up the flyers. "There's no one out shopping in this miserable weather."

"The point is that we're doing something. You never know, the next person who comes in could be the one with a clue to Gabe's whereabouts. Come on, we're going to put up the rest."

We work our way toward the front door.

"How can Dad be so upbeat when his grandson is still missing?" I stick a flyer on a toaster.

"Maybe Paul's letting God drive his church bus. So why didn't you tell me you fought the devil and won?"

"I didn't."

"Put a flyer on the vacuum."

I tape one on the handle. "I still don't remember anything after the sea lion reared up and barked."

"You remember a sea lion?"

"Yes, I guess I do."

"Did he push you in the river?"

"I don't know." I think back. I remember the dock rocking, the sea lion on the other end of it. "I don't think so. He surprised us. That's all." I try to remember more, but I can't.

We tape the last flyer to the door and she swings it open. "Look." She cups a hand over her eyes. The power lines are dripping silver, the store's awnings are. The clouds have blown through, leaving a deep blue sky.

"The sun will bring people out," I say.

We stop at the car for more flyers and I check for messages on my phone. Dad left one a half hour ago – where are you Noah? The meeting starts at ten.

"Any news?" Charlee asks.

"No."

We walk over to the main road. Hand out flyers out to a couple of joggers, a family getting out of a minivan, the UPS guy. We stop on the sidewalk across the street from Rolling River. The doors are propped open and people are streaming inside. I hear singing – "would you be free from your passion and pride?" One of Dad's favorites and he's belting out the words. "There's pow'r in the blood, wonder-working pow'r –"

"Paul's Expect Miracles service has begun," Charlee says.

I look at my watch. It's after ten.

"Think there will be a miracle today?" she asks.

"I want there to be a miracle."

I think of the time when the church was newly built and Dad took me out the backdoor to the pier. The day was much like today, after a hard rain and everything was wet and the glare hurt your eyes. Dad shaded his and pointed up. He said Rolling River's cross is Jesus' beacon to guide His lost lambs home.

"Do you want to go?" she asks.

"Go where?"

"Your Dad's meeting. I'll go with you."

"Did I hear right? You will go to Dad's meeting with me?"

"Yes. Bigfoot Hunters stick together, right?" She holds out her hand and I slap it.

Dad pounds across the stage and back, the microphone – thwonk thwonk – against his palm. "All things work together for good for those who love God. We love You Lord; we're expecting mighty miracles today." Dad points to the big screen with the mike. He says the words. Expect Miracles. Under the words is a larger than life photo of Gabe, the same photo that's taped to every post in town. "My grandson is coming home today. I believe in miracles, do you?" People shout they do believe.

In the photo, Gabe's grin seems off and I wonder if enlarging the photo distorted it or if Gabe didn't feel like smiling when the picture was snapped. Say cheese and you smile because it's expected.

Dad wipes his mouth with a handkerchief. "Who loves Jesus?"

My hands fly up with everyone else's, an automatic response, and I put them down. The people shout. "We do, we love Jesus."

It never takes Dad long to fire up a congregation.

Charlee loops her arm through mine and points out a space here in the back of the chapel we can squeeze into. People I don't know make room and we slip in without Dad seeing.

"Of course you love the Lord," Dad says. "God bless you all for coming. For where two or three are gathered together in my name, there I am in the midst of them. I testify to you. Jesus is with us now. Do you feel Him?"

They shout – "we feel You, Jesus, Jesus Jesus."

I don't feel Him now and I didn't last night. I would remember if I had. I saw a light before I succumbed to the river. Jesus wasn't in it.

Charlee slips an arm around my back. "Do you need some air?" she whispers.

"No." I unzip my coat and she helps me out of it.

"With Jesus, all things are possible to him who believeth. Who believes?"

"We believe," the congregation says.

Dad cups his hand to his ear. "Who believes?"

Their replies shake the floorboards.

"I'd like Pastor Noah to come up and join me now." Dad points the mike at me.

My stomach clenches. Of course Dad saw us come in. Dad sees everything. People are turning around in their seats and I see many faces I know.

I didn't see Satan's face in the river. I remember going under. He wasn't there. A life preserver ring was. I couldn't reach it at first.

"I'm not coming up. Go on with your meeting."

"Trust Jesus, Son. Come forward and we'll call on Him for strength and understanding."

"No."

Dad breathes heavy into the microphone. "The events of the last few days are weighing heavy on the heart and mind of our young pastor. This year has been Noah's hell. I'm telling you. God has tested him to the core. It wasn't easy to stand by and watch." Dad's voice cracks and he pauses to wipe his eyes. "I'd like you to come forward now, Noah, and report to the good and faithful people who've come to pray your son home. Tell them about last night on the dock. Tell them how you wrestled with the devil."

The congregation stirs. They whisper, sit up straighter. Dad cradles the mike and paces.

"Do you want to leave?" Charlee asks and I say I don't.

"Satan's a cunning fellow, is he not?" Dad asks. "Satan with the blood red eyes, horns that can pierce a man's heart, oh, I know him well."

I remember last night on the dock. Our surprise when a second sea lion squirted out of the river. I heard trumpeting. Dad stumbled.

I rub my forehead and Charlee lays her hand over my shoulder and asks if I'm all right and I tell her I am.

"It was you the devil came for this time, Pastor Noah," Dad says. "Satan himself leaped out of the river and glommed on to you, same as he did to me on the same dock 36 years ago." People turn around in their seats to look at me. Dad mops his face with the handkerchief. "My son fought for his life last night. He is the chosen one and Satan is well aware that Pastor Noah will become a spiritual giant in God's church. Satan knows Pastor Noah will lead the good and faithful believers back to Jesus. Satan wants him bad. He will do anything to stop you Noah."

I lean into Charlee and whisper. "The second sea lion flopped onto the dock in front of Dad and Dad stumbled back and bumped into me."

"So your dad freaked out, and in a desperate attempt to get away from the devil sea lion, he knocked you in the river?" she whispers.

"I don't think so."

"You understand, Noah, what it's like for a father to lose a son," Dad says. "I watched you take your last breath. I pleaded with Jesus to pull you out of the river, like He did me. I testify to you, Jesus listens. He came straight away, in a beam of white light, and wrapped you in His arms and washed you clean. I bear witness. He carried you out of the water. He said go Pastor Noah, go and lead my church, Rolling River Ministries of JESUS Church of the Mighty Miracles, in righteousness, and you and your posterity will be called blessed. Come up here now. Tell your flock the good news. You've had your miracle. You've been called. God wants you."

I think of all the years I imagined the day when Dad would call me forward and pronounce me as the leader of God's church. It was supposed to be a proud day for me and Dad.

"Please Son." Dad extends his arms. "Please come up here now."

Dad wants me. Dad wants me bad. I remember now. The sea lion didn't need rebuking. Jesus came on a flashlight beam. And Dad didn't stumble into me. Before the splash, came a nudge.

"You're telling it wrong," I shout. "I remember."

"You remember?" Dad with the steel blue eyes, the jaw set, looks out over the river of his people. A hush has come over them.

Dad holds out the mike. "Then come up here

and tell it right. Who would like to hear Noah tell us about his miracle?"

A couple of Amens and several praise the Lords come out of the crowd.

"There's nothing to tell. What you call my miracle is another one of your stories." I take in a ragged breath. "Here's my story. I lost my son and I can't find him. I'm scared Dad. I'm really scared."

Charlee reaches for my hand and Dad runs his through his white mop of hair. "Oh Noah. Times like these try a man's soul, do they not?" Dad turns off the mike, bends down and sets it on the stage.

I imagine him jumping off the stage. I imagine him running. He can't run fast enough. He pulls me into his arms. He says I know you're scared. I know.

"Jesus, Jesus, how I trust Him." Dad is still on the stage and he's singing. "How I've proved Him o'er and o'er –won't you sing with me Brothers and Sisters? Jesus, Jesus –" The congregation sings. "Precious Jesus. O for grace to trust Him more."

In the pause between stanzas, a new voice breaks in. "O how sweet to trust in Jesus." Grace breezes down the aisle.

"Just to trust His cleansing blood." She jogs up the stairs and scoops the mike off the stage. "And in simple faith to plunge me."

Charlee looks at me. "What's she doing?"

"I don't know."

"Your dad's eyes are about to pop out."

"Clearly, Grace isn't on the program."

She looks like a movie star in heels, a dress, top coat and a shimmery red scarf. She belts out the last of the hymn. Unties the scarf and slips it off her head revealing wet, stringy hair. Charlee and I exchange glances.

"Brothers and Sisters," she cries, "I've come to publicly confess my sins. To tell you first hand that Jesus saves wretched sinners like me. Yes. I was an unrepentant sinner. I sinned against God and my husband. I sinned against you."

People whisper and lean into one another and I wonder just how much Grace is planning on saying.

"I was an adulteress, a whore, chasing after gratification and pleasures of the flesh." Grace pats her eyes with the red scarf. "I was the vilest of sinners. I couldn't get enough sex."

"This is just great," I whisper. "She couldn't get enough?"

Charlee tugs on my arm. "You don't have to listen."

"I was hanging by a single thread," she says, "over Satan's frigid bottomless sea. God was ready to cut me off. Snip – and all would be lost. I was full aware of my imminent demise, and yet, I went back to my lover, my desire unquenchable."

"You said you strayed once," I shout and heads turn. "Once, you promised it happened once, and never again."

"I lied," she shouts back. "I'm sorry. I couldn't stop lying. Then my precious baby went missing. Last night, I stayed in Gabriel's bedroom to be close to him and pray. His room filled with darkness, so dense I couldn't see my own praying hands. With the dark came a frigid cold straight from the abyss of hell. I was so cold. I believed God had forsaken me." She paces in front of Dad, tapping the mike in her palm. "Then

I felt a flutter in my heart and God told me to go into the woods behind the school. I thought to find my son, but God had other plans. I didn't search for long, before God struck me down. Paralyzed, I laid on my face in needles and moss and rotting leaves and there I pleaded for mercy and begged God to unchain me from the shackles of sin. Noah – I betrayed you." She has stopped on the edge of the stage to talk to me. "I betrayed us. I'm so sorry. I hope you can find it in your heart to forgive me." She turns and walks deeper onto the stage. Charlee slips her arm around me.

"The blood of the Lamb set me free, Brothers and Sisters." Grace whirls around. "I turned my back on Satan and God poured the heavenly waters of baptism down on me. They soaked me to the bone, to my very soul, I testify." She pushes a strand of hair out of her face. "My egregious sins have been washed away and God remembers them no more. Thank you Jesus."

"Thank you Jesus," the congregation shouts.

"God lifted me to my feet. He said, Sister Grace, you were caught and bound in Satan's net. You have learned firsthand the terrible power he wields. You have been called to the work. Your story will free the hearts of many and you will guide them back to the fold, for you shall be a wise and mighty leader in my kingdom. Go now and sin no more."

"Thank you Jesus," Dad cries and he takes Grace by the hand and walks her to the front of the stage. "Brethren, God has spoken."

"Praise Him," they shout. "Praise God."

"Sister Grace," Dad says, "Jesus has made you and Pastor Noah fishers of men. You will serve together in righteousness. This is your flock. This is your church – Rolling River Ministries of JESUS Church of the Mighty Miracles." Dad raises his hands to heaven. "Thus saith the Lord. Now come up here Noah and pray with us and we'll ask Jesus to bring Gabriel home to the flock."

"No, I'm leaving. I have a son to find." Charlee and I start pushing our way through the wall of people who came in after we did.

"This is a church of mighty miracles, is it not?" I hear Dad loud and clear. "Sister Grace has returned to the fold. God, we pray for Pastor Noah's change of heart. We pray for his safe and apt return. Brothers and Sisters, as long as we believe, God will keep the miracles coming. Do you believe?"

"We believe!"

Charlee and I break out into the foyer where more people are gathered and listening to the meeting over the loudspeakers.

"Yes, we believe, Lord," Dad says. "Do you hear us? We believe. Jesus, oh sweet Jesus, bring our lost lamb home to the flock."

"I'll race you to the street," I say to Charlee.

"You're on."

"My baby," Grace screeches and Charlee and I come to an abrupt halt. We hear Grace weeping. "My baby, oh dear God, my baby's home, thank you Jesus, thank you."

Charlee and I start pushing our way back through the wall of people.

"Dad – Dad!" I hear his voice over the loudspeaker. "Where are you Dad?"

"Dad's here. I'm coming," I shout and the wall opens like the Red Sea.

Chapter Twenty

Anthony carries in a pizza box. "Special delivery for Gabe Cathcart."

"Over here." Gabe leaps off the couch. "I'm Gabe Cathcart."

"This pizza must be yours," Mark says and Anthony sets it on the coffee table.

Gabe's mouth falls open. "A whole pizza just for me?" He kneels, lifts the lid and inhales a deep breath of pepperoni.

Anthony high fives him. "All yours, my man. Welcome home." Anthony plops down on the couch next to me and I scoot into Charlee to make room for Mark.

Hercules sticks his snout in the pizza box and Gabe pushes him away. "This is all mine." He chooses a piece and eats a big bite.

We cheer.

"So Gabe, did you know Uncle Mark drove a Coast Guard boat all over the river looking for you?" Anthony asks and Gabe shakes his head. "So where were you anyway?"

Gabe stares at his pizza slice. His eyebrows knit together. "Uh. I don't know," he says, which is what he told the police.

"You don't know where you were?" Anthony asks.

"I don't remember." He slaps the pizza down on top of the box and folds his arms.

My mother grabs him around the waist and pulls him into her lap where she's sitting cross-legged on the floor. "You've answered a million questions today, haven't you?"

"No, Grandma Libby, I answered a trillion – jillion."

"Oh my. In that case, how about no more questions for now?" She looks at us. "Sound good?"

We nod. Officer Walker told us it's common for a child to forget or be reluctant to discuss a traumatic event. Give him time, she said. Don't pressure him.

Gabe leans back, resting his head under my mother's chin. "I bet nobody at school ever got a whole pizza to eat for themselves."

"I never did," Charlee says.

"You are not eating a whole pizza, young man." Grace comes in with Dad.

"But Uncle Anthony said the pizza is all mine."

"You had three helpings of spaghetti for dinner." The red scarf is still tied around Grace's neck.

I put the half eaten slice back in the box and close it. "We'll put your pizza in the fridge and you can eat more tomorrow."

"Somebody will eat it."

"No one will."

"How do you know?"

"Listen up folks, this is Gabe's pizza." I point to it. "Hands off or you will be forced to contend with my wrath."

"Your wrath, Bro?" Anthony laughs and snorts.

"What's so funny?" I ask.

"Uncle Anthony, Dad has wrath, believe you me," Gabe says and turns to me and asks what wrath is and everyone breaks out laughing.

"I have to be going," Dad says. "Come over here Gabe and give Granddad a hug."

Gabe leaps out of my mother's lap and flies into Dad's arms and he lifts him off the ground and holds him for the longest time. "Thank you God for bringing our boy safely home." He puts Gabe down and stretches his back. "I'm on my way to visit Brother Richards in the hospital."

"Don't go Granddad."

"The Lord's work is never done. You sleep tight, Gabe. We'll talk in the morning, Noah. I'll see myself out."

I heard him ask Grace earlier if she'd tell her miracle of forgiveness story on Sunday – again.

"Paul's right." Grace sinks into the chair. "The Lord's work is never done." She rests her bare feet on the ottoman. "We have so much to do to prepare for this Sunday, don't we Noah?"

"Good thing you're on top of it," I say and she scowls.

Anthony and Mark stand. "We also have much to do," Mark says.

Anthony sings – we're getting married in the morning – and waltzes Mark across the room.

Gabe waves his hand. "I'm gonna try and come to

your wedding."

Grace offers Gabe a pointed look.

"Okay, my man. I'll see you when I see you. Remember, Noah, the invite is still good."

"Thanks." We bump fists and they leave.

"You didn't tell him you were going to the wedding, did you?" Grace asks.

"No," I say.

"Grandma Libby and Aunt Charlee are going and Dad wants to, I heard him telling Uncle Anthony." Gabe holds out his pleading hands. "Please, pretty please, let me and Dad go."

"God tells us it's a sin for a man to marry another man," Grace says and Charlee rolls her eyes. Grace continues. "We've talked about this. We follow God's rules. Whatever God says, goes, and that's final. Dad and I have to be especially diligent about obeying God, because now we set the example for all the good people of Rolling River."

"God made a dumb rule," Gabe says.

"Gabriel!" Grace says and flashes me the help-me-out-here look and I shake my head.

"You're not being fair. I'm old enough to go if I want."

"This topic isn't up for discussion. Tell everyone goodnight now." Grace gets up and slips her arm around his shoulders.

He pulls away. "You're mean." He stomps up the stairs.

Gabe conks out in the middle of Grace's bedtime

prayer. She pulls his door shut and turns to me. "I'm so grateful this nightmare is over."

"Yeah."

Her eyes narrow. "You could try to act a little happier. This is a joyous time for our family. God brought our son back."

"I'm happy Gabe's safe and home." I turn to go downstairs and she stops me.

"We witnessed mighty miracles today. I'm grateful and you should be too. We've been given a brand new start. You and I are working together for the Lord now. I'm going to bed. Why don't you get rid of Charlee and Libby and hurry back? Maybe I'll still be awake." She pecks me on the mouth.

The Valentine's Day outfit comes to mind, but doesn't linger there for long. "I'm sleeping on the couch."

"Why on earth would you?"

"How is it that you're shocked? After I discovered via public confession that you had a secret life, am I supposed to be fine with it?"

"I know my confession was shocking. I feel a great remorse for what I did. I'm lucky God gave me a good shaking and I'm grateful I didn't lose everything that's dear to me. I've been forgiven and washed clean. God doesn't remember what I did and you shouldn't either." She goes in the bedroom and shuts the door.

On the way downstairs, I imagine Sunday's church meeting. I'm pretending. Smiling when I don't feel like smiling. Saying things I don't believe. Grace steps up to the pulpit. She says Brothers and Sisters, God forgave me. My husband won't. He won't forget either. He remembers that my lover wore sheepskin. He won't forget that my lover knew how to pleasure a woman like me.

I find my mother and Charlee in the spare bedroom, where my mother keeps most of her belongings, and she's holding a dress that's on a hanger up to herself.

"Look out, Rivers Edge, here comes one hot mama of the groom," Charlee says and they giggle.

"I'd better come back later," I say.

"Come in," my mother says, "I was picking up a few things for the wedding."

Charlee is lying across the bed on her stomach going through a jewelry box. "How would this look with the dress?" She shows my mother a necklace.

"It's perfect."

Charlee fingers it. "What are the beads made out of?"

"Moroccan agave silk, every bead is hand woven; it is beautiful, isn't it? A very nice man, Youssef was his name, gave it to me on my 50th birthday."

"I see, so, Libby, just how nice was Youssef?" Charlee asks, a sinister grin.

"I lived with him for six months in Morocco. Those were some good times. We were happy."

"Then why did you leave?" Charlee asks.

"Oh, I had other things to do." She slips a garment bag over the dress and zips it. "One thing I've learned is that it's important to take care of yourself and do what you want. It's not selfish like so many think."

"When Grace told her confession story today, I felt a piece of me leave."

Charlee and my mother turn and look at me for

several moments.

"Oh honey." My mother comes over and wraps her arms around me. "I'm sorry."

"Mom, I'm so unhappy."

I plop down in my office chair and an air horn blasts. The blast rattles the bones in my ears. I spring to my feet and Hercules climbs up my leg.

I hug him close to my chest. "That was a big scary noise for such a little guy. Know what? I think we've been pranked again." He shivers and I rub his ears. He likes that.

I close my eyes for a second. I didn't sleep last night. I stared at the ceiling. Thinking about my – about Mom, about my son and job and future. Hercules licked my chin occasionally. He's licking it now.

"Feeling better buddy?"

He barks and I set him on the floor and look under the chair. I find an air horn rigged underneath, activated by the pressure of sitting down, along with an envelope addressed to Pastor Noah from Naomi. I chuckle. "Good one, Naomi." I stand, lean my back against the desk and read.

She has started loving herself better. My Valentine's Day sermon helped give her the courage to stand up to her mom.

I bet Dad gets a call from Sister Monk, if he hasn't already. Last night, Mom asked when I was going to start loving myself better. She remembered my words from my River Street sermon the day she slipped in the back wearing the red poncho.

"What's the racket?" Dad bursts in without knocking.

I look down at the note. Naomi withdrew her application from Oral Roberts University and applied to UC Berkeley for a degree in Public Health. I look up at Dad and smile.

"That racket was my wakeup call. Take a seat, Dad." I point to the metal chair.

Naomi is finally doing what she wants, she says, and she's pretty happy about it. Her mom's pretty mad, but Naomi is confident she'll get over it.

"You've had a wakeup call all right." Dad settles into the chair and smiles.

"Not the wakeup call you think. "

"What do you mean?"

I sit on the corner of my desk. "I should be happy, right? I mean I have my son back and my wife, I have a job and a home and a future."

"Yes, you have a good life ahead."

"But I'm not happy."

"What do you mean, not happy? You have everything."

"I don't have the life I want."

"Your mother's been filling your head with these sinful thoughts, hasn't she? I warned you about her." Dad runs his hand through his miraculous white hair.

You make your own happiness is what Mom said. If you're happy, you can make the world a better place.

"You don't know anything about Mom. But that's not the matter at hand. I've decided it's time to start making my own happiness. One thing I want is to start a new River Street. I've been thinking. I want to help realize a community for the underserved where they can find hope. Where no hate is spoken, only love and acceptance and inclusiveness and where community members work together helping and supporting each other, where they can find job training, education, legal help, enough to eat, dry places to sleep and where no one ever has to die alone in the woods."

"There's no money in charity."

"This isn't about money."

"What on earth are you thinking?"

"Uh – I'm thinking I quit. Yeah, I quit."

"You can't –"

"No, I can."

"I've built Rolling River for you. It's all yours, Son."

"No disrespect, Dad, but Rolling River is yours. I don't want it." He looks at me slack jawed, the steel blue eyes blink.

"Look, sorry to run off, but I have to be somewhere."

I think of the PS Naomi added to her note – see you at the wedding Pastor Noah. I grab Hercules and leave Dad sitting.

Grace is sitting at the dining room table reading her Bible. "I have some exciting news," she says without looking up.

I thought about my news on the way home, which order to tell it in, and decided first thing first. I'm taking Gabe to the wedding and then I'll tell her I quit the ministry. She's going to flip out.

"Noah, are you listening?" She's peering over the Bible.

"Uh, yeah, what's your news?"

"I found a home for Hercules."

I stand here dumbfounded. "You've been looking?"

She sets the open Bible on the table, folds her hands and rests them on it. "I know how much trouble you've had finding him a proper home. The new family at church, the Lake's, adopts disabled dogs. Who knew? They have a houseful of dogs on wheels." She chuckles. "Sister Lake showed us pictures at Bible study. I told her about Hercules and she phoned this morning. They'd love to add him to their pack. They're a Godsend, a perfect match. I left their number next to the coffeepot."

"Hercules doesn't need wheels."

"Honestly Noah, you said you'd find him a home in two weeks and it has been over seven months. Seven." She flashes seven fingers. "You have to give them a call. He'll be happier with dogs like himself."

"He won't be happier without me." I pick him up and he licks my chin. "He has a home."

"You can't keep him."

"Yes, I believe I can. He's my dog and I'm keeping him."

"Hooray!" Gabe jumps off the fourth stair from the bottom. "Did you hear that Hercules?"

"The dog's not staying." Grace shuts her Bible and eyes me. Then she flashes Gabe the eyes. "What have we told you about jumping off the stairs, mister?"

"Sorry Mom." Gabe reaches for Hercules. "You're our dog now, for reals." He lifts him out of my arms and kisses his nose. "No one can love you better than me and Dad."

"Gabe, go to your room while Dad and I finish this conversation."

"No stay," I say. "I also have exciting news. I've decided to go to the wedding."

I watch Gabe's face brighten. Grace pushes away from the table.

"And I'm taking Gabe with me."

"Really Dad? That's so cool."

"No," Grace says.

"Yes. Gabe, go upstairs and change into Sunday clothes."

"Hey boy, we're going to see Uncle Anthony get married. Won't that be fun?" Hercules licks his face and Gabe sets him down. "I'll get Hercules ready too, okay, Dad, okay?" I say okay and they scramble up the stairs.

Grace pokes me in the chest. "What do you think you're doing?" She shouts after Gabe, "You aren't going to the wedding, young man."

Gabe's door shuts.

"Why did you tell him he's going, because he isn't and you know it?"

"By not letting him go, don't you see what we're teaching him?"

"Yes, I do see. We're teaching him to follow God's laws."

"Jesus didn't teach intolerance and hate. Gabe loves his uncle. He wants to go to the wedding."

"He's too young to understand."

"He's old enough to understand love."

She breathes out her nose. "I understand how

hard this day is for you. Of course you want to go. You love your brother." She clutches me by the arms. "Let's pray. I'll pray with you."

"Praying won't change how I feel."

"Together, we'll pray for understanding. God will open your eyes and lead you back to the path."

I shake my head. "No. I quit the path."

"No, honey, you don't mean it."

"I do." I step back out of her grip. "Look, I don't want Rolling River."

Her eyes narrow. "Are you telling me you quit the church?"

I breathe in and out. "Yes, that's what I'm telling you. I don't want Dad's church. I told him before I came home. I don't want that path."

"But I'm on the path – God's path."

"I'm not asking you to get off."

"We're on it together. We've been on it for ten years and we vowed to stay on it until the day we die."

"We aren't the same people we were when we made those vows." My stomach clenches and I lay my hands on the counter, lean over the black crumbs from the toast I burned this morning, the half mug of cold coffee, and try to gather my thoughts. What am I saying?

She clutches my wrist. "Of course we aren't the same, we grew up. Together, we changed. Yes, we've had growing pains, but God is on the path with us – though the waters thereof roar and be troubled, though the mountains shake, God is our refuge and strength. Psalm 46."

"I'm talking about you and me, not God."

"It's never been just you and me," she says like I'm

being ridiculous. "God is part of our marriage and He always will be."

"I want to talk about us. We started out in our marriage wanting the same things. Children, a house, a garden, a dog and a fence, I wanted to be Rolling River's pastor and you wanted to be a pastor's wife. We were willing to do whatever God asked with no questions, no hesitation. But that was ten years ago. Come on, Grace, admit it, you and I haven't been on the same path for a long time. Do you even love me?"

"Of course I do."

"I mean me, do you love Noah James Cathcart, your husband, not pastor, with all your mind and heart and soul?"

"God witnessed to my heart and mind and soul that you were the man for me and you know it – for this cause shall a man be joined unto his wife, and they two shall be one flesh. One flesh, Noah. One path until death do us part."

"Why can't we be on separate paths? You have Rolling River and I've been thinking about what I want to do in the future."

"What we want doesn't matter. Our future is in God's hands. The straight and narrow path is the only way."

"I ought to have a say about what path I follow."

"You do have a say. Are you on God's side or not?" She raises her eyebrows and waits for my answer.

"This sounds like an ultimatum."

"What's an ultimatum?" Gabe asks. He's standing at the top of the stairs.

Grace sighs. "A choice."

"It's more final than a choice," I say.

"Oh." Gabe starts down the stairs, Hercules prancing behind, dressed in the rainbow striped sweater. "Hercules wanted to wear the new black and white sweater, but I told him it was drab, like a funeral, so he decided on the rainbow, because it's really happy and really bright like getting married is, even though I've never been to a real wedding before. Hercules looks handsome, don't you think?"

"Yes, he does," I say. "You spent all that time dressing him and not getting yourself ready?"

"Sorry, Dad, he's wiggly and slippery and wouldn't hold still. I'll go change now." Gabe's wearing a Mario Brothers' sweatshirt, jeans and the bright green rain boots.

I glance at the clock. "No time." I pull the keys out of my pocket. "Take Hercules out to the car. I'll be out in a minute."

"Gabe isn't going anywhere." Grace steps in front of me.

"He's almost nine and old enough to choose whether he should go to his uncle's wedding or not."

"I choose yes," he says and jumps, punching the air.

"The sin will be on your shoulders, Noah. Think about the consequences."

"He's going with me."

She pokes me in the chest. "You are treading on the edge of a slippery, broken-down dock. Hanging by a thread, and believe you me, Satan is there lurking beneath the water's skin waiting for you to fall in. I know firsthand and so do you. You fell in the river and God pulled you out. You may not be so blessed the next time. Do you really want to risk drowning in

Satan's frigid bottomless sea?"

"Believe you me, Grace, God wasn't in the river and Satan wasn't either. I know firsthand."

"It's a grievous sin to deny God."

"I'm telling it like it is."

She folds her arms and scowls.

"Grace, you hurt me. You hurt me like I've never been hurt before. You don't know how hard it is to come back from a betrayal. Right now, I don't feel like I ever will. It takes a long time for a heart to heal. But that's only a part of what's wrong with you and me. I'm through pretending to feel things I don't feel, pretending to believe when I don't and I'm through being afraid – though the earth be removed, and though the mountains be carried into the midst of the sea, there is a river. I will not fear. Psalm 46. I choose a new path. I'm going to do what makes my heart happy."

"Bigfoot Hunters Code Number 10." Gabe grins.

"Have you been reading our Bigfoot Journal again?"

Grace grabs my arm and pulls me around. "I thought I knew you. I thought you had a compassionate and loving heart, a heart big enough to forgive my transgressions."

"You know what? God never gave my heart or mind or soul confirmation that you were the woman for me. That's the truth." We stand here in silence for a very long moment. "I'm through lying to myself. I'm not happy on the path you and God are on. I quit." I toss the car keys to Gabe and he jumps and catches them overhanded.

We turn onto the bridge. Traffic is stopped. "That's just great," I say and Gabe announces that the wedding starts in 18 minutes. Since we left the house, he has been giving me a minute to minute update – the wedding starts in 25, 20, 19.

I power the window down, peer around the line of cars. Lights are flashing at the other end of the bridge. We're going to be here for a while.

Now seems as good a time as any to explain to Gabe what just happened between me and Grace. My stomach clenches. I don't want him to hear it from anyone else, but adding this on top of the ordeal he has already been through seems a lot for a little boy. Will he cry? Yell, turn quiet, blame himself? Will he hate me?

"I have something to tell you, but before I do, I want you to know how much me and Mom love you."

"I know. Look at Hercules. He's waving at seagulls."

"Uh-huh. Listen, Gabe, Mom and I –"

"You're getting an ultimatum, like the divorce Aunt Charlee and Uncle Michael got." He fiddles with his fingers.

"Yes, we are."

"Uncle Anthony and Uncle Mark are going to be so surprised when they see us."

"Yes, they certainly are."

"You aren't going away like Grandma Libby did when you were a little boy, are you?"

"No. I'm staying right here."

"Will you and Mom still be pastors of Rolling River?"

"I won't be, but Mom will, I suppose."

"Are you gonna sleep on the couch from now on?"

"No. I'll stay with Aunt Charlee and Grandma Libby for a while. I'll only be five minutes away from you."

"Can I come over and watch TV on Aunt Charlee's big screen?"

"If your homework's done."

"Oh."

"I'll be checking from now on."

"Okay. The wedding's in five."

"Yes, it is. You know nothing will change between me and you, right?"

"Yeah, yeah, I know. Hercules, guess what, we get to be the ring guys at the wedding. Isn't that so cool?"

"I don't think so, buddy. Uncle Anthony made other arrangements when he thought we weren't coming. We'll sit in the back and be happy to watch. Okay?"

"I guess. Is Mom gonna ground me for going to the wedding?"

"No, you're not getting grounded."

"She was mad."

"She'll get over it."

"Are you happy now?"

"Mostly," I say.

"Just mostly? I thought you did what made your heart happy."

"I did and my heart is happy. But I feel a little sad too."

"Why?"

"When you marry somebody you expect you'll be married forever and when it doesn't work out like that, you feel bad. But in the long run, Mom and I will be much happier."

"You don't have to fight anymore and that makes me really, really, really happy."

"Me too."

"Will there be cake at the wedding?"

"Yep and dinner and dancing. It will be a night Uncle Anthony and Uncle Mark will always remember."

"Do you remember your wedding with Mom?"

I think back. I remember eight months before the wedding, after Grace announced I was who God wanted her to marry and I waited for my own confirmation. Dad said what are you waiting for? Grace is a perfect pastor's wife.

"Dad- Dad? Do you remember?"

"Oh. Yes. Mom was beautiful in her wedding dress. I remember a ginormous cake with tons of white frosting, a plastic bride and groom on top and when Mom and I fed each other a piece of the cake –"

"She smooshed hers in your face." I look at him and he giggles. "I've seen the pictures. Are you going to cut Mom's head out of them?"

"No, I'm not going to do that."

"Good." He smiles and gazes out the window.

I get out my phone and write Charlee a text. I tell her I quit my job. I make a smiley face. And I quit my wife. Today is a new beginning, I say, for Anthony and Mark, and me and Gabe. I'll tell you everything after the wedding. Gabe and I are on our way, stuck in bridge traffic. See you soon. Don't tell anyone we're coming.

Someone lays on their horn and I look up. Cars

are moving, a slow crawl, but moving. I send the text.

"Who'd you write to?" he asks.

"Aunt Charlee."

"Why?"

"Why?"

He nods.

"Because I wanted to let her know what's going on with me. I tell her everything."

"Does she tell you everything?" I nod. "Everything like what she ate for breakfast or when she washes the dishes or puts on socks?"

"No. Everything like what we're thinking about or how we feel, if we're happy or sad. I don't know. We've talked to each other like that since we learned to talk."

"Do you and Mom talk like that?"

"No."

"Bigfoot Hunters never lie, right?" Gabe asks and I flash him a look. "I didn't read it. I'm not lying. I promise. I was just checking."

"Okay." I give him a sideways glance. He's looking out the window. I pass what's left of the flares and turn onto the highway.

"The wedding started five minutes ago," Gabe says.

"We won't miss much."

Ten minutes later, I turn onto the street the chapel's on. I pass three protestors on the side of the road waving their signs. Sister Monk is one of them. I power down my window and say hello, it's a great day for a wedding, and pull in the driveway.

We stop in the back of the chapel and I hold my finger up to my lips. Gabe nods, a stealthy grin, while Hercules, his chin resting on Gabe's shoulder, snoozes. The chapel is filled with fall color. Flowers Grace would know the names of, if she were here, are attached to the pews, lining the aisles and clustered in corners.

A cello and three violins are playing Pachelbel's Canon and the grooms are walking a slow pace to the front, the tassel on Anthony's Chullo hat swinging. Row by row the guests stand. They're all oohs and aahs. There's Mari Yew on the other side of the chapel. She raises a thumb.

Anthony and Mark take their places facing Pastor Green. He tells the guests to be seated. A hush falls over the chapel. Charlee, a small bouquet in her fist, spots us and breaks out in smiles.

"We are here today in the presence of family and friends to share with Anthony and Mark the most important moment in their lives," Pastor Green says, "the joining of heart, of mind and soul. Won't you join us in prayer?"

Now Mom sees us and I signal her not to tell, though Hercules may give us up if he snores any louder.

After the amens, Pastor Green lays a hand on Anthony's shoulder and the other on Mark's. "Brothers, love bears all things. Love believes, hopes, and endures all things. Love will not fail you."

I've said the same thing to couples I married. Right out of 1Corinthians. A romantic notion. Love isn't that simple.

"Let's stand over there on the side where we can

see better," I whisper to Gabe and reach for his hand, but he raises it high over his head and waves.

"Uncle Anthony, it's us. We came!"

Hercules shoots out of Gabe's arms, zooms up the aisle and Gabe goes clomping after him.

I walk a quick clip up to the front. Gabe is already there.

"Did we surprise you?" he asks and Mark and Anthony burst out laughing.

"Yes, my man, you certainly did." Anthony high fives Gabe.

"Sorry about all this," I say and scoop up Hercules, who is dancing on his hind legs between the grooms.

"What are you apologizing for?" Anthony asks. "You're here, Bro. You're here." He pulls me and Gabe and Hercules into a bear hug.

I walk up a short gravelly path to where Charlee is sitting on top of a picnic table rubbing her hands up and down her bare arms. She looks over her shoulder and I raise my hand, the one with her coat hanging from it, and she smiles.

Over the loudspeakers I hear – "All well drinks are on the happy couple. Drink up, chaps." They hoot and cheer.

"The party's just beginning to rock," she says.

I sit beside her on the splintery tabletop and drape the coat over her shoulders. "I needed some air."

"You okay?"

"Yeah, are you?"

She nods. Slips an arm into a sleeve and I hold the other side while she shrugs into it. We gaze out over the vista, the sun's last rays casting a warm glow over the river and hillside, over the big firs and cedars, and we say at the same time – isn't it beautiful up here?

We chuckle.

"Let's hear it for the Rivertown Boy Band." A woman's voice and a drawn out whistle.

"Mari Yew," I say.

"No mistaking that whistle."

The drummer bangs the cymbals and the band starts playing.

"That's some sound system they have," I say.

"It's got to be blaring inside."

"We sound like old fogies."

"We are a few years older than most of the guests. Hey, nice job stepping up and finishing the wedding ceremony when Anthony asked."

"I was not prepared to do that. I mean, look at me." I point out the rip in my jeans.

"I saw that. And what's this?" She rubs my three days of stubble.

"Nothing. I meant to shave, but I ran out of time."

"You didn't come dressed for a wedding, but the advice you gave the wedded couple, in direct contrast to Pastor Green's Bible advice, was quite insightful."

"You think?"

"Yes, I think. No matter how much a couple believes or hopes or endures, love will fail if they don't talk heart-to-heart or if they talk more than listen. How'd you get so smart?"

"I took that bit of advice from some ten year olds."

"We were wise beyond our years, were we not?"

"Yes, we were." I chuckle. "Grace and I didn't talk past our schedules, whose turn it was to pay bills and clean house."

"I know. Michael talked more than listened."

"I know. If we were so wise, why didn't we follow our own advice?"

"Who listens to kids?" she asks and I shrug. "It must have been hard speaking today, considering you left your wife before you came."

"I don't think the whole impact of leaving my wife has sunk in."

"I have a peach pie and a half gallon of ice cream in the freezer."

"Your half, my half?"

"Exactly what I had in mind."

"The wedding was hard for you too."

"A little – all those happy people, but I'm glad Anthony found his happiness. I hope it lasts forever."

"Me too."

"So, has quitting your job sunk in?"

"It's beginning to. Before I came out, Pastor Green told me about a coffeehouse ministry he visited in P-Town."

"Coffee and a prayer?"

"A bit more. It's a community meeting place open seven days. They serve coffee and sandwiches. People drop in to chat, hang out and warm up. They recently started a food bank and they work with social services providing resources like housing referral and job counseling, legal help and mental health, right there on site. They provide spiritual counseling for those who want it."

"Sounds like your vision of River Street."

"Yes, it is, and more. Pastor Green said he'd been mulling over the idea for River Street, but he hadn't thought much past the concept, because he doesn't have time to take on a project like it."

"But now he knows someone who does."

I smile. "While Pastor Green and I were discussing options, Annabelle, you know, the –"

"Your dad's strip lady –"

"Yeah, she overheard us talking. She likes the idea. She said her building was still empty and if we were interested, she'd talk to her attorney about donating it for a tax write-off."

"You made quite an impression on her."

"Must be this stubble, you know, the rugged manly look."

Charlee breaks out laughing.

"What's so funny?" I ask and she shrugs.

"That's not all. Naomi and Finn walked into the conversation. He offered to hold daily prayer meetings, optional, not required, for those who want a little spiritual pick-up to start their day. Naomi wants to come back after she gets her degree and work with us."

"What more do you need?"

Pastor Green said if I was interested and had the time to head up the project, he could help find grants and donors."

"Do you want to do it?"

Do I want to? Not does Dad want me to, not does Grace want me to. Do I?

"Yes, I want to. This feels right. I feel right. Pastor Green and I are meeting first thing Monday morning to discuss it. I was also thinking about going back to school to finish my degree, not in theology, but something in social services."

"You're finally going to do what makes your heart happy."

We slap hands.

"Ladies and Gentlemen, may I have your attention please?" Mari Yew whistles. "All right folks, the new Anthony and Mark Cathcart Dickerson are ready for their first dance. Please, everyone gather around. You don't want to miss this."

The guests cheer and clap and hoot.

"Want to go inside?" Charlee asks.

"No, they won't miss us."

"Are you sure?" Charlee asks and I say I am.

"*Because you Loved Me*, by Celine Dion," a band member announces.

"Anthony loved that song when he was like five, remember?" Charlee asks.

"I remember. He knew all the words."

"We did too, because little Anthony sang it incessantly."

"Bet we still do." I get down off the picnic table and offer Charlee my hand. "Will you dance with me?"

"You've never asked me to dance before." She takes my hand.

"We've danced before."

"Yeah, the Hokey-Pokey."

We laugh and lean into each other.

"For all those times you stood by me," we sing.

We've never danced like this, but our arms seem to know where to go.

The smell of salmon fish and chips has wafted outside. They announced dinner. I see a long line of people.

"Hungry?" we ask at the same time.

"Dad – Dad." Gabe clomps out with Hercules trotting beside him. "I've been looking all over for you."

"Is something the matter?"

"We need to talk."

"Right now?" He nods his head up and down.

"I'll save you a place in line," Charlee says.

"No, you can't go," Gabe says. "I have to talk to you too."

She and I exchange glances. Who knows what he's thinking.

"All right," I say. "What do you want to tell us?"

Gabe scratches his head, kicks at the gravel.

"We're listening," I say. "Go on."

"Remember when I went missing?"

"Well, yeah," I say. "I doubt I'll forget that anytime soon."

"I ran away because you and Mom were fighting all the time."

I sigh and Charlee offers a sympathetic look.

"But I didn't know where people went when they ran away. Do they go live in the woods and eat huckleberries or stowaway on a big ship? Or hide in Safeway where the food is? I walked around for a really long time trying to decide where to go and I got really tired." Gabe looks at us.

"You remember what happened to you?" I ask.

He picks up Hercules and scratches him behind the ears. "I never forgot, please don't be mad."

"Where were you? Did somebody hurt you?"

"Nobody hurt me. I made sure. I took the Golden Bullet with me for protection."

Charlee looks at me wide-eyed.

"I hope Mom isn't mad about that." Gabe stabs his toe into the ground.

"Don't worry about it. Just give it back to her, okay?"

"Okay."

"So where were you?" I ask.

"Granddad said not to tell."

"Granddad?" Charlee asks.

"Uh-huh. Granddad said I was the miracle you needed to be happy." He smiles. "Granddad said God sent me."

"Did Granddad tell you to run away?" I ask.

Hercules licks Gabe's face and Gabe giggles. "He didn't know I ran away until he found me. Stop it Hercules." Gabe puts Hercules up on his shoulder and pats his back. "I decided to go home because I didn't want to sleep in weeds or garbage like a homeless guy." I nod. "But I got kind of lost. Then I remembered Granddad said Rolling River's cross guides people home. I could see it from where I was, so I walked to it. Granddad was wrong. His cross took me to Rolling River, not home. But I know the way home from church and I would have walked, but it was dark and Mom said never to walk home in the dark. If I had my own cell phone, I would have called you." He pauses and offers me a pointed look.

"Go on."

"I decided to sleep on the church bus and walk home in the morning."

"When did Granddad find you?" I ask.

"In the morning before I woke up. That was when he called me a miracle."

"I see."

"Granddad said God had a plan to make you happy. He took me to his office and told me what it was. He even gave me his bagel with jam and cream cheese on it because I was really hungry. Wasn't that nice of Granddad?"

"Sure Gabe, then what?" I ask.

"Granddad made me promise not to tell anyone about the miracle, because if I did, it would mess up God's plan and the miracle wouldn't be a miracle anymore and you wouldn't ever be happy."

I glance over at Charlee. She's scowling same as me. I'm surprised Dad would stoop to this, but then, he came close to drowning me for a miracle.

"I wanted you to be happy. That's why I told you I didn't know where I'd been," Gabe says. "I didn't want to ruin your miracle. Am I a liar?"

"Of course not."

"You only did what your Granddad told you to do," Charlee says.

"Whew, I'm glad. I was worried, because I'm not a liar. Really, I'm not."

"I know you aren't," I say.

"I think God told me to run away so Granddad would find me. God works in mysterious ways, you know. He told Granddad to have an Expect Miracles Prayer Service. God's plan was for me to wait behind the choir place during the service. Granddad told me to listen real hard and when I heard him pray for Jesus' lost lamb to come home, I was supposed to come out. I did just like He said. Baaaaaaa." Hercules barks and Gabe giggles. "I thought the miracle worked, because everybody was so happy."

"We were happy because you came home." I hold Gabe by the shoulders. "Listen to me. This is important. Don't ever run away again, even if you think God told you to. Instead, come to me or Mom, Aunt Charlee or Grandma Libby and we'll talk about it."

"Okay. Are you mad?"

"No."

"From now on, I'll talk to you guys instead of Elmer. He was no help when I ran away. Do you think he'll mind?"

"You know him better than I do. What do you think?"

"He's getting old like Granddad and wants to retire."

"I'm sure he understands that you're growing up. Did Mom know anything about Granddad finding you on the bus?" Gabe shakes his head. "Did Granddad tell her that you were a miracle or that you'd come out on stage when he said to?"

"Granddad didn't know where Mom was. He didn't tell her anything. Should I tell her?"

I think of Grace whisking by in her heels and her scarf on her way up to confess. Grace was once a vile sinner. Then God took her son away. She repented. God returned him. This is Grace's miracle, the story that will become the backbone of Rolling River, a story that will turn hearts with every telling.

"Dad?"

"It's your call. Whether Mom knows how her miracle came about or not won't change the fact that she had one."

I wrap my arms around Gabe and Charlee and Hercules. "Know what? I'm really happy right now."

"Me too, but there's more." Gabe wriggles away.

"More?"

"Uh-huh. Grandma Libby said if I really wanted something, I should ask for it and maybe I wouldn't get it, but I might."

"What do you want?" I ask.

Gabe folds his hands and pleads. "I really, really want to be a Bigfoot Hunter like you and Aunt Charlee."

Charlee and I exchange glances. I remember the day Mom said – you can't blame Gabe for wanting in on what you and Charlee have.

"Will you take me in, please, pretty please?" Gabe asks. "I memorized the Bigfoot Code and I can say it if you want and I'll be the best Bigfoot Hunter, I know I can."

I look over at Charlee and she gives me a nod.

"Being a Bigfoot Hunter is not to be taken lightly, right, Charlee?" I ask.

"Absolutely. You'll have standards to live up to."

"That's right. Being a Bigfoot Hunter isn't really about hunting for Bigfoot."

"I know. It's about the code." Gabe grins.

"You may never see Bigfoot."

"Maybe Bigfoot is a myth," Gabe says.

"Maybe," I say. "Or maybe not."

"He works in mysterious ways," Gabe says.

"He does, indeed. You have to understand, being

a Bigfoot Hunter isn't an easy road."

"It's a lifetime commitment," Charlee says.

Gabe thinks for a moment. "I have a lifetime. I promise I'll try my best to follow the Bigfoot Hunter's code."

I take Charlee aside and we whisper as if we're conferring. I tell her I'm ready for dinner. She tells me she's ready for a beer. We step apart and Gabe beams.

"We have reached a decision," I say and Charlee nods. "By the power vested in Charlee and me as Bigfoot Hunters, we pronounce you, Gabriel James Cathcart – Bigfoot Hunter."